Edward Walford

Londoniana

Vol. 1

Edward Walford

Londoniana
Vol. 1

ISBN/EAN: 9783337428839

Printed in Europe, USA, Canada, Australia, Japan

Cover: Foto ©Andreas Hilbeck / pixelio.de

More available books at **www.hansebooks.com**

LONDONIANA.

BY

EDWARD WALFORD, M.A.,

FORMERLY SCHOLAR OF BALLIOL COLLEGE, OXFORD.

AUTHOR OF

"THE COUNTY FAMILIES," "OLD AND NEW LONDON,"
"TALES OF OUR GREAT FAMILIES," ETC.

IN TWO VOLUMES.

VOL. I.

LONDON:
HURST AND BLACKETT, PUBLISHERS,
13, GREAT MARLBOROUGH STREET.
1879.

PREFACE.

THE sketches which compose these volumes have been written by me at various times within the past few years, and for the most part have appeared in the columns of the *Times, Builder, Once a Week, City Press, Queen,* and *Globe.* They have no sequence or connection with each other, each one being complete in itself; their point of unity being simply this, that they treat of persons, places, and things now or heretofore connected with that Great Metropolis, in the growth, progress, annals, and fortunes of which it is impossible for an educated Englishman or Englishwoman not to feel an interest. If it be true, as Dr. Johnson tells us, that the full tide of human life flows in the main streets of London as it does no where else, I venture to

hope that these efforts of mine to record some
phases of London existence in the past as well as
in the present, may meet with acceptance, if not
with favour. They are mostly of an antiquarian
cast; but they do not pretend to treat the remains
of antiquity in anything but a popular manner;
and if they contribute to the amusement of leisure
hours, which else would hang heavily, I shall be
gratified. In a few cases where the matter of my
sketch has been put out of date by the lapse of
time, or by the course of changes and improvements, a note to that effect has been added for
the guidance of the reader.

E. WALFORD.

Hampstead, N.W.
   April, 1879.

CONTENTS

OF

THE FIRST VOLUME.

period, yet, as these are not readily accessible to the public, a few words upon the subject of their contents, and on the irregular marriages which marked the earlier half of the "Georgian era," may not be wholly void of interest, at all events in the eyes of our fair readers, to whom marriages, whether "à la mode" or not, are deemed matters of some concern, however lightly they may be thought of by the "lords of the creation."

It was not until the time of the Council of Trent that the presence of a clergyman was held to be actually necessary to the performance of marriages, or to their validity; but the practical evils which were found to result from secret unions were so great that it was then resolved by the Western Church that they should not be performed but by a priest, and in the presence of two witnesses. The canon law, however, not being received in this country, all matters matrimonial were regulated by the common law, under which, " whilst, in virtue of domestic institutions, a form was enjoined for the more solemn celebration of matrimony, and persons departing from these regulations were liable to ecclesiastical censure; still other and more private modes of contracting a marriage were tolerated by the law." *Fieri non oportebat; facta valebant.* Hence marriages *per verba de præsenti*, and even *per verba de futuro*, though informal and irregular, if followed by cohabitation, were regarded as valid, and the ecclesiastical courts refused to annul them.

But, in spite of all efforts on the part of the Church and the State* to prevent clandestine unions these informal marriages continued to take place in London under the Tudors and the Stuarts too. Within a few years previous to 1686, many thousands of such unions were celebrated in London alone, many of them in churches and chapels exempt from the visitation of the Bishop as ordinary. These were called " lawless churches," and the clergy who performed there, "lawless parsons ;" but, in spite of hard names and censures, it appears that they drove a thriving trade and amassed large fortunes accordingly.

In the Bishop of London's Registry there is an entry showing that the Commissioners for Ecclesiastical Causes, in February, 1686, suspended for three years *ab officio et beneficio*, one Adam Elliot, the Rector of St. James's, Duke's

---

* Banns were first directed to be published by Hubert Walter about A.D. 1200 ; and the constitution of William la Zouch, A.D. 1347, states that "Some, contriving unlawful marriages, and affecting the dark, lest their deeds should be reproved, do procure every day, in a damnable manner, marriages to be celebrated without publication of banns duly and lawfully made, by means of chaplains that have no regard to the fear of God and the prohibition of the laws."

Place, for solemnizing marriages without banns or licence. This suspension, however, was withdrawn in the following May (on the technical ground, it would seem, that his church was extraparochial, and not subject to the ordinary); on which the rector resumed his friendly offices, and married parties, on an average, at the rate of sixteen couples a day. It appears from the register of this chapel that between 1664 and 1691 there are nearly 40,000 entries, and that on special days the worthy high-priest of Hymen made happy—or miserable—between thirty and forty couples.

The old chapel in May Fair, however, is that with which we have more particularly to deal just now; so let us return *à nos moutons*. This chapel, which earned the reputation of being second only to that in the Fleet in respect of what we may be pardoned for styling "Cryptogamia," or secret unions, was built about the year 1730, in consequence of the increase of new streets and squares on the north of Piccadilly. The person chosen to officiate there was the Rev. Alexander Keith, who is described by Horace Walpole as having "constructed a very bishopric of revenue" by his weddings at May Fair, which he had the impudence to advertise in the public papers. His practices, however, gave offence, not without good cause, to Dr. Trebeck, then Rector of St. George's, Hanover Square, who, in 1743, instituted against him proceedings in the Ecclesiastical Court, the result of which was his excommunication* and committal to the Fleet, or to Newgate —it is not certain which; though he certainly died in the Fleet Prison in 1758, after fifteen years' imprisonment. The secret weddings, however, did not cease at May Fair, where Keith fitted up a house as a chapel, and continued to work by deputy, as appears from the following advertisement:—

" To prevent mistakes, the little new chapel in May Fair, near Hyde Park Corner, is in the corner house opposite to the city side of the great chapel, and within ten yards of it; and the minister and clerk live in the same corner house where the little chapel is; and the licence on a crown stamp, minister and clerk's fees, together with the certificate, amount to one guinea, as heretofore, at any hour till four in the afternoon. And that it may be the better known, there is a porch at the door, like a country church porch."†

---

* Keith resolved to give tit for tat, "excommunicated" in turn at his chapel Dr. Gibson, Bishop of London, Dr. Andrews, Judge of the Court, and Dr. Trebeck.

† *Daily Post,* July 20, 1744.

The author of an interesting and scarce work on the " Fleet Registers," states that Dr. Keith's curates here, after his imprisonment, were the Rev. Peter Symson,* the Rev. Francis Denevan (both "Fleet Parsons"), the Rev. John Grierson, and a Rev. Mr. Walker. While in prison Keith seems to have had a keen eye to lucre, having kept his wife's corpse embalmed and unburied for many months—a circumstance which he ingeniously contrived to turn into an advertisement of his trade. At all events we read the following in the *Daily Advertiser*, January 23, 1750:—

"We are informed that Mrs. Keith's corpse was removed from her husband's house in May Fair the middle of October last to an apothecary's

* The following is a copy of one of Mr. Symson's handbills:—

G. R.

At the true Chapel
at the old red Hand and Mitre, three doors from Fleet
Lane, and next door to the White Swan,
Marriages are performed by authority by the
Reverend Mr. Symson, Educated at the University
of Cambridge, and late Chaplain to the Earl of
Rothes.
N.B. Without Imposition.

in South Audley Street, where she lies in a room hung with mourning, and is to continue there till Mr. Keith can attend the funeral. The way to Mr. Keith's chapel is through Piccadilly, by the end of St. James's Street, and down Clarges Street, and turn on the left hand. The marriages (together with a licence on a five shilling stamp and certificate) are carried on for a guinea as usual, any time till four in the afternoon by another regular clergyman at Mr. Keith's little chapel in May Fair, near Hyde Park Corner, opposite the great chapel, and within ten yards of it; there is a porch at the door like a country church porch."

The *Craftsman* for August 6th, 1748, tells us that Keith turned to a like good account the death of his son, whose corpse "he had carried on a bier by two men from the Fleet to Covent Garden Churchyard. In their progress," says the writer, "they made several halts, and crowds of people assembled to read the inscription, which referred to the father's persecution."

In 1753, while a prisoner in the Fleet, Keith had the hardihood to publish a pamphlet styled "Observations on the Act for preventing Clandestine Marriages," with a portrait of himself prefixed. The following extracts from the pamphlet, which is now extremely scarce, will serve to amuse our readers :—

" Happy is 'the wooing that is not long a-doing ' is an old proverb and a very true one; but we shall have no occasion for it after the 25th day of March next, when we are commanded to read it back-wards, and from that period (fatal indeed to Old England!) we must date the declension of the numbers of the inhabitants of England."—" As I have married many thousands, and consequently have on these occasions seen the humour of the lower class of people, I have often asked the married pair how long they had been acquainted; they would reply, some more, some less, but the generality did not exceed the acquaintance of a week, some only of a day, half a day," &c.— " Another inconveniency which will arise from this Act will be, that the expence of being married will be so great that few of the lower class of people can afford; for I have often heard a Flete-parson say, that many have come to be married when they have had but half-a-crown in their pockets, and sixpence to buy a pot of beer, and for which they have pawned some of their cloathes."—" I remember once on a time. I was at a public house at Radcliff, which then was full of sailors and their girls, there was fiddling, piping, jigging, and eating: at length, one of the tars starts up, and says 'D——m ye, Jack, I'll be married just now; I will have my partner, and be spliced;' the joke took, and in less than two hours ten couple set out for the Flete. I staid their return. They returned in coaches; five women in each coach; the tars, some running before, others riding on the coach-box, and others behind. The cavalcade being over, the couples went up into an upper room, where they continued the evening with great jollity. The next time I went that way, I called on my landlord and asked him concerning this marriage-adventure: he at first stared at me, but recollecting, he said those things were so frequent, that he hardly took any notice of them; 'for,' added he, 'it is a common thing when a fleet comes in, to have two or three hundred marriages in a week's time among the sailors.'" He humorously concludes: "If the present Act in the form it now stands should (which I am sure is impossible) be of service to my country, I shall then have the satisfaction of having been the occasion of it, because the compilers thereof have done it with a pure design of suppressing my *Chapel*, which makes me the most celebrated man in this kingdom, though not the greatest."

It would appear that Keith's troubles did not

end with his imprisonment, for another " Fleet Parson," named Wyatt, set up an opposition " Marriage shop" in May Fair, not, however, very successfully, if we may judge from the following, in the *Craftsman*, November 26th, 1748.

" The town being informed by this paper for some months past of a Fleet Parson that had opened a chapel in May Fair in order to supplant Mr. Keith, we think it not improper to acquaint the Public that we shall not trouble them on that score any more for the future, he having decamped on Thursday last, and returned to his own place, the Fleet."

It seems however that he had managed to net £57 12s. 9d. by his ministrations within the previous month.

It was not until 1753 that the subject of these clandestine marriages was taken up seriously by the Parliament, when Lord Hardwicke brought in a Bill (26 Geo. II. c. 33), enacting that any person solemnizing matrimony in any other than a church or public chapel, without banns or licence, should, on conviction, be adjudged guilty of felony, and be transported for fourteen years, *and that such marriages should be void.* It did not pass into law, however, without the most violent opposition. Mr. Fox, afterwards Lord Holland, who had himself found a wife in the Fleet, gained such popularity from his fierce resistance to the Bill that (if we may believe Wilkinson's Memoirs) his chariot was dragged along for many days by the populace. He was supported by Nugent and Charles Townshend in the Lower House, and by the Duke of Bedford in the Upper, as we learn from Horace Walpole's Correspondence. At length, when he found that all further open resistance was in vain, Fox changed his tactics, upheld the Bill with all the additions, alterations, and erasures which had been made to it and in it, and, to the infinite amusement of the House, pronounced over it a parody of Antony's oration over the mangled body of Julius Cæsar.

"It appears," says the compiler of the Fleet Registers, "that the alterations made in the Bill were made in order to defeat it when returned for the Lords." Be this, however, as it may, the tactics of Fox and his friends failed; as, in order to out-manœuvre the opposition in the House of Commons, the House of Lords consented to pass the Bill, even though it appeared before them like Banquo's ghost, "with twenty mortal murders on its head." It appears that, while the Bill was under debate, it created great popular excitement; and our regret is great that we have no contemporary *Punch* to refer to, in order to show the actual state of feeling in town and country. Handbills, however, on the subject were distributed, both pro and con., those in favour of the Bill urging that secret marriages had been the ruin of many families, that the religious respect for marriage was entirely subverted by them, and that the legal evidence of them was imperilled; while those on the other side contended that Lord Hardwicke's Bill would discourage marriage altogether, and that it was brought in for the protection of the fortunes of noble and rich persons against alliances with the middle classes. These latter handbills endeavoured, like Lord Russell in 1850, to make political capital out of the hereditary national hatred of Popery, declaring that it was the Council of Trent which had first annulled* clandestine marriages, and made the presence of a priest a necessary condition of every marriage, and that it was " after that *excellent* precedent " that the Bill in question was drawn.

As may be easily imagined, the Act for Preventing Clandestine Marriages gave no quarter to the marriages at May Fair, which were effectually stopped from that day forward. It is

* This is not a true accusation. The Council declared them " vera et rata," but condemned them as informal.

clear, however, that "marriage *not* à la mode" did not die without a struggle, and that Hymen's high-priest was "game to the last;" for it is on record that, on the very day before the Act came into force (the 24th of March, 1754), no less than sixty-one couples were married in the little unpretending chapel.

We learn from more than one allusion in Horace Walpole's Letters that this Marriage Bill was the subject of common talk in West End circles for many months before it arrived at the dignity of becoming actual law, Thus, in a letter to George Montagu, under date of the 17th of July, 1753, he writes : "Lady Anne Paulett's daughter is eloped with a country clergyman. The Duchess of Argyle harangues against the Marriage Bill not taking place [effect] immediately, and is persuaded that all the girls will go off before next Lady Day." In another letter, Horace Walpole relates the follow *bon mot* of Dr. Keith, the marriage-broker, who, to do his memory justice, appears, in his anger, to have spoken words prophetic of the future glories of Kensal Green, and the cemeteries of Highgate, Nunhead, and Norwood :—" ' God bless the bishops,' said he (I beg Miss Montagu's pardon); ' so they will hinder my marrying [trade]. Well, let 'em. But I'll be revenged : I'll buy two or

three acres of ground, and, by God, I'll under-
bury them all!'"

In the *Connoisseur* for October, 1754, we find
the following witty and satirical remarks upon
the effects of the recent Act on Dr. Keith's
chapel :

" I received a scheme from my good friend Mr.
Keith, whose chapel the late Marriage Act has
rendered useless on its original principles. The
reverend gentleman, seeing that all husbands
and wives are henceforth to be put up on sale,
proposes shortly to open his chapel on a more
new and fashionable plan.   As the ingenious
Messrs. Henson and Bever have lately opened in
different quarters of the town repositories for all
horses to be sold by auction, Mr. Keith intends
setting up a repository for all young males and
females to be disposed of in marriage.   From
these studs (as the doctor himself expresses it),
a lady of beauty may be coupled to a man of fortune, and an old gentleman who has a colt's
tooth remaining, may match himself with a tight
young filly. The doctor makes no doubt but his
chapel will turn out even more to his advantage
on this new plan, than on its first institution,
provided he can secure his scheme to himself, and
reap the benefits of it without interlopers from

the *fleet*. To prevent his design being pirated, he intends petitioning the Parliament that, as he has been so great a sufferer by the Marriage Act, the sole right of opening a repository of this sort may be vested in him, and that his place of residence in May Fair may still continue the grand mart for marriages."

Then follows a "Catalogue of Males and Females to be disposed of in Marriage to the best bidder, at Mr. Keith's Repository, in May Fair:—

"A young lady of £100,000 fortune—to be bid for by none under the degree of peers, or a commoner of at least treble the income.

"A homely thing who can read, write, cast accounts, and make an excellent pudding—this lot to be bid for by none but country parsons.

"A very pretty young woman, but a good deal in debt—would be glad to marry a member of parliament, or a Jew.

"A blood of the first-rate, very wild, and has run loose all his life, but is now broke, and will prove very tractable.

"Five Templars—all Irish.—No one to bid for these lots of less than £10,000 fortune."

And the article concludes with the following advertisement:

"Wanted, four dozen of young fellows, and

one dozen of young women, willing to marry to advantage—to go to Nova Scotia."

It is as well known that the first Lord Holland,[*] as said above, was married in the Fleet, as that Lord Brougham and Lord Eldon were married at Gretna Green. But the following random extracts from the May Fair register-books at St. George's, Hanover Sqnare, will serve to show that, at all events, a private marriage in the little chapel at the corner, with a porch like that of a small country church, was not the low and plebeian thing which at the first blush it might appear to be:

"1753, June 29.—Lord George Bentinck and Mary Davies, Hanwell."

"1748, March 23.—Hon. George Carpenter and Frances Clifton."

"1749, September 14.—William, Earl of Kensington, and Rachel Hill, Hempstead."

"1751, July 21.—Edward Wortley Montagu and Elizabeth Ashe, St. Martin's Fields."

"1752, June 30.—Bysshe Shelley and Mary Catherine Mitchell, Horsham."

"1752, June 15.—Henry Trelawney, Esq., and Mary Dormer, St. Margaret's,"

---

* His wife was Lady Georgiana Caroline Lennox, eldest daughter of Charles, second Duke of Richmond.

"1751, May 25.—Hon. Sewallis Shirley and Margaret, Countess of Oxford."

"1753, March 7.—William Shirley, Esq., and Madalane Julie Le Blanc, St. Margaret's."

"1753, March 15.—James Stewart Stewart, Esq., and Catharine Holloway, of St. Matthew's, Friday Street."

"1753, August 31.—George Montague Martin, Esq., and Elizabeth Berkeley, St. George's, Hanover Square."

"1752, February 14.—James, Duke of Hamilton, and Elizabeth Gunning."

Of the above, it may be remarked that the fifth entry refers to the grandfather of Percy Bysshe Shelley, and that the last entry records an event with which Horace Walpole has made all the world familiar.* He writes to Mr. (afterwards Sir Horace) Mann, under date of the 27th of February, 1752:—"The event which has made most noise since my last is the extensive wedding of the youngest of the two Gunnings;" then describes an assembly at Lord Chesterfield's, where the Duke of Hamilton made love to Miss Gunn-

* Letters, Vol. VIII. p. 51. It is not a little remarkable that his great-uncle, another Horace Walpole, was married clandestinely at St. James's, Duke's Place, on the 26th of March, 1691, to Anne, daughter of Thomas, Duke of Leeds, and widow of Robert Coke, of Holkham, in the county of Norfolk, Esq.

ing; and proceeds to give an account of the whole transaction in terms which we quote below.

This Miss Elizabeth Gunning was the second of three fair sisters, of Irish extraction, without fortune, but nearly related to the first baronet of the same name. Two out of the three were far-famed beauties in their day—twin stars in the world of fashion and rank, as every reader of Horace Walpole will remember. He says that they are generally declared to be "the hand-somest women alive," and is willing to admit the truth of the statement if they are regarded as a pair, though he adds, "singly, I have seem much handsomer women than either." They could not walk in the Park or go to Vauxhall without being followed by such mobs, that they were generally driven away. One day, when the sisters went to Hampton Court, the housekeeper showed the company into the room where the Miss Gunnings were, instead of into the Beauty Room. Mary, the eldest of the sisters, became Countess of Coventry. The story of the second, Elizabeth, shall be told in Horace Walpole's own words :—

"About six weeks ago, Duke Hamilton, the very reverse of the Earl, but debauched, extra-vagant, and equally damaged in his fortune and person, fell in love with the youngest at a

masquerade, and determined to marry her in the
spring. About a fortnight since, at an immense
assembly at Lord Chesterfield's, made to show
the house, which is really most magnificent, Duke
Hamilton made violent love at one end of the
room, while he was playing at pharaoh with the
other; that is, he saw neither the bank nor his
own cards, which were of £300 each; he soon lost
a thousand. I own I was so little a professor of
love, that I thought all this parade looked ill for
the poor girl; and could not conceive, if he was
so much engaged with his mistress as to disre-
gard such sums, why he played at all. However,
two nights afterwards, being left alone with her,
while her mother and sister were at Bedford
House, he found himself so impatient that he sent
for a parson. The doctor refused to perform the
ceremony without license or ring. The Duke
swore he would send for the Archbishop. At
last, they were *married with a ring of the bed-
curtain*, at half an hour after twelve at night, at
Mayfair Chapel. The Scotch are enraged; the
women mad that so much beauty has had its
effect; and, what is most silly, my Lord Coventry
declares that now he will marry the other. The
Duchess was presented on Friday. The crowd
was so great that even the noble mob in the
drawing-room clambered into chairs and tables to

look at her. There are mobs at their doors to see them get into their chairs, and people go early to get places at the theatres, when it is known they will be there. Such crowds flock to see the Duchess pass, that seven hundred people sat up all night in and about an inn in Yorkshire, to see her get into her post-chaise the next morning."

It may be added, by way of conclusion, that Miss Elizabeth Gunning was not content with a single dukedom, but, after the death of the Duke of Hamilton, married John, Duke of Argyll, and was eventually created a peeress of Great Britain in her own right, as Baroness Sundridge and Hamilton. She was the grandmother of the present Duke of Argyll.

PLANTAGENET LONDON.
(1868).

THOUGH in a certain sense it is true that "God made the country, but man made the town," and, consequently, that the study of nature must rank higher than that of man's handiwork—the material fabric of any town or city—yet there is a certain sense in which the study of cities and city life is the higher and nobler pursuit of the two. For, as Thucydides tells us, "it is men, not walls or ships, that constitute a city," in the sense of the Greek word "Polis," which, as we need scarcely remind our readers, denotes the moral city, including that idea of common social existence, with its common ties and interests, its common laws and customs, to which the Republics of Northern Italy in the Middle Ages seem to approach most nearly, but which idea was also realised in great measure by our own London in the age of the Edwards and their immediate successors—in other words, from the close of the thirteenth century to the early part of the fifteenth.

The Corporation of London, as it happens, have had in their possession for centuries, stowed away in their Guildhall Library, a variety of cotemporary records, in the shape of a series of folio volumes, written on parchment, containing manuscript entries of most of the current matters of the day in which the City and its citizens have been in any way interested, from the early part of the reign of the first Edward downwards. The entries have been made by regular scribes, under civic authority, from week to week and month to month, in every possible handwriting, good, bad, and indifferent, and in a way which, if not very scientific in the higher sense, at least " speaks well," as Mr. Riley observes,* " for the business habits of our City Chamberlains and Common Clerks in the time of the Plantagenets."   Hitherto these records have been guarded with great care and jealousy as the apples of the Hesperides; and though such well-known antiquaries as Stow, Fabyan, and Strype had access to them in their

---

* " Memorials of London and London Life in the Thirteenth, Fourteenth, and Fifteenth Centuries," from the archives of the City of London. By Henry T. Riley, M.A.

respective days, yet the City was so disgracefully plundered—we cannot use a milder term—by Sir Robert Cotton, the collector of the Cottonian MSS. and founder of the Cottonian Library in the British Museum, that we cannot wonder these literary treasures were kept safely under lock and key until times of greater literary honesty should arise. Hence it comes to pass that from Strype's day these treasures have lain forgotten and unheeded down to our own age, when attention was called to their high historical value by the late Sir Harris Nicolas, Sir Francis Palgrave, and Sir T. D. Hardy, the late worthy custodian of our Record Office in Fetter Lane. Since public attention has been drawn to this subject, we believe that these treasures have been consulted by M. Augustin Thierry, Dr. Lappenberg, and Mr. Froude; but we are not exaggerating at all when we say that their existence has been hitherto almost unknown even to the literary public; and we are not at all sure that they have been made available to any great extent either by Lord Macaulay for his " History," or by Mr. Timbs for his " Curiosities of London."

But, thanks to the general revival of a taste for antiquarian studies in their more useful form as the best aids to historical inquiry, the Corporation of London have not only withdrawn the dragons with which they kept watch and ward over the golden apples in their Guildhall, but, either in a sudden fit of generosity, or led on by the good example set by the Master of the Rolls, they have resolved to place the contents of their library—at all events, such portions of it as are of general interest—at the service of the public; and they have carried this resolution into effect, thus far at least, with Mr. Riley as their interpreter. Accordingly, this "Series of Extracts, Local, Social, and Political," is now given to the world at the cost and expense of the Corporation of London; and it is a boon for which all students of mediæval history and of domestic manners in the Middle Ages—to say nothing of our future Macaulays—will feel abundantly grateful.

In a volume of 700 pages, all full of quaint and curious matter, it is difficult to know where to begin, in order to give our readers a good idea of its contents. It is, indeed, a *dubia cœna*, as Terence or Plautus would have called it. The dishes are most varied, and nearly everyone will be able to able to find something or other to suit his taste. The City antiquary, for instance, will be glad to learn more about the early history of Leadenhall than he can gather even from the laborious chronicles of Stow—how that upwards of five centuries ago a court of justice was held

there, and how it was used as a poultry-market
as far back as the reign of Edward III. At that
time, where Gracechurch Street and Leadenhall
Street meet, instead of a constant cross-current of
omnibuses, there was a "Carfakes" or "Carfax"
(in which latter form the name will be familiar to
Oxford men), a fountain with four sides or faces
(*quatre faces*), and probably surmounted with a
cross, the erection of some worthy citizen whose
name is long forgotten, five centuries before the
Drinking Fountain Association was born or
thought of. But these are dry—at all events, dull
—affairs, and too retrospective to concern us at
the present day. Let us, then, turn to other
matters.

The work of an alderman of London at the
present day is easy enough. He wears a gown
of state, has a voice and a vote in the delibera-
tions of his fellow City magnates; presides, in
his turn, as a magistrate within the City, and
is bound to eat a certain number of public
dinners yearly, including a fit proportion of
haunches of venison and basins of real turtle.
But let Mr. Alderman Moon or Mr. Alderman
Mechi of our own day go back in memory some
five hundred years, and what will he find among
the duties of his office? Mr. Riley shall tell us, in
his capacity of interpreter of the civic edicts. In

the first place, he was not allowed a country-house at Richmond, or Clapham, or Hampstead, much less to go down to a seaside mansion at Brighton, but was bound to reside within the City walls. And the reason is plain. He was a conservator of the public peace, and had to take an active part in the administration of civic discipline, which, it must be owned, was of a very personal character, and troubled itself immensely with the most trivial details of everyday life. For instance, he had to set, arrange, and arm the sturdy fellows who kept watch in his "ward" both by day and night, and sometimes to take part in this duty in person, as being responsible for the peace of the City within that district, which then not only gave him a nominal title, but saddled him with active work enough to keep down his fat. With the same object in view, he had to inspect all the "hostels" in his ward, to see that they did not harbour any evil or suspicious characters; to take care that the several gates of the City were watched, "every gate, by day, by twelve men, strong, vigorous, well-instructed, and well-armed, and by night by twenty-four men;" and to see that the gates were closed at sunset, and the lesser or wicket-gate at the last stroke of curfew; after which, until the bell rang for "Prime" in the early morning, no one was to be allowed to go in or out without special leave from the mayor, or an alderman at least. When to these duties we have added those of looking well to the weights and measures of City tradesmen, of fining, imprisoning, and sending to the pillory all who were guilty of cheating and defrauding their neighbours, and all women who were brought before him as "common scolds," or as walking abroad at night with doubtful objects in view, or as not adhering strictly to the prescribed dress of the Paphian sisterhood, if they belonged to it, we think that we have succeeded in showing our aldermanic and non-aldermanic readers, by the help of Mr. Riley, that an alderman's gown in the olden time was no sinecure, and that, if a civic magnate ate turtle soup, he earned it by hard labour first, and had very little chance of attaining our ideal of aldermanic obesity in middle life.

The discipline to which we have alluded was carried out by the mayor and corporation over the citizens of London in a way which seems to show that the City was regarded but as an extension of the family; and it partook consequently of a modified and parental despotism. Thus when William Anecraft, of "Botulveswharf," was accused, not of selling, but of housing "putrid and unwholesome wine," it was adjudged by the mayor and aldermen that eight vessels of one tun each should be poured out in the street and thrown away; the sentence was carried out by the sheriff, and John Wallingtone, the City crier, got the empty vessels as his fee. But more amusing and cleverer by far was the punishment inflicted by Adam de Bury, Lord Mayor, upon John Penrose, taverner of the parish of St. Leonard in Eastchepe, who, being found guilty of selling bad wine, was condemned to drink a draught of it himself, to have the remainder of it poured over his head, and to give up his trade as a vintner. This was summary and speedy justice with a vengeance. Still more summary would seem to have been the penalty inflicted by the alderman on a woman found guilty of a robbery in " the hostel of the Bishop of Sarum, in Fletestrete," Desiderata de Toryntone—what a grand name for a felon !— of whom we read, " The jurors say that the said Desiderata is guilty of the felony aforesaid. Therefore she is to be hanged. Chattels she has none." Whether her life would have been spared if she had been possessed of " chattels " is more than we can say, and Mr. Riley does not inform us. *O infelix Desiderata!*

We have said that the discipline of the aldermen was carried very extensively into the arcana of social and almost of domestic existence. As

Mr. Riley observes in his introduction, hardly a feature of the City life of the middle and lower classes is passed over in these records—the tricks of trades, card-sharpers, dice-sharpers, the rules and usages of the various trades, from the merchant to the rag-dealer, the regulations of the markets, the drainage and roofing of houses, the fitting out of ships, the sale of Yarmouth herrings, the supply of fuel, of eggs, of fowls, of fruit, the setting of the City watch—now represented by Colonel Fraser and his merry men—the munitions of war, the rates of wages, the relations of master and apprentice, the arts and frauds of mendicants and swindlers, and the impostures of soothsayers.

On two subjects, however, which closely concern all men at the beginning and end of life—namely, the duties of midwives and " wise women," and those of undertakers, as Mr. Riley observes, this volume throws little or no light. To these we must add a third desideratum; in the index at the end of the volume we can find no reference to dogs 'and dog-life; and, after a tolerably careful perusal of the work itself, we discover in it no allusions to the canine species. Now, when all our four-legged pets, from " Nero " and "Neptune" down to " Tiny " and " Fido," are forced to go about with muzzles on their noses, we should have been glad to learn how the Walworths and the Whittingtons in the old Plantagenet days would have dealt with the great canine question ; but, alas ! to our disappointment, " the oracles are dumb," like the dogs.

We are sorry to perceive, from a perusal of Mr. Riley's book, that the character of the London clergy did not stand quite so high in the days of Bishops Lovel and Gravesend as it does in those of Bishops Tait and Jackson. In spite of the fact that these " Memorials " show the most obvious intention of screening clerical offenders, still it is quite clear that some of the " chaplains " of the City, as they were then called, must have been anything but a credit to their cloth. To a very great extent they seem to have been " night-walkers," " brawlers," and " bruisers;" and, if the reader will turn to pp. 484-6 of Mr. Riley's book, he will see that they sometimes did not scruple to indulge in other peccadilloes which are usually thought more pardonable in laymen than in those who are invested with the cure of souls. The careful profession of ignorance, on the part of Elizabeth Moring and her serving-woman Joanna, as to the name and residence of the " chaplain " whose name is the subject of a " delicate inquiry " in these pages, can scarcely fail to raise a smile, and to remind us that great was " the benefit of the clergy," in one sense at least, in the good old Plantagenet days.

In another aspect Mr. Riley's work is curious, as throwing light on the vexed question of the origin of surnames, and useful, too, as illustrating one feature of the Normans and Saxons in respect to the change which came over Christian names soon after the Norman Conquest. As might be expected in a work of this kind, nearly every surname and Christian name that was in use five hundred years ago crops up in its pages. First, as Mr. Riley observes, we have the surname derived from the country, birthplace, or old home of the new comer to the little world of London; such as John de Sevenoakes, John Francis (*i.e.*, of France), William Waleys (*i.e.*, of Wales), Walter Norris (*i.e.*, of Norway), John de Langmede, Alice atte Lane End, Christian atte Felde, Walter atte Watre, William atte Stile, from which come respectively the Longmeads, or Langmeads, the Lanes, the Fields, the Waters, and the Styles of our own day. Then comes a long catalogue of names taken from a man's own or his parent's calling, such as Chaucer (the Norman equivalent of our " shoemaker " and the German " Schuster "), Slatter, Taylor, Plumer, Butler, Walker, Corder, Vintner, Scrivener. Next follow those derived from some personal quality good, bad, or indifferent, including such names as Long, Strong, White, Brown, Black, Green, Longman, Panyfader, Le Curteys (now Curtis), Pork, Smaltrot, Vigors (*i.e.*, Vigorous), Tyler, Podifat (*i.e.*, lover of children), and Clenhond or Cleanhand—the last, curiously enough, the name of a Member of Parliament, &c. Nay, to such an extent did this habit of calling names proceed that we find mention here of John Outlawe, and Matilda and Alice Strumpet, names which must have had their origin in that rough kind of re-tributive justice which was dealt out by the *vox populi*, and which seems determined, as it were, to set a brand on persons known to be of bad repute. Among other noteworthy names which occur here, we may here mention in passing those of Whit-tington, Caxton, and Walworth—all well known to history; and that of Canynges or Canning, then, as in our day, honourably connected with the City.* We find, also, Walter de Cavendishe, citizen and mercer, Richard de la Pole, Alderman

* Mr. Riley mentions John Canynges as residing at Bristol, but a freeman of London, assessed to the King in 1379, and another John Canynge, of Aldersgate, in 1393. He reminds us of William Canynge of this family, the founder of St. Mary Redcliffe's Church at Bristol. He might have added that the father of the present Lord Stratford de Redcliffe was a mer-chant in the City, and that his lordship was born at his father's office, not a stone's throw out of Lombard Street.

of Billingsgate, and Richard de la Pole of Edel-
meton (Edmonton), vintner, Adam de Walpole,
of Cripplegate, John de Pulteney, and, last, not
least, a certain William de Wykham, whose
connexion with the great bishop of the same
name is more than problematical, as there are
half-a-dozen Wykhams in England. Among the
more curious and outlandish names that occur are
Cockow (or Cuckoo), Strokelady, Puppe, Citron,
Padecryst, Pettejoie, Pelkeshanke, Freshfyssho,
Piggesflesshe, and Killehogge.

Turning next to the kindred matter of Christian
names, we are struck by the fact, to which Mr.
Riley also refers in his introduction, that, while
the old Saxon names still held their ground in
the provinces, or the " Highlands," as the country
then was called, the City populace followed in
the wake of the Norman aristocracy, and christened
their children by the names of John, William,
Thomas, Richard, Robert, Henry, Joanna or Joan,
Christine, &c., in the place of the good old
names of Edward, Edmund, Emma, Edith, and
Ethel, of the Saxon age. Radulf or Ralph is
nearly the only Saxon name that meets our eye,
and that but rarely. It is strange to find that,
even in the Roman Catholic age with which these
books are concerned, the name of Mary was in use
only among the higher classes, and that the other

female names of most frequent occurrence are
Isabel, Matilda, Juliana, Alison (Alice), Lucy,
Petronilla (often abbreviated into Pernel or
Parnell), Agnes, Idonia, and Avice. Among
those less frequently, but still often met with,
are Clarice, Anabella, Theophania (or Tiffany),
Desiderata, Massilia, and Auncelia. Godiyeva
(Godiva), as Mr. Riley remarks, is perhaps the
only female Christian name to be found in these
books that recalls the purely Saxon times.

The Norman Conquest, then, it is clear, worked
pretty effectively inside the gates of the city of
London. There must naturally have been a large
stream of Saxon recruits from the provinces flowing
into London ; but within a hundred, or at the most
two hundred years, from the day when the Saxon
was humbled in the dust before the Conqueror,
the dear old familiar names of his childhood had
been almost wholly laid aside. This result, no
doubt, would be largely helped on by the constant
influx into London of a most motley group of
colonists from Normandy, Guyenne, Spain, Flan-
ders, Lorraine, Picardy, Norway, Denmark, and
Italy, whence the free and unfettered port of
London was ever ready to welcome all new
comers with open arms. As, however, besides
these foreign countries, there was scarcely a town
or village from Berwick to Dover or the Lands'-

end, which did not contribute its quota toward
the ever-growing aggregate of the Cockney population, it is singular, to say the least, to find how
soon the old Saxon names became extinct when
the parents got within the sound of Bow Bells.
The real fact is that the same spirit which
insisted on substituting in general parlance the
Norman "beef," "mutton," "veal," and "pork,"
for the Saxon "oxen," "sceap," "cealf," and
"swyne," would not rest content until such
rough and rural names as "Uilfrid," "Eadberht,"
"Aelfgar," and "Sigbert" had been fairly superseded by the more congenial and courtly appella-
tions of "William," "Robert," "Richard," and
"John."

We have neither time nor space to enter into
such other curious questions as the signs of
taverns and other public houses of London, or
the various trades of its citizens; but, if there be
any truth in the old homely proverb which tells
us that "there are as good fish in the sea as ever
came out of it," we are sure that we have said
enough to prove that Mr. Riley's work must be a
repository of antiquarian information of the most
novel and singular kind, and one for which not
only the scholar but the general reader will have
reason to thank him, and also the Corporation who
have placed their treasures at his disposal.

CURIOSITIES OF THE POST OFFICE.

(1868.)

WHAT is that which makes the Post Office the most popular of all the departments of Her Majesty's Civil Service? Why is it that we like the daily visits of the official with blue coat and red collar so much more than those of the official with blue coat and black helmet? Why is it that in every neighbourhood John Wilkins, the postman, is so much more acceptable, both to Emma, the parlour-maid, at the front door, and to Mary Anne, the cook, at the area gate, than even the much adored policeman X 99? The fact is that we are a homelike and home-loving people, and that the postman, in nine cases out of ten, is the bearer of "home tidings." As individuals, we know but little of the Excise, unless we happen to have a relative in the "smuggling line," and the minister of that branch of the service seldom or never favours us with a visit. It is otherwise with the tax-gatherer, he is only an occasional nuisance; but the Post Office is brought home almost daily to every householder among us by the double rap of its *employé*. For him "Betty" and "Sally" wear the brightest of smiles as he passes along our street, the object, if not of adoration, at all events of curiosity; for may he not be the bearer of some good news or tender message, some not "unwelcome tidings," for the kitchen as well as for the parlour?

But there is also another point of view from which "Paterfamilias" regards the Post Office with affectionate pride. It is nearly the only one of our public departments that "burns its own smoke," and costs nothing to John Bull. "Bother the Admiralty and the Horse Guards," he says; "only see what they cost the British householder in taxes year after year! If we have a war, and beat Russia, or lick Abyssinia into fits, we never make Russia or Abyssinia pay the cost: it all comes out of my breeches pocket, and I have to 'pay the piper.' But, thanks to Sir Rowland Hill, the benefits of the Post Office are mine, daily if I live in the country, and hourly if I live in London. What a benefactor, then, that man must be to the human race! For all this, I say, bless the name of Sir Rowland Hill, and his successor the Duke of Argyll!"

But before we get down to Rowland Hill's day,

it is as well to remember that there are a good many other people also whom we ought to bless; Plantagenet kings; Tudor and Stuart sovereigns, and more especially Charles I.; some half-dozen speculative adventurers in postal matters; sundry Postmasters-General in succession; and then the great Postal Reformer whose name we have mentioned above.

Though it is right and proper to consider Charles I. as the founder of our postal system, it must not be supposed that that same system, even in its ante-reform days, leaped all perfect and ready for action from the brain of an English king or his minister, as Minerva sprung full armed out of the head of Jupiter. On the contrary, though it now spreads its arms across whole continents, and embraces the two hemispheres in its grasp, the Post Office came from a very humble beginning. We will not attempt, as some dreary antiquaries have attempted before us, to base it on the eastern practice of employing relays of mounted couriers, who ran, or rather galloped, their set course with tidings or instructions, which they handed forthwith to another horseman, leaving him to hand them to a third, and so on, till they reached their destination. All this is very pretty, and sounds charming in poetry; but in treating this subject we have to do with the plain sober prose of matters of fact. For our sources of information we will refer to one or two of our most popular Cyclopædias, and to the first " Report on the General Post Office," issued by Lord Canning, if we remember rightly, in the year 1855. There may be, and indeed there is, some dispute as to the actual source of the Thames; but there can be no doubt about the origin of that system which now has its head-quarters in St. Martin's-le-Grand.

Yet for the *fontes remoti* of the British Post we must travel back in our memories as far as the Wars of the Roses; and it is well to find some good thing resulting from them, for they brought us evils in plenty. During those troubled times, special messengers carried tidings backwards and forwards between camp and court, but it was not long before they gave way to a settled staff of regular letter-carriers. Till writing, however, as well as reading became general, the need of a regular post was felt but slightly; and, when the " carrier "* came into being, it is quite clear that,

* Our readers will scarcely need to be reminded that Shakespeare uses the terms " post " and " carrier " as synonymous. Here, as in other matters, he was singularly true to every day life, as is proved by the fact which we learn from the old Records of the city of Bristol, that the Corporation paid a penny to the " carrier " for conveying a letter to London.

as he had only his own horses to rely on, his speed was limited by their powers; he could go no faster than his legs, or those of his horses, could carry him along roads, rugged, rutty, and un-macadamized, such as those with which the pen of Macaulay has made us so familiar.

In course of time, these messengers came to be kept, not only by the king and his court, but by wealthy nobles and men of importance in the state, who would seem to have adopted the plan of expediting messages by taking a leaf out of Persian history in the early ages, and establishing relays of men and horses much as we said before. The words, " Haste, post haste !" which, as we are told, are still to be found endorsed on the covers of important public and private letters of the fifteenth and sixteenth century, show the near balance of hope and fear with which the " post " was regarded, if not in their own day, at all events in that of their fathers, by those who entrusted that agent with their messages. We say this, for the custom of inscribing those three mystical words was kept up long after all necessity for them was at an end.

Lord Canning, in his first Report on the Post Office, to which we have already alluded, tells us that " Edward IV., when at war with Scotland, established relays of horses between Edinburgh and York ;" and he sees reason for believing that these horses were "posted" at intervals of about twenty miles, in such a manner as to accomplish 200 miles in three days. An amusing contrast certainly to the present year of grace, when a letter dropped into the box at Charing Cross or St. Martin's-le-Grand at 7 p.m. appears on our friend's breakfast-table at Glasgow or Edinburgh at 9 next morning.

It is only fair to the credit of foreign cities to say here that, if we may believe some antiquaries, our "postal system" is not of English origin, though we have improved upon the idea we imported from abroad. They tell us that the first establishment of a letter post was the work of the Hanse towns, early in the thirteenth century ; that these were followed by a line of posts connecting Austria with Lombardy, in the reign of the Emperor Maximilian ; and that another line of posts from Vienna to Brussels joined together the most distant parts of the dominions of Charles V. The representatives of the noble house which was mainly instrumental in establishing these posts, we are told by a writer in " Chambers' Cyclopædia," still continue to enjoy certain rights with regard to the German postal system, their posts being entirely distinct from those established by the crown, and sometimes proving rivals to them.

We hear little of the post during the times of the earlier Tudors; and it is just possible that, as they had succeeded in sweeping away nearly the whole of the Barons who served in the Wars of the Roses, and treated their subjects as serfs and helots, though the printing press had been set up, men had but small use for their pens, or had too many of their own matters to mind, to have leisure to spend on correspondence. Curiously enough too, the post figures but little in the reigns of Edward and Mary, or even in the early part of Elizabeth's reign,* when we should have supposed that the approach of the Spanish Armada would have called it into active play. We glean but scanty notices of its existence, except the fact that a horse-post was established in Ireland during the wars against O'Neill. It would seem that this service ceased with the occasion that had called it into being; but, if it was established temporarily in Ireland, one would fancy it must have been first permanently at work in England.

It appears that as early as 1514 the alien mer-

---

* Camden mentions the office of "Master of the Postes" as existing in 1581, but his duties probably related to the supply of horses only.

chants in London had an office for the transit of their own letters from London to the out-ports; but these gentlemen quarrelled among themselves, and were viewed with great jealousy by the English merchants of the metropolis, for whose benefit Charles I. set on foot a Post Office of his own. This office had at first no connection with our inland towns; and special messengers, called crown couriers, were still employed to carry letters of State.

Afterwards, however, this omission was rectified, and an inland post was organized; and in 1635 the rates of postage for a letter were fixed at twopence under eighty miles, fourpence under one hundred and forty, sixpence for any longer distance in England, and eightpence for the transit of a letter from England to Scotland.

No doubt, in establishing this branch of the civil service, the King saw, or thought he saw, the opportunity of securing a lucrative monopoly to himself, while he conferred a boon upon the people. His faithful Commons, however, do not seem to have regarded the matter wholly in the latter light, for they subjected it to the ordeal of a Parliamentary inquiry; but the new institution came bravely out of this trial, and in 1640 we find a weekly post at work along all the chief lines of road between London and the larger towns. Some four years later, a Mr. Edmund Prideaux was fully established in the chair of control, and at this period the revenue of the department is said to have reached no less a sum than £5,000 a year.

The King, his ministers, his court, and eventually his "trusty and well-beloved cousins" of the Upper House, and the knights and burgesses of the Lower House, successfully claimed—though not without a struggle—the right of sending their letters "free." Hence arose the Parliamentary privilege of "franking," of which we shall have more to say presently. It should be mentioned that in this reign the Common Councilmen of London started a rival post of their own,* but the royal monopoly carried the day against it, and the Londoners were foiled in their attempt.

Many improvements, as might have been expected, were introduced into the Post Office by Oliver Cromwell; but it was only at the Restoration that the system was settled by Act of Parliament, and gained what is called its Charter. The nation at large, however, appears to have got anything but the lion's share in this arrangement; for, though the county gentlemen of Cheshire, or

---

* It appears that even under Charles II. the two Universities and the Cinque Ports were allowed to have "Posts" of their own.

Cornwall, or Northumberland, and the merchants of Bristol and Norwich, received their letters one day in every seven, still the profits of the Post Office, which were £21,000 in 1663, and had risen in 1685 to £65,000, were not carried to the credit of the nation, but were quietly settled, by a right regal job, on the Duke of York, after-wards James II., and his issue.*

In 1710 a further step towards the existing state of things was made by the appointment of a regular "Postmaster General," whose office, though largely modified in succeeding reigns, has remained, on the whole, the same down to the present day, increased of course, both in dignity and salary, as befits a Privy Councillor, and generally a member of Her Majesty's Cabinet.

Up to Queen Anne's time, the headquarters of the Post Office had been Bishopsgate Street,†

* At the time of Lord Canning's first "Report" (1855), the Post Office was still chargeable with three annual pensions to the illegitimate descendants of Charles II., which for more than a century and a half had been a heavy drag on its in-come; viz.: £4,700 to the Duke of Grafton, as representative of the Duchess of Cleveland; and £4000 to the heirs of the Duke of Schomberg; besides these there was a pension of £5000 to the Duke of Marlborough. These had been regu-larly drawn since 1686, 1694, and 1708 respectively. We believe, however, that they are now at an end, having been repurchased for those families by the nation.

† Mr. Timbs, in his "Curiosities of London," tells us that

but now they were transferred to more commodious premises in Lombard Street, where they
remained until our own day. The machinery
at this time may be easily and briefly described.
The London establishment consisted of a Deputy
Postmaster General and seventy-seven clerks;
England and Scotland were worked by one hundred and eighty-two Deputy Postmasters, besides
Sub-postmasters; Ireland, too, had a chief office,
with eighteen clerks, at Dublin, and forty-five
" deputies " scattered over the country; making
in all, at a rough guess, about three hundred and
fifty hands for the whole of the three kingdoms.
The service afloat comprised seven packet-boats
for the Continent, three for Ireland, and two at
Deal for the Downs. Communications were kept
up with some parts of the Continent three times
a week; with others twice; with all parts of

"The General Post Office has had five locations since the
Postmaster of Charles I. fixed his house in Sherborne Lane in
1635, from which dates 'The settling of the Letter Office of
England and Scotland.' The office was next removed to Cloak
Lane, Dowgate; and then to the Black Swan, Bishopsgate
Street. After the great fire in London, the office was shifted
to the Black Pillar in Brydges Street, Covent Garden; thence
early in the last century, to the mansion of Sir Robert Vyner,
in Lombard Street, close to Sherborne Lane. The chief office
was removed to its present site in St. Martin's le Grand in
1829."

England and Scotland three times; with Wales twice; with Ireland once; and with Kent and the Downs daily. All those parts of the Service which involved a sea-passage were most uncertain as to time, being dependent on wind, tide, and weather. The inland Post went night and day at an average rate of five miles an hour, except in bad weather, when the pack-horse tracks across the country, and not unfrequently the great high roads as well, became impassable.

Coming down from that day to the present, we find the total staff of the Postal Establishment estimated at some 25,000 hands, of whom above 4,000 are employed in London; the number of post offices and letter boxes exceed 15,000; the cost of the packet service amounts to more than a million; and that of the railway service to half a million more; while the sea service—thanks to steam—is performed at an average of ten, and the railway service at forty miles an hour.

The advance made in this period is "prodigious," as Dominie Sampson would say; but, after all, it is insignificant when compared with the progress made in the first sixty years after the accession of the first Stuart to the English throne. As Mr. Robert Bell remarks, "When once the idea of a Post Office was developed and set in motion, its expansion was an inevitable corollary from the increase of population and the march of popular knowledge. The wonder really would have been if the Post Office, the heart of our system of circulation, had not kept pace with the progress of other things. But the advance from the absence of all postal institutions to the establishment of a regular system by which communication was opened up, not only throughout all parts of the kingdom even before the interior was intersected by roads, but with the whole continent of Europe, was an advance entirely different in kind. It was not an improvement upon anything that had existed before, as the Post Office of Victoria is an improvement on the Post Office of Charles II., but the absolute creation of something never previously known to exist in the country; like the introduction of gas to light our houses, in place of the miserable oil-lamps and tallow candles with which our grand-fathers were content."

It is strange to think that, while the Post Office was employed in keeping up a connection between distant parts of England and the Continent, no one thought of applying it to the internal traffic and intercourse of our large cities.

It is the opinion of most persons that Sir Rowland Hill was the inventor of the Penny Post, but this idea is not correct. He took up the invention at second hand, when it was just a century and a half old. The merit of making this obvious application, or at all events of carrying it into practice, belongs to a *par nobile fratrum*, Messrs. Murray and Dockwra, who, about the year 1680, set up a " Penny Post " in London. We are not sure where its head-quarters were, though Mr. Timbs places them in Lime Street and Wood Street; but certainly they were not connected with the royal establishment in Bishopsgate ; and the Duke of York was induced to appeal to the English law against the invaders of his monopoly. Murray appears to have quarrelled with his partner, or to have abandoned the scheme in alarm; but Dockwra stood his ground manfully; he resisted at law the action by which it was hoped that he would be crushed; and, by taking one or two partners into a share of his venture, he was enabled to gain a victory.

He undertook to forward not only letters, but small packages, several times a day, between all parts of London, Westminster, and the suburbs; and he appears to have carried pill-boxes and doses of medicine " within the Bills of Mortality " for about the same price charged by his Stuart rival for conveying a letter from London to Oxford. It is probable that what saved Mr.

Dockwra from being annihilated by the jealousy of Royalty was the fact that his seven "district offices" acted as feeders to the great postal system, which had no collecting boxes about the town· It is said that Mr. Dockwra collected the letters every hour, and delivered them at the extremities of his district four or five times a day, and at more central places six or seven times; while at the Inns of Court, particularly during term and in the session of Parliament, he had no less than ten deliveries daily. In order to make the public sensible of the advantages which he offered, he had placards hung out at his receiving houses with the words "Penny Post Letters taken in here;" prepaid letters were stamped with the word "Paid," and with the hour at which they were dispatched.

At last, however, religious bigotry effected what the law alone could not do; it enabled the public to gain a triumph over the enterprising individual who had risked his fortune in its service. A report was spread abroad by some amiable Whalley or Murphy that Dockwra's office was in the pay of the Jesuits; a case was brought before the Court of King's Bench; and it was ultimately ruled that Mr. Dockwra had infringed the royal patent. He was also accused of "hazarding the lives of patients many times

when physic is sent by a doctor or apothecary."
He was therefore not only stripped of his property, but cast in heavy costs and damages,
leaving behind him a moral to others to " Be careful how they do anything to benefit their fellow-
countrymen."   In the end, however, he got from
the Government, if not justice, at all events some
recognition of his services in the shape of a pension of £200 a year, and the office of Controller
of the London District Post.   A few years later,
in 1708, a halfpenny Post Office was started in
the metropolis, but, like its precursor, it was put
down by the high hand of the law.

The next person whom history connects with
the Post Office is Ralph Allen—of Prior Park,
the friend of Pope—one who deserves to be
called, in more senses than one, a " man of
letters ;" as he spent his gains in works of charity
and hospitality, especially to men of learning.
Up to this time the internal postage communication of this country had been confined to the
work of connecting London with the largest and
most important country towns, such as Bristol,
Chester, and Exeter, while there were no means
of sending a letter direct from Oxford to Buckingham, from Canterbury to Margate, or from
Salisbury to Southampton.   It was Ralph Allen
who suggested the the idea of " cross posts," as

they were called; and being a man of capital, and of sound sense, into the bargain, he obtained a government contract, under which he "farmed" them at a profit of some £12,000 a-year. This scheme was first adopted about the year 1720, and it was only at the close of the last century that the "cross posts" were absorbed into the general postal system. It was calculated that at that time their income was some £200,000 a-year.

The third and last person of whom we have to speak in connection with the Post Office is Mr. John Palmer, the well known manager of the Bath Theatre, who, about eighty years ago, first broached to Mr. Pitt the idea that the "Post," instead of being carried by boys on horseback, might be sent long distances by coach. It may sound strange to our ears that such an idea should have been a novelty to our grandfathers, and that for the work of accelerating the said post from an average speed of less than four miles to over six miles an hour, Mr. Palmer should have been first told that he was not wanted any longer, and afterwards should have received a reward—though only after many memorials and petitions, and a long weary struggle with the nation—in the shape of a Parliamentary grant of £50,000. Such however, was really the case.

We have alluded to the "franking" monopoly, which commenced with the era of the Civil War. It was not conceded, in the first instance, without much demur and a squabble between the two Houses of Parliament, and it was always unpopular with the nation. The loss to the revenues of the office arising from it was estimated in the reign of Queen Anne at £17,000, and at £38,000 in that of George II. In 1764, a public complaint being made that the signatures of members of both Houses of Parliament, on blank half-sheets of paper, were sold at a fixed tariff by peers' and members' servants, and that a regular trade was carried on in them, it was ordained that the entire address should be written by the same hand with the signature; and in 1784, with a view to limiting the loss to the revenue arising from this privilege, an Act was passed compelling each letter to bear, in addition, the date of the month, day, and year, and also the place at which it was posted, all in the same handwriting; the franker being limited to the right of sending only ten "franks" per diem, and receiving fifteen letters free of cost.

A host of stories are told about this franking privilege. At one time a noble Lord would send a haunch of venison* "free" to his brother

* We have seen a letter cover addressed by Lord Maynard

or his solicitor; another peer would dispatch his wife's silk gown "free" to her ladyship's dress-maker for alterations; while a third, who held the office of Postmaster-General, and therefore could "do what he liked with his own depart-ment," dispatched a whole pack of hounds, at the rate of a brace a day, at the cost of the nation. In like manner George Canning is said to have sent all the volumes of Clarendon's "History of the Great Rebellion," to a friend in Ireland.

The signatures of the various members of the Houses of Lords and Commons being written in the corner of all "franked" letters, the covers in the course of time came to be objects of interest as autographs; and just before the aboli-tion of the privilege in 1840, almost as many young ladies were employed in collecting "franks" as have since been busied in collecting foreign postage stamps. At all events, the fair collectors had an admirable guarantee of the genuineness of each signature, in the shape of the "free" post mark impressed on every franked letter which passed through St. Martin's-le-Grand. The penny Post system of Sir Rowland Hill knocked this pretty mania for ever on the head; and "franks"

about 1740, in the corner of which is written, "This free with a Buck."

are now sought after by none but antiquaries and "worshippers of relics."

It will be within the remembrance of very many of our readers that when, some thirty years ago, the public clamoured so loudly for the adoption of Rowland Hill's "Penny Post System," there were persons sanguine enough to declare their belief that the change would be found to show a profit from the very first year, while a large number of grumblers and prophets of evil declared that the nation was throwing away a sure source of income for the chance of most uncertain gain, and that very many years—perhaps a century—must elapse before it would stand, financially, where it stood before. As usual, the truth lay between the two extremes: the author of the scheme himself augured that the change would pay, but not immediately, and pay handsomely, too, if the country only had the courage to wait.*

It is pleasant to look back upon this result as long since acheived, and to be able to tell our readers that it was achieved in fifteen years ; that the net profits of the department, which in 1858 were £347,000, had risen in 1862 to nearly £832,000 ; and that, showing a steady annual rise with scarcely a single drawback, last year they exceeded £1,421,000, and this year or next

* This augury has long since been verified. (1879.)

will probably touch a million and a-half. When
we add to this the fact that a corresponding steady
increase is to be noticed in all the various
branches of the service; that the correspondence
of the nation at large had risen from about 24
letters per head in 1865 and the following year,
to 26 last year; that the Money Order Office
has opened 271 additional local offices in the last
two years, and that its issues in 1867 were nearly
£565,000 against £417,000 in 1865; that the
number of receiving houses and pillar-boxes has
been growing in a greater ratio than the increase
of either inhabited houses or the population; that
the gross total of articles carried by the post,
rose from 851,000,000 in 1866 to 877,000,000 in
1867; that the number of post towns and of free
deliveries during the same time has been largely
increased, while the rates of foreign postage, in
several cases, have been reduced, we cannot but
congratulate the Postmaster-General on the "tottle" of financial results which he is able to chronicle, and cry aloud again, "God bless the Dukes
of Argyle and Montrose!" In one single item,
only, so far as we can discover, the last Post
Office Report shows a falling off, and that—
strange to say—is a matter for congratulation·
The letters compulsorily registered as containing
coin had fallen from 33,000 in 1866 to 28,000

in 1867; and it is to be hoped that the silly and wicked practice of tempting our postmen and Post Office clerks to acts of dishonesty, by enclosing coin in letters instead of using Post Office orders, will shortly be a thing of the past.

If we were in Italy, instead of in England, the Post Office, like every other department of the state, would be sure to be put under the protection and patronage of some saint or other, real or imaginary. We shall not be suspected of any tendency to Popery if we suggest that St. Valentine should certainly be established as the guardian saint of our postal system, and be honoured with a statue in St. Martin's le Grand.

Twenty years ago, not 20,000 valentines were sent annually; but in 1865, no less than 820,000 valentines, or letters presumed to be such, were delivered in London alone; in 1866 this number rose to 997,000; and in 1867 to 1,119,142.

The return for 1868 is not yet made public. Valentines sent *from* London to the country are in the proportion of two to one sent from the country to London; this may be explained by the cheap manufacture of such articles, and their large and ready sale among the servant girls and milliners' and dress-makers' apprentices; but it is curious, and not so readily to be accounted for at first sight, that the valentines posted in the Western district of London are greatly in excess of those posted in any other of the postal districts. The real fact, we suppose, is that the butchers and grocers of Whitechapel, and the small shopmen of Lambeth and Southwark, have less time on their hands than the dwellers in Marylebone and St. George's, Hanover Square. It is satisfactory to know that this St. Valentine is a profitable saint, and will have no grounds for many a long year for sending round a begging box, having brought into our coffers, in London alone, £9,354 in 1866, and £11,242 in 1867. If we go on at the present rate of increase, in a century or so we shall have swept off the heavy incumbrances which the Post Office has had to pay to the Fitzroys and other descendants of Charles II. and his many mistresses.

Let us now pick up from Lord Canning's Reports, and from other sources, a few scraps of information respecting the Post Office, past and present; desultory they may be, but they will not on that account be wholly void of interest. For instance, we find that the loss to the revenue by franking, which in Queen Anne's time was £17,000, and in that of George II. £38,000, was estimated by Sir Rowland Hill, in 1838, two years before its abolition, at little short of a million; the letters thus sent free amounting to about seven millions, or about thirty per cent. of the whole number that passed through the post.

Again, we learn that in [the early part of the last century, a "despatch" from London to Plymouth took nearly three days on the road; and even as late as between 1730 and 1740, the mail for Edinburgh left London only three times a week, and was equally long in performing the journey, which now, thanks to steam, is performed in twelve hours with ease and certainty. How much less in bulk the mails were then than now, may be gathered from the fact that, if we may believe Lord Canning, the Scottish mail once set out on its journey with only a single letter in the bag!

This sounds like a bit of quiet waggery on the part of the Postmaster-General; but it is to a great extent authenticated by the publication of a reward offered in 1779 for the arrest of certain footpads who had robbed the postboy of the contents of the entire northern mail—in other words, of the letters for Birmingham, Shrewsbury, Chester, &c., which then were easily packed up in a little leathern valise, slung across the bearer's shoulders, though now, some ninety years later, they would probably weigh little less than three tons. Scarcely less wonderful, though quite true, is the fact recorded by Macaulay, that the whole revenue of the kingdom, at the accession of William III., fell short of the sum collected by the Post Office in pennies only, within a year or two after the death of William IV.

There are some other stray matters of information and of counsel to which it may be well to direct the attention of our readers before we close this article. It is obvious to remark the close analogy between the daily working of our postal system and the arterial system of our bodies.

London is practically the heart of the world of commerce, and daily it sends forth and receives back into itself again the flood of correspondence on which commerce and trade depend, and which pulsates through every vein and artery of the social fabric from the Land's End to John o' Groat's House, and from Great Yarmouth to Galway and Cape Clear. It may have been, and it probably was, a trifling and unimportant matter for the mail to be stopped on its road to Edinburgh or Birmingham in the days of our fathers or grandfathers, as we have mentioned above; but think for an instant what would be the effect of a like stoppage of that mail now-a-days, even for a single twelve hours !

A century ago the work of the Post Office in London could be discharged by one Postmaster-General, one Accountant-General, and one Receiver-General, each of whom had under him a staff of three clerks—twelve persons in all. Compare this staff with that army of secretaries, assistant-secretaries, surveyors, assistant-survey-ors, inspectors, clerks, and supernumeraries, to say nothing of a host of sorters, stampers,* and letter carriers, who all look up to the Postmaster-General as their Field-Marshal, and to whom his word is law.

As the whole staff of the Post Office work so steadily and industriously for the comfort and pleasure, and for the profit also, of ourselves, who, after all, are but a "nation of shopkeepers," it is but fair to lend them a helping hand wherever we can.   And we can do so easily.

It is quite possible for every English man, woman, and child to *write a legible hand* if he or she will take the trouble.   As Lord Palmerston so sensibly told us, we can look to our "up-strokes " as well as our "down-strokes," and form

---

* These "little regicides on a large scale," as we have heard them called, can destroy from 6000 to 7000 "Queen's heads " in an hour.

our letters large, plain, and distinct, as he did. It is quite possible, also, with only a very moderate knowledge of geography, to put the right *post town* on our address instead of contenting ourselves with stating the county. It is quite as easy to write " Preston, Brighton," as " Preston, Sussex," or " Lexden, Colchester," as " Lexden, Essex ;" and, when we address a letter to Newport, or Yarmouth, or Bradford, we can mark which of the two or three towns so named we mean ; for instance, whether " Newport in the Isle of Wight," or " Newport in Cornwall," or " Newport in Essex," or " Newport in Monmouthshire," or " Newport in Shropshire." Then, again, we can send our letters to the post carefully sealed or gummed down, and *addressed* in some way or other. This looks like nonsense; but it really is by no means a superfluous warning ; for the Postmaster-General tells us in his report that " many letters, and even registered letters, are received open, and, in several instances, postage stamps and bank notes are forwarded in registered packets in so careless a manner that they might easily have escaped or have been abstracted." It may be added here that the utter carelessness of correspondents and would-be contributors to magazines and periodicals is notorious, and thoroughly bears out the

implied censure passed on many of our country-
men and countrywomen by the Postmaster-
General in the above remarks.

What will our readers think when we tell them
that, "in the year 1866, no less than 10,400
letters were posted in England and Wales *without
any address at all*;" and that "276 of these were
found to contain cash, notes, bills, and cheques to
the amount in all of £3,670!" Worse even than
this, one old report tells us that about fifteen
years ago a single undirected letter was found to
contain £1,500 in notes.* It is satisfactory to
know that most of this missing property ultimately is restored to its stupid senders, through
the medium of the Dead Letter Office, to which
we venture to suggest, for the consideration of the
Postmaster-General, that such property ought to be
made to pay a toll of five per cent. on the amount,
for the trouble so needlessly caused. We learn that
the sums which cannot be so returned, and remain
unclaimed, are ultimately carried to the credit of
a benefit fund for the working members of the
service. Another piece of advice that we can
give our readers, and for which we shall be much
surprised if we do not receive an autograph letter

---

* It is a matter of congratulation that the 10,000 and odd
persons so exceedingly stupid show what may be called a
sensible decrease on the previous year.

of thanks from the chief of the Department, and possibly a basket of grouse as well, is, that they should use envelopes of an adequate size. Ladies are especially fond of using tiny, toy envelopes, just as they cherish toy terriers and tiny spaniels. Avoid tiny envelopes. "In a single week," says a writer in the *Quarterly Review* (No. 173, June, 1850), "no less than 727 notes had 'pigged' into larger envelopes or newspapers;" and of course they were carried to 727 different and wrong destinations: One toy note—it was only a note of condolence, most fortunately—which ought to have reached Cavendish Square on a Saturday, came back from Ireland, after some four days travelling, just in time for a funeral; but the fate of another tiny and delicate bit of rose-tinted paper, three-cornered in shape, was more serious. It was addressed by Lady ——, from Belgravia, to a gentleman at the —— Club, St. James's, asking him to come next day and help his lordship and herself to eat a haunch of venison. We do not know whether, when in due course the said missive returned from somewhere beyond Inverness, the absent guest got absolved by her ladyship, and came in for the venison when hashed; but we are quite sure that he brought no action against the Postmaster-General for the loss of his dinner; though we would not for the world repeat what he said about her ladyship's stupidity, in the way of blessing or otherwise, when the letter reached him in the smoking-room of his club.

Another rule that we would lay down is, " when practicable, post your letters early." Do not leave all your letters to be thrown into the box just as the mail is being made up. A little thought on this head will save an immense deal of trouble within the office. Again, those who wish to save the letter-carrier's time and trouble should have letter-boxes to their doors.

Of all rules, perhaps the most important, however, is that of " spelling correctly." The *Times* told us not very long ago, that a letter addressed " Sromfredevi," once reached Sir Humphrey Davy, and another, directed " Nerth Ewysis," found its owner in the neighbourhood of Devizes. So, too, we have heard of a letter addressed, " March 25th, London," reaching a certain Lady Day, though the story may be apocryphal; as may also be that of the little boy who was successful in his object when in the simplicity of his heart he inscribed his envelope, " For my mamma, London." But really it is not just to ride a willing horse to death; neither is it fair to add to the work of a department to whose clerks Lord Palmerston's jest concerning those of Downing Street will *not* apply, namely, that, "like the fountains in Trafalgar Square, they play from ten till four, and then do nothing for the rest of the day." To express one's self in the words of the *Times*, " Enigmas of this kind are an unnecessary addition to the labours of a department of the public service, even though it is kind enough to keep at hand an Œdipus to read the riddles which every careless and ill-taught Sphinx may choose to set before him to be solved."

A SUMMER DAY IN HYDE PARK.
(1865.)

NOW that the inhabitants of Belgravia and Tyburnia have betaken themselves to the moors to look after the grouse and the partridges, let us, gentle reader, take a quiet stroll in Hyde Park, without as much fear of being ridden down by Miss Di Vernon, or driven over by Lady Aspasia, as we might have felt a week or two ago. Hyde Park has a past as well as a present; and let us see if we cannot dress up its past history into a pleasant and readable paper, for the Park has seen many great scenes and many great personages since it first obtained its name.

Everyone, we imagine, is aware that Hyde Park lies, as the London guide-books tell us, " in the county of Middlesex, and hundred of Ossulston, within the liberties of the city of Westminster, about four miles west of St. Paul's

Cathedral;" but all may not be equally aware of
the fact that the ancient Roman military way, the
"Watling Street," passed across Hyde Park, and
thence through St. James's Park, to the Thames
close by Old Palace Yard; nor may they know
that the park derives its name, not from Hyde,
Earl of Clarendon, but from the manor of Hyde,
which belonged to the abbot and monks of St.
Peter's, at Westminster, from a date which carries
us at all events back nearly to the Conquest.
Among the records of the Abbey there are to be
found court rolls of the manor of Hyde during the
reigns of the Edwards; but little else is known of
it till the time of Henry VIII., when, like many
other places, it reverted to the Crown. As soon
as it was enclosed, it appears to have been pro-
moted from a manor into a park, with a "keeper,"
who eventually was dignified with the title of
"ranger." The first keeper on record was George
Roper, Esq., whose pay was sixpence a day! In
1554 the office was divided, and the salary raised
to fourpence a day, with pasturage for twelve
cows, one bull, and six oxen. The keepership
appears to have been held successively by Carey,
Lord Hunsdon; Robert Cecil, Earl of Salisbury;
Sir Walter Cope; Sir Henry Rich; and the Earl of
Newport. This was before the Rebellion; but three
years after the death of Charles, it was "re-

solved that Hyde Park be sold for ready money."
The Park, as we learn from the printed particulars
of the sale, was put up in three lots, the whole
621 acres which it then contained realising
£17,068 6s. 8d.   At the Restoration, the Park
came back into royal hands, and Charles II. gave
the keepership, with the title of ranger, to his
brother, the Duke of Gloucester; and he was succeeded by Colonel James Hamilton, one of the
grooms of the bedchamber, after whose widow,
Mrs. Elizabeth Hamilton, the houses built near
Park Lane were called Hamilton Place.   It
appears from an indenture still extant that this
Colonel Hamilton was anxious to do a little business with the King on his own account, as he
states that he has undertaken to plant fifty-five
acres of the ground with choice and fit apple-trees
—pippins and red-streaks—in order to supply
His Majesty with cider.

King Charles I., it appears, had been anxious
to have had Hyde Park surrounded with a
wall, " as well for the honour of his palace and
great city as for his own disport and recreation ;"
but it was not till his son's days that it was
stocked with deer and walled round.   The list of
subsequent rangers includes William Harbord,
Esq., ancestor of Lords Suffield; the Earls of
Bath and Jersey; Mr. Portman; the Earls of

Essex, Pomfret, Ashburnham, Oxford, and Euston ; Viscount Weymouth, Lord Grenville, Viscount Sydney, the Duke of Sussex, and the Duke of Cambridge.

Our readers may be interested at learning that Hyde Park once was strongly fortified. At Hyde Park Corner stood a large fort with four bastions, erected in 1642, when the city and suburbs were fortified by trenches and ramparts, in anticipation of an attack by the royal army ; another fort was also erected at Oliver's Mount, close to Mount Street· The enthusiasm prevailing at this period was carried to such an extent that the whole population appear to have assisted in the trenches ; detachments from all trades relieved each other at intervals. The work proceeded night and day without intermission : even women and children partook of the general feeling, which is facetiously alluded to by Butler, in " Hudibras," Part II., Canto 2 ; and in a note by Nash it is stated that " ladies of rank and fortune, not only encouraged the men, but worked with their own hands ; Lady Middlesex, Lady Foster, Lady Anne Waller, and Mrs. Dunch having been particularly celebrated for their activity."

During the reigns of James and Charles I., Hyde Park appears to have been a place of fashionable amusement ; but although the Park was in 1632 said to be " then lately thrown open," it does not appear that the public were admitted indiscriminately. The amusements provided for the company comprised horse-racing, foot-racing, morris-dancing, &c.; refreshments were also to be procured, such as wines, syllabubs, &c., at the lodge, which bore the sign of the " Grave Prince Maurice's Head." In one of Shirley's plays entitled " Hide Park," licensed in 1632, first printed in 1637, and dedicated to Henry Rich, Earl of Holland, at that time Keeper, the following allusion to the sports occur in various scenes :—

Act II. Scene 2.

LACY. Prithee stay; we'll to Hide Park together.

BONAVENT. There you may meet with morriss-dancers.

Act. III. Scene 1.

LORD B. Lady, you are welcome to the spring ; the Park
  Looks fresher to salute you ; how the birds
  On every tree sing with more cheerfulness
  At your access, as if they prophesied
  Nature would die, and resign her providence
  To you, fit only to succeed her !

JUL. You express
  A master of all compliment; I have
  Nothing but plain humility, my Lord,
  To answer you.

BONAVENT. Be there any races here ?

LACY. Yes, Sir, horse and foot.

BONAVENT. You'll give me leave to take my course then.

And again, in a comedy called the "Merry Beggars, or, Jovial Crew" (1641), we find the question asked, "Shall we make a fling to London, and see how the spring appears there in Spring Garden, and in Hyde Park to see the races horse and foot?"

Though horse-racing was voted sinful by the Puritan party, yet Hyde Park appears to have been still a centre of attraction, such profane sports being superseded by athletic exercises. The ring also—the entrance to which may still be traced—was even then the favourite resort of equestrians, male and female; and elegant carriages were driven there by irreligious cavaliers and their ladies, in spite of the severe and canting criticisms of the press, as will be seen by the following paragraphs:—

"HYDE PARK, May 1.—This day there was a hurling of a great ball, by fifty Cornish gentlemen on the one side, and fifty on the other; one party played in red caps and the other in white. There was present, His Highness the Lord Protector, many of his Privy Council, and divers eminent gentlemen, to whose view was presented great agility of body, and most neat and exquisite wrestling, at every meeting of one with the other, which was ordered with such dexterity, that it was to show more the strength, vigour, and nimbleness of their bodies, than to endanger their persons. The ball they played withall was silver, and designed for that party which did win the goal.—*Moderate Intelligencer, 26th of April to the 3rd of May, 1654.*"

" MONDAY, May 1, 1654.— This day was more observed by people's going a Maying, than for divers years past, and indeed much sin committed by wicked meeting, with fiddlers, drunkenness, ribaldry, and the like ; great resort came to Hyde Park, many hundreds of rich coaches, and gallants in attire; but most shameful powdered-hair men, and painted and spotted women ; some men played with a silver ball, and some took other recreation. But His Highness the Lord Protector went not thither, nor any of the Lords of the Council, but were busie about the great affairs of the Commonwealth, and among other things, had under consultation how to advance trade for the good of the people with all speed that might be, and other great affairs for the good of the Commonwealth.—*Several Proceedings of State Affairs, 29th of April to the 4th of May, 1654.*"

In defiance of the puritanical cant displayed in the above account, it is well known that the wily

Cromwell paid great attention to the breeding of
race-horses; he possessed a celebrated stallion
named White Turk; and he had also an equally
famous brood-mare, afterwards called the coffin-
mare, from the circumstance of her being concealed in a vault during the search for his effects
after the Restoration; the name of his stud-groom
was Place, a conspicuous character in those days.

Hyde Park was the scene of an accident which,
by all accounts, nearly cost the Protector his
life, though the papers give different versions of
the matter, some asserting that his Highness
was inside his coach when it upset, while
others declared that he had got upon the box in
a frolic, and suffered severely in consequence.
The Dutch Ambassador, quoted in Thurloe's
" State Papers," Vol. II. p. 652, says that he was
" flung out of the coach-box upon the pole . . . .
and afterwards fell upon the ground . . . . during
which time a pistol went off in his pocket . . . .
He was presently brought home and let blood."
The " Faithful Scout," a journal of the day, thinks
it necessary to apologise for His Highness being
seated on the box, which it justifies by the examples of the heroes of old. The following lines,
which we take from a " Collection of Loyal Songs
printed at the Restoration, and reprinted in
1781," (Vol. II. p. 281), refer to this event.

"Nol, a rank rider, got fast in the saddle,
  And made her shew tricks, and curvet, and rebound;
She quickly perceived he rode widdle-waddle,
  And his coach-horse His Highness it threw to ground.
Then Dick, being lame, rode holding the pummel,
  Not having the wit to get hold of the rein;
But the jade did so snort at the sight of a Cromwell
  That poor Dick and his kindred turned footmen again."

There would seem to have been some fatality about Oliver Cromwell's visit to Hyde Park; at all events in February 1656, we find Myles Syndercombe tried for high treason and sentenced to be hanged at Tyburn, for an attempt to assassinate the Protector in Hyde Park; an attempt which was prevented only by the merest accident from being fatal.

Five years later, in 1659, we find Hyde Park thus described by a foreign gentleman in "The Characters of England," a "Letter to a Nobleman in France," p. 54.

"Did frequently accompany my Lord N—— into a field near the town, which they call Hyde Park; the place is not unpleasant, and which they use as our course, but with nothing of that order, equipage and splendour; being such an assembly of wretched jades and hackney-coaches, as, next to a regiment of carmen, there is nothing approacheth the resemblance. This parke was, it seems, used by the late King and nobility for the freshness of the air and the goodly prospect; but it is that which now (besides all other exercises) they pay for hire in England, though it be free for all the world besides; every coach and horse which enters buying his mouthful and permission of the publican who has purchased it, for which the entrance is guarded with porters and long staves."

From chance expression in Evelyn's and Pepys' Diaries, too, we learn that money was at this time taken for admission into the Park, and that the character of its amusements was not a whit more reputable than those of the last century at Belsize or Marylebone Gardens, or of our own century at Vauxhall and Cremorne.

It should be mentioned that at one time Charles II. contemplated the erection of the National Observatory in Hyde Park, though his design was set aside by Sir Christopher Wren, who recommended Greenwich Park as a better situation.

We are not going to inflict on our readers a history of all the springs and water-pipes in Hyde Park which have been the subject of grants and litigation at various times; but we will remind them that the broad lake which is now named or misnamed the " Serpentine " was originally a narrow winding brook, which drained the uplands of

Hampstead through Kilburn and Paddington, and was gradually widened into its present expanse of water by order of Queen Charlotte, who took the greatest interest in this ornament of the Park.

It is not very long since a circular basin or reservoir of water stood on the east side of the Park, nearly opposite to the entrance of Mount Street; but it has lately been drained off and the site converted into a flower-garden. The ugly engine-house which adjoined the basin was taken down as far back as 1835, when its materials were sold by auction. Between this reservoir and Grosvenor Gate stood the Duke of Gloucester's Riding School, which having been occupied by leave of the Government as the head-quarters of the Westminster Volunteer Cavalry, was taken down about the year 1824. After that its site was occupied by a temporary wooden building, in which some of our readers may remember to have seen exhibited a picture of the battle of Waterloo by Sir John Pieneman, principal painter to the King of the Netherlands.

Walnut-tree walk, which extended nearly the whole length of the Park from Hyde Park Cor-ner towards Cumberland Gate, consisted of two rows of magnificent walnut trees, shading a broad gravel walk near Grosvenor Gate; these trees formed a circle, the area of which will be readily imagined when the reader is informed that the reservoir of the Chelsea Water-Works, which was placed in the centre of this circle, stood ninety feet from the nearest tree. This splendid grove was consigned to the axe during the war against Napoleon about the end of the last century, the wood being required by Government to be used in the manufacture of stocks for soldiers' muskets.

It is said, and most probably with truth, that the gate at the corner of Piccadilly is the oldest entrance into the Park; Grosvenor Gate was opened in 1724, Stanhope Gate about the middle of the last century, Cumberland Gate in 1774-5, and Albert Gate in the present reign.

The inhabitants of London have always been especially jealous of any encroachments on the part of the Crown and the Government on the Parks, which, though in theory they belong to Her Majesty, are regarded by the people at large practically as national property, and therefore not to be profaned by surveyors and builders. Accordingly we find that when, in 1808, it was recommended to raise about £2,500 by ground-rents, giving building leases for nine handsome houses on the west of Park Lane, between Grosvenor Gate and Brook Street, so great an outcry was raised against the proposal, both in the House of Commons and outside, that the plan was abandoned. It is quite recently, comparatively speaking, that the stone wall which ran along the north side of the Park, shutting it off from the Uxbridge Road, has been superseded by light iron rails, though that improvement was suggested so far back as 1826; and it is only within the last ten or twelve years that flower-gardens have sprung up in the place of dull and dreary groves of elms with wet soil beneath them, wholly bare of grass, and soppy with perpetual puddles.

It is well known to all our readers, no doubt, that Tyburn turnpike stood close to the north-east corner of the Park, and that consequently the latter has been the scene of the death throes of many a distinguished criminal besides Lord Ferrers and Dr. Dodd. At all events, in the "Particulars of Sale" already alluded to, we find mention of a parcel of ground, "formerly used as a meadow," and called "Tyburn Meadow," which was the scene of the execution of two individuals—one of them no less a personage than the Chief Justice of the King's Bench—for high treason. Many a poor "seminary" and "missionary" priest of the Catholic Church breathed his last at Tyburn under the Tudors and Stuarts as a traitor, in consequence of the severity of the penal laws against papists, and the intense jealousy felt against foreign ecclesiastics. It is perhaps less generally known that all military criminals who were sentenced to death by court-martial were taken to a spot just within the wall of Hyde Park, and there suffered death by being shot; this spot is identified by a stone, against which the delinquent was placed when about to pay the forfeit of his life, and which was visible till within these last few years. The situation of this stone is laid down in a Plan of Hyde Park, which was once, and perhaps still is, at Kew Palace; it was situated only a few yards from Cumberland Gate; and when this entrance to the Park was enlarged for public convenience, by the munificence of a private individual, and it became necessary to raise the ground for that purpose, this stone was found to be so deeply embedded in the earth that, to prevent trouble, the earth was carried over it, and it now lies buried on the spot where it was originallly placed.

Military punishment, by flogging, was also inflicted in Hyde Park. In 1716, the fear of the "Pretender," and the rigid measures adopted for punishing his suspected adherents, were carried to great excess; even the wearing oaken boughs on the 29th of May, in commemoration of the Restoration, was construed into an insult to the reigning Government, and several persons were apprehended and committed to prison for indulging in this display. On the 6th of August of that year, two soldiers were flogged almost to death in Hyde Park, and turned out of the service with every mark of infamy and disgrace, for having worn oak-boughs in their hats on Oak-Apple day !

Our readers must not forget that " Tyburn Meadow" was also the ultimate destination of Oliver Cromwell himself, though the fact of his interment here is denied. At all events, we take the following from a MS. diary of Mr. Edward Sainthill, a Spanish merchant of the middle of the seventeenth century :—

" The 30th January, being that day twelve years from the death of the King, the odious carcases of Oliver Cromwell, Major-General Ireton and Bradshaw were drawn on sledges to Tyburn, where they were hanged by the neck, from morning till four in the afternoon; Cromwell in a green seare-cloth, very fresh, enbalmed; Ireton having been buried long, hung like a dried rat, yet corrupted about the body ; Bradshaw, in his winding-sheet, the fingers of his right hand and nose perished, having wet the sheet through; the rest very perfect, insomuch that I knew his face when the hangman, after cutting his head off, held it up; of his toes, I had five or six in my hand, which the prentices had cut off. Their bodies were thrown into a hole under the gallows, in their seare-cloth and sheet. Cromwell had eight cuts, Ireton four, being seare-cloths; and their heads were set up on the south end of Westminster hall."

Hyde Park has also been used at various times for the purposes of military encampments, as we learn from history. Thus, for example—

"1648, Dec 2—The Parliament army marched up to London, and were encamped in Hyde Park; and St. James's.

"1665.—The troops under the command of General Monk were encamped in Hyde Park. The General remained in London during the whole year of the Plague.

"1715.—His Majesty's regiments of Horse and Foot Guards, with a train of Artillery from the Tower, were encamped here, extensive preparations being made in various part of the kingdom, in anticipation of an invasion by the Pretender.

"1722.—The Household troops encamped here were reviewed by His Majesty George I. on the 11th of June, who was afterwards magnificently entertained by General the Earl of Cadogan, the commanding officer, in a pavilion which had been formerly taken from the Grand Vizier by Prince Eugene. His Majesty was accompanied on this occasion by the prince, a numerous staff, and a majority of the nobility.

" Troops, both horse and foot, were encamped here in March, 1739; other forces were also encamped at the same time on Hounslow Heath and Blackheath, in pursuance of an order issued from the Horse Guards on the 8th of February preceding.

" Troops of the line were also encamped in Hyde Park, in the year 1780, in order to assist in suppressing the riots which had been excited by the fanatical intemperance of Lord George Gordon, and which by the pusillanimous conduct of the Lord Mayor and constituted authorities, had been allowed to increase to such an alarming extent that the executive Government found it necessary to draw troops from the provinces to the amount of 30,000 men, before order was restored in the metropolis and the suburbs."

The Park has also been used from time immemorial for reviews and other military spectacles, and although there is not sufficient room for the execution of manœuvres on a large scale, yet these reviews have frequently been graced by the presence of Royalty. The earliest instance of the Park being put to this use is to be found in the year of the Restoration.—" The Commissioners of the Militia of London, in pursuance of an order of the Council of State, appointed on Tuesday the 24th of April, to rendezvous their regiments of train-bands and auxiliaries at Hyde Park, Major Cox, Quarter-Master General of the City, hath since, by their order, been to view the ground, and hath allotted a place to be erected for the reception of the Lord Mayor, the Court of Aldermen, and the Commissioners for the militia. The Lord Mayor intends to appear there with his collar of esses, and all the aldermen in scarlet robes, attended with the mace and cap of maintenance, as is usual at great solemnities.* The household troops also are continually exercised there, as being the most convenient spot close to the metropolis and the Palace. Evelyn's " Diary" and Pepys' " Memoirs" will supply abundant other instances of these military spectacles being held in Hyde Park. For instance :—

" 1663, July 4.—I saw His Majesty's guards, being of horse and foote 4000, led by the General, the Duke of Albemarle, in extraordinary

* *Mercurius Publicus*, 19th April to 26th April, 1660.

equipage and gallantry, consisting of gentlemen of quality and veteran soldiers, excellently clad, and mounted and ordered, drawn up in battalia before their Majesties in Hide Park, where the old Earle of Cleveland trail'd a pike and led the right-hand file in a foote company commanded by the Lord Wentworth his son, a worthy spectacle and example, being both of them old and valiant souldiers. This was to show the French Ambassador, Monsieur Comminges; there being a greate assembly of coaches, &c. in ye park."—*Evelyn's Diary*, Vol. II. p. 208.

" 1663, July 4—To the King's Head Ordinary. Thence with Creed to hire a coach to carry us to Hide Park, to-day there being a general muster of the King's Guards, horse and foot."—*Pepys' Memoirs*, Vol. II. p. 68.

" 1668, September 16.—When I came to St. James's, I find the Duke of York gone with the King, to see the muster of the Guards in Hide Park; and their Colonell, the Duke of Monmouth, to take his command this day of the King's Life Guards, by surrender of my Lord Gerard. So I took a hackney coach, and saw it all: and indeed it was mighty noble, and their firing mighty fine, and the Duke of Monmouth in mighty rich clothes; but the well-ordering of the men I understand not. Here, among a thousand coaches

that were there, I saw and spoke to Mrs Pierce."
—*Pepys' Memoirs* Vol. IV. p. 170.

"1676, March 16.—I was at a review of the
army about London, in Hide Park, about 6,000
horse and foote, in excellent order; His Majesty
and infinity of people being present."—*Pepys'
Memoirs*, Vol. III. p. 205.

Pope also, in the following notice, shows that
the taste of the ladies a century and a half ago
was the same as in our own days, when they go
off to Aldershot or Shorncliff.

"Women of quality are all turned followers of
the camp in Hyde Park this year, whither all the
town resort to magnificent entertainments given
by the officers, &c. The Scythian ladies that
dwelt in the waggons of war were not more
closely attached to the luggage. The matrons,
like those of Sparta, attend their sons to the field,
to be witnesses of their glorious deeds, and the
maidens, with all their charms displayed, provoke
the spirit of the soldiers. Tea and coffee supply
the place of Lacedemonian black broth. This
camp seems crowned with perpetual victory, for
every sun that rises in the thunder of cannon,
sets in the music of violins. Nothing is yet
wanting but the constant presence of the Princess

to represent the *Mater Exercitus.*"—*Letters to Digby, No. XII.*

There are perhaps some few Volunteers still living who remember King George III. reviewing the Volunteer troops in Hyde Park, in October 1803, a display of which the daily and weekly press gave full accounts. More recently, the same place was the scene of a magnificent review of the cavalry and infantry, and Volunteer troops, in 1814, in the presence of the Prince Regent and the Allied Sovereigns; and we ourselves have more than once seen a similar spectacle within its boundaries. At coronations, public victories, and on other grand occasions, Hyde Park has always been the great centre of festivities in the way of fireworks and fairs.

One kind of adventures the Park has happily long ceased to witness; we allude to those duels which disgraced the age of our fathers and grandfathers; and when we have given a passing notice of some of the most celebrated of these, we shall bring this paper to a conclusion.

It appears that between the years 1760 and 1821, one hundred and seventy duels have been fought (including three hundred and forty-four individuals), that sixty-nine persons were killed; that in three of these, neither of the combatants survived; that ninety-six were wounded, eight of them desperately, and forty-eight slightly, and that one hundred and eighty-eight escaped unhurt. It will thus be seen that rather more than one-fifth of the combatants lost their lives, and that nearly one-half received the bullets of their antagonists. It appears also that only eighteen trials took place; that six of the arraigned were acquitted, seven found guilty of manslaughter, and three of murder; that two were executed, and eight imprisoned during different periods.

In November, 1712, the Duke of Hamilton and Lord Mohun "met" in Hyde Park. They fought with swords, and with such ferocity that Mohun was killed on the spot, and the Duke expired before he could be conveyed to the keeper's house. The cause of the duel was said to be a dispute on the subject of a law-suit between the rival families; but violent party politics no doubt produced a termination so sanguinary. The Duke of Hamilton was leader of the Tories, and suspected by the Whigs of favouring the Stuart cause; he had also been appointed Ambassador Extraordinary to the Court of France, at which the Whigs were much exasperated. Lord Mohun was an experienced duellist, and had killed two antagonists in previous combats; he was, moreover, called "the Hector of the Whig party;" and it was generally believed had been selected to pick a quarrel with the Duke, and thus to prevent him from proceeding on his mission. The Duke of Marlborough, who was also publicly blamed as the author of all this mischief, immediately retired to the continent, whither he was shortly followed by his Duchess.

In 1773, John Wilkes fought with pistols, in Hyde Park, with Mr. Samuel Martin, M.P., the duel having arisen out of a paragraph, written by Mr. Wilkes, in the *North Briton*, the author of which Mr. Martin denounced in the House of Commons as "a stabber in the dark, a cowardly and malignant scoundrel." Mr. Wilkes was severely wounded, receiving his adversary's shot in the belly, with which—no wonder!—he "declared himself satisfied."

In 1770, we read of a more harmless duel fought in Hyde Park, between George Garrick and Mr. Baddeley. Mr. Garrick having received the fire of his antagonist, fired his pistol in the air, which produced a reconciliation between the principals. Mr. G. Garrick was the brother of the celebrated tragedian, David Garrick ; and the memory of Mr. Baddeley is preserved by a sum of money which he bequeathed for the purpose of a Twelfth-cake, to be drawn for annually by the performers at Drury Lane Theatre.

In 1780, we find Lord Shelburne engaged here in a duel with Colonel Fullarton, M.P. for Plympton, by whom he was severely wounded; and a " student at law," whose name is not given, fighting with the Rev. H. Bate (afterwards Sir Henry Bate-Dudley), with whom he had quarrelled on account of some circumstances connected with the *Morning Post.* Two years later, in 1782, another clergyman, the Rev. Mr. Allen, fought with and mortally wounded Mr. L. Dulany, for which he was afterwards tried at Newgate, and sentenced to a fine of one shilling and six months' imprisonment. Here, also, the cause of strife was an article penned by Mr. Allen in the *Morning Post* some three years previously.

In 1786, General Stewart and Lord Macartney fought at the end of Hyde Park next Kensington Gardens. The duel arose out of personal ill-will on the part of the General. Lord Macartney was severely wounded, but subsequently recovered.

In October, 1797, was fought perhaps the most celebrated of all duels, the scene of which was laid in Hyde Park, between Colonel King and Colonel Fitzgerald; the circumstances of it are recorded as follows in an account published a few years afterwards.

" The distressing circumstances attending this

duel caused a great sensation at the time in the public mind. The facts are as follows :—It appears that Colonel Fitzgerald had seduced the Hon. Miss King, daughter of Lord Kingsborough, at the same time being married to a lady who was second cousin to Miss King, and had caused her to elope with him from Lady Kingsborough, her mother, who resided at Windsor. The lady, having been discovered after great difficulty, was forcibly taken home to her friends.

" As soon as Lord Kingsborough, who was in Ireland, heard of the fate of his daughter, he came to England with his son, Colonel King, determined to call Fitzgerald to a personal and severe account. A meeting was appointed near the Magazine in Hyde Park; Colonel King was accompanied by Major Wood as his second, but Colonel Fitzgerald came alone. After exchanging six shots without effect, Colonel Fitzgerald's powder and balls being all expended, it was agreed that they should meet again the next morning. Both Colonels were, however, put under arrest the same day.

" The sequel to this extraordinary affair is most tragical. It appears that the young lady was removed to her father's residence at Mitchelstown, near Kilworth in Ireland. A discarded servant became the bearer of a letter to Colonel

Fitzgerald, which induced him immediately to
follow her. Colonel King, now Lord Kingsborough, his father being created Earl of Kingston, having received intelligence of his arrival,
immediately proceeded to Kilworth, and went
to the apartment in which the Colonel lodged.
Having demanded admittance, and being refused,
the enraged young nobleman forced open the
door, and running to a case of ,pistols lying in
the room, seized one, and called on the Colonel
to defend himself; they instantly grappled, and,
while struggling, the Earl of Kingston entered
the room, having come in pursuit of his son,
and seeing that his life was in danger, immediately fired upon the Colonel, and killed him on
the spot. Colonel Fitzgerald thus fell a victim
to the most horrible infatuation and depravity,
lamented by no one who reflected on his dishonour-
able conduct in this affair." He was the terror of
the West End Clubs, and of Society at large,
who knew him as " fighting Fitzgerald."

But happier and brighter, because more peaceful, days have dawned upon us, and the green
turf of Hyde Park is no longer periodically dyed
red with the blood of men anxious to vindicate
their position as " gentlemen." Let us turn from
the scene of such savage deeds, and saunter idly
to the " drive" along the banks of the Serpentine,

or the "ride" in Rotten Row, and gaze upon the fairest and the loveliest of our countrywomen, all emphatically declaring that the reign of Mars in these quarters has given way to that of Venus, and that their motto, re-echoed from Belgravia to Tyburnia, is " *Cedant arma togæ !*" Let us congratulate ourselves that the gallows-tree no longer stands by Tyburn Meadow, foul with the bleaching bones of highwaymen, forgers, and Catholic priests. Happily a milder code of laws and a more sensible standard of honour prevail than under the Stuarts, or even under the first three of the Georges. With such thoughts in our minds, let us, gentle reader, turn our backs quietly on the gay and giddy throng who still, though in lessened numbers, are haunting those rides, or resting, as idle spectators, beneath the trees ; thence let us stroll quietly and leisurely up Piccadilly, and having dined on good substantial fare at my club near Pall Mall, let us wend our way back to my chambers, where, at all events, whether you be more or less of an antiquary, you, reader, shall receive at least a hearty welcome.

NORTHUMBERLAND HOUSE.

(1874.)

NOW that a clean sweep is about to be made of the last of those historic residences of our nobility which lined the banks of the Thames from Blackfriars to Westminster, a short notice of the house which, with but slight intermission for two centuries and more, was the home of the Percies, Earls, and Dukes of Northumberland, may not be unacceptable to our readers. The best and fullest description of the house is to be found in "The New History of London," by John Noorthouck, published in 1773. He describes the street front as "magnificent," though irregular in style; with its "grand arched gate in the centre," and its piers "continued up to the top of the building, with niches on each side decorated with gothic carvings." These piers are connected at the top in such a way as to form a central arch, opening from the top of the house to a circular balcony, which surmounts a bow-window over the gateway, and itself in its turn supporting the crest of the Duke of Northumberland, a "lion passant," an object well known to every country cousin who comes up to see the sights of London. The walls on each side of the central tower are of brick, pierced with two series of ten windows, and ending on either side in towers with rustic stone corners, which rise to a slight elevation above the rest of the front. The centre is connected with the turrets, not by a regular balustrade, but by a breastwork of solid piers and open lattice-work alternately corresponding with the windows beneath.

The Strand front is 162 feet in length, and to the west of the central gateway there is an ingenious contrivance by which a portion of the wall is made to open for the egress of carriages upon state occasions. Along the *façade* at the top of this front was formerly a border of capital letters, one of which—" S"—fell down at the funeral of Anne of Denmark in 1619, and killed a spectator in the street below, as recorded in the register of St. Martin's parish. The date A.D. 1749 on the *façade*, as it stands at present, refers to the work of restoration which was commenced in that year, the letters "A.S.P.N.," denoting "Algernon Somerset, Princeps Northumbriæ."

Horace Walpole, in his "Anecdotes of Painting," tells us that in a frieze near the top of the central gateway there used to be in large capitals the letters "C. Æ.," which were long a puzzle to to the curious, but that Vertue found out that they stood for "Christmas Ædificavit;" Christmas being an architect and carver of high repute, who "gave the design of Aldersgate, and cut on it the *bas relief* of James I." He concludes that Jansen in reality built the house, but that the front of stone was added by Christmas.

The gateway can scarcely be described correctly, for, handsome as it is as a whole, the ornaments are scattered about it in the utmost confusion from the base to the summit, which supports the Northumberland lion, the crest of the Percies; this is said to be a copy of the celebrated lion of Michael Angelo. Double ranges of grotesque pilasters inclose eight niches on the sides, and over the gate is an open arch and a bow window. The basement of the whole front contains fourteen niches, in which are imitations of ancient weapons crossed; and the upper stories have twenty-four windows in two ranges, with pierced battlements. Each wing terminates in a cupola, and the angles have rustic quoins.

The inner court is quadrangular, 81 feet square, faced with Portland stone, and architecturally an improvement on the outer front. Beyond this are the chief dwelling apartments of the family, looking across the garden to the river, with wings of about 100 feet in length. Speaking of the "new front" towards the garden, Evelyn in his Diary, in 1658, remarks that it would be "tolerable were it not drowned by too massive and clumsy a pair of stairs of stone without any real invention"—he means, of course, in the way of balustrade to relieve the effect. Of this front, with the said heavy stairs, there is a view by Whale in Dodsley's "London." But it is time to enter. "The principal door of the house it-self," says Northouck, "opens into a vestibule about 82 feet long, ornamented with columns of the Doric order. Each end of it communicates with a staircase leading to the principal apartments, which face the garden, and which have ceilings embellished with copies of antique paintings and fine ornaments in stucco richly gilt. The chimney-pieces consist of statuary and other curious marble-work, carved and finished in the most correct taste. The rooms are hung either with tapestry or with damask, and are furnished with

large glasses, chairs, settees, marble tables, &c.,
with frames of exquisite workmanship, all richly
gilt. They also contain a very large and very
valuable collection of pictures by the greatest
masters, among them works by Raphael, Titian,
&c., not to mention those by more modern
masters." The "Cornaro Family," painted by
Titian, as is known to every visitor who has seen
the interior of Northumberland House, forms by
far the most valuable item in the entire collection. Hugh, Earl (and afterwards Duke) of
Northumberland, as appears from Horace Walpole's "Letters," ordered for his gallery at Northumberland House copies of some of the finest
pictures in Italy. Horace Walpole alludes to
one, "The Triumph of Bacchus;" but he adds,
with his usual cynicism, that he "never approved
the thought of them," and has consequently
"adjourned his curiosity on the subject till the
gallery is thrown open with the first masquerade."
Dr. Waagen, in his list of the pictures at Northumberland House, dwells especially on the "St.
Sebastian Bound," by Guercino; the "Adoration
of the Shepherds," by Bassano; "A Fox and a
Deer Hunt," by Snyders; the "Holy Family," by
Jordaens; an excellent copy, by Mengs, of "The
School of Athens," after Raphael; and three half
figures, portraits, in one picture, by Vandyck.

The boast of the interior of the house, however, is the double state staircase with marble steps, rich ormolu balustrades, chandelier and lamps, and carved marble podium. In some of the rooms are several magnificent chests, curiously embellished in old genuine Japanese work. The left wing contains the gallery, or ball room, 105 feet in length by 26 feet in breadth. This, with its adjuncts, forms what we may call the state apartments of the palace, and when lit up for a grand evening reception the suite must be truly magnificent. Northouck adds that the rooms in Northumberland House are 140 in number; that they contain " two libraries of well-chosen books on the most useful and curious subjects;" and that, while "the apartments of the Duke and Duchess are very commodious and elegantly furnished, her grace's closet itself is a repertory of curiosities which will afford a most pleasing entertainment to a connoisseur."

The state gallery is gorgeously gilt with groups of eagles, boys, and foliage in high relief, and decorated in compartments with paintings after the Roman school; the chimney-pieces are supported by figures of Phrygian captives in marble; and the room will hold 800 guests. On the walls are copies of some of the best paintings of Raphael, Caracci, and Guido; but they are copies only. There are two cabinets of marble and gems, which once belonged to Louis XIV., and are valued at £1,000 each. In the centre is a Sèvres china vase, nine feet high, exquisitely painted with Diana and her Nymphs disarming Cupid. This was presented by Charles X. to Hugh, the second Duke of Northumberland of the present line, when Ambassador at the Court of Versailles. Our lady readers may be interested by learning that just beyond the principal drawing room is a small boudoir hung with tapestry, which was designed by Zuccarelli, and was worked in Soho-square in 1758.

The mansion itself is deserving the fuller notice as being almost, if not quite, the last house remaining in town where the ancient magnificence of the old English nobility is upheld. Within its walls, we should say, his grace of Northumberland is more truly and completely "the Duke" than their graces of Norfolk or Devonshire are, in St. James's Square and Piccadilly respectively. In the back buildings of Norfolk House is still to be seen the room in which George III. first saw the light, his father having rented the house from the then duke for a term of years. But Northumberland House can boast that it has never yet been let, even to royalty; and we should be much surprised to find that the proud porter at Charing

Cross would acknowledge himself in any degree inferior in rank or dignity to the corresponding official at Norfolk or Devonshire House, or even at Marlborough House or Buckingham Palace.

"As regards Northumberland House," writes a lady who has frequently been a visitor within its walls, "I always thought it one of the dullest and stiffest houses that I ever knew. The furniture—I speak of some twelve years ago—was of no special style, and certainly far from modern; there was not a light or comfortable chair in the place, but only large ottomans and very large sleepy chairs, covered with red silk, and all arranged in harmony with one another; but they were so huge and so heavy that you could not move them if you wished and tried. There was a long ball-room, in which were given a very splendid dinner, and afterwards a very pretty *fête*, to the Prince and Princess of Wales just after their marriage; but this, I fancy, was a modern addition to the house itself, and I don't think that it could be said to have any special style of its own. The picture of the Cornaro family, by Titian, in the dining room, was in my eyes always the pleasantest object in the house, and it was regarded by judges as the gem of all. There were other good pictures, however, including some Dutch specimens, in the dining and anterooms. The drawing-rooms were hung with silk. and adorned on every side with mirrors, and the walls of one drawing-room were of red glass. This had a handsome and curious appearance, but, for lighting, a very heavy and dark effect—forgive the double Irishism—and I always thought it rather of the Birmingham than of the Venetian school. I imagine that the house still is very much as it was when I knew it best. I must not imply that the interior was not handsome in a certain sense, for it *was* that; and fifty years ago, I suppose, everybody would have been quite satisfied with it, and even have voted it unsurpassed. But tastes have altered, and things are so much more decorative now, and so many more *objets d'art* are introduced to make life pleasant and amusing, that a room which has remained untouched since our grandmothers' days strikes me as depressing, however rich and gorgeous its silken hangings may be." I fancy that few persons who have seen the inside of Northumberland House will dispute the verdict of my fair correspondent.

And now a few words about its early history. This, it may be owned, has nothing about it either particularly interesting or romantic. It may be summed up in a very few lines. It covers some five or six acres of ground which was formerly the site of a chapel and hospital dedicated to St. Mary, founded by William Marischal, Earl of Pembroke, as a cell to the Priory of Ronceval, in Navarre, in the reign of Henry III. This house, however, appears to have been suppressed, along with the alien priories, by Henry V., though subsequently revived by Edward IV. Such, at all events, is the testimony of Speed, the antiquary.

After the dissolution of the monasteries at the era of the Reformation, the site appears to have been granted by Edward VI. or his ministers to one Edward Carwarden, or Carwardine, to be held in free soccage of the honour of Westminster; from his hands it passed into the possession of Henry Howard, Earl of Northampton, a son of the gallant and noble Earl of Surrey, who erected on it, out of the ruins of the hospital, a magnificent mansion, which was known as Northampton House.*

* According to Maitland, the early residence of the Northumberland Percies stood upon a site "contiguous to the church of St. Catherine Coleman's, in the City, on the east of where the East India Company's warehouses are now (1739) situate;" and afterwards for a time the Earls of Northumberland, according to the same authority, had a house "near to the west end of Aldersgate, in Bull and Mouth Street." In due course of time, however, like the rest of the fashionable world, they moved in a westerly direction; but it was not until the year 1642 that they actually obtained, by marriage,

The garden between the house and the Thames is sadly hemmed and closed in by walls and by buildings of an inferior class, and makes us regret that it has not been preserved intact down to the riverside, as it appears once to have been, for a view of London in 1543 shows its gardens reaching down to the Thames. It consists now, just as it did in Northhouck's day, a century since, of a "fine lawn surrounded with a neat gravel walk, bounded by a border of curious shrubs, flowers, and evergreens."

The edifice itself, at the present time, in the main is the same as when it was first built in the reign of our first Stuart king, and its architecture may be most fitly described as neither Gothic nor classical, but " Jacobean." Of this somewhat anomalous style it is a very fair and even handsome specimen. It then consisted of three sides only, according to the prevailing fashion of the day. At Lord Northampton's death, in 1616, it was bequeathed to his nephew Thomas Howard, Earl of Suffolk, after whom it came to be called Suffolk House, until 1642, when Algernon Percy, the tenth Earl of Northumberland, and Lord High Admiral of England, became its proprietor in right of his wife, Elizabeth Howard, the

possession of the house which has since been identical with their name.

daughter and heiress of Theophilus, second Earl of Suffolk. From that date down to the present it has continued to bear the name of Northumberland House.

It was the first of its Percy owners who added a fourth side to the building, completing the quadrangle by the erection of the south side facing the river; and it is worthy of record (though the fact is doubted by some persons) that his architect was no less a person than the celebrated Inigo Jones.

Northumberland House is thus quaintly described in Seymour's "Survey of the Cities of London and Westminster" in 1735: –"It is a noble and spacious building, having a large square court at the entrance, with buildings round it, at the upper end of which is a piazza, with buildings over it, sustained by stone pillars; and behind the pillars there is a curious garden, the which runneth down to the Thames, all which makes it a stately habitation, fit to receive such a person of quality as is the owner therefore, viz., Charles, Duke of Somerset. This house came to him in right of his first lady, viz., Elizabeth, heiress of Jocelyn, late Earl of Northumberland. It is a magnificent building, and the furniture within is equal to it, among which, it is said, there is one picture valued at thirty thousand

pounds—the Family of the Cornaros, an ancient
Venetian family, and painted by the celebrated
Titian."

We learn from Northouck that, in order to
secure privacy for his dwelling apartments, Earl
Algernon erected the side parallel to the street
front, employing the assistance of Inigo Jones.
The street front, he adds, was much altered
about the year 1750 by Algernon, Duke of
Somerset, the alterations being completed by his
son-in-law and daughter-in-law, the first Duke
and Duchess of Northumberland of the present
creation.

In 1682, Charles, Duke of Somerset, better
known to the readers of anecdote as "the proud"
Duke of Somerset, began to rebuild the street
front and to alter the apartments in various
ways; but he died before his designs were accomplished, leaving the completion of the house,
pretty nearly as it now stands, to his daughter
and heiress, the wife of Sir Hugh Smithson, afterwards first Duke of Northumberland of the present line. The old Duke of Somerset was as
proud a man as ever lived; but, as Horace Walpole says, he "tendered his pride even beyond
his hate, for he has left to the present Duke all
the furniture of his palaces, but to his Duchess,
who has endured a long slavery with him, he has

left nothing but £1000 and a small farm, besides her jointure, giving the whole of his unsettled estate equally between his two daughters." The Duchess here alluded to was the sole heiress of the house of Percy, Lady Elizabeth Percy*—in her own right Baroness Percy—only surviving child and heir of Algernon, eleventh Earl of Northumberland ; and she made a settlement of her estate, in case her sons died without heirs male, on the children of her daughters. Her eldest daughter, Catharine, married Sir William Wyndham, whose son Charles, by the death of Lord Beauchamp, son and heir of the Earl of Hertford, afterwards Duke of Somerset, succeeded to the greater portion of the Percy estate, in preference to her sister Elizabeth, who married Sir Hugh Smithson. Horace Walpole writes to Sir Horace Mann in December, 1748 :—" The famous settlement is found which gives Sir Charles Wyndham about £12,000 a year out of the Percy estate, after the present Duke's death; the other five, with the Barony of Percy, must go to Lady

---

* This lady was twice a widow and three times a wife before she was seventeen years old. Her first husband was Henry Cavendish, Earl of Ogle, who died before she was of age to leave her parents' roof for that of his lordship ; and her second husband, Thomas Tynne, of Longleat, Wilts, was barbarously murdered in his coach in Pall Mall, on Sunday, February 12th, 1681-2.

Betty Smithson. I don't know whether you ever heard that in Lord Granville's administration he had prevailed with the King to grant the Earldom of Northumberland to Sir Charles; Lord Hertford represented against it. At last the King said he would give it to whoever they would make it appear was to have the Percy estates; but the old Duke of Somerset refused to let anybody see his writings; so the affair dropped, everybody believing that there was no such settlement."

So thoroughly has the family of Percy been identified with this house for the last two centuries that Horace Walpole, writing to Lady Ossory, in 1774, speaks of her Grace of Northumberland as "the Duchess of Charing Cross."

Northumberland House is rich in social and political associations. Evelyn, who visited it in 1658, has left in his Diary not only an account of the mansion, but a critique on its contents, including some of its pictures. Horace Walpole, too, in his amusing correspondence, makes constant allusions to its state-rooms and its inmates. He attended a fête here in the time of the first Duke of the "Smithson" line. It was from Northumberland House, as he tells us, that he sallied forth with a gay party to visit the scene of the "Cock-lane Ghost." A century before that time, however (in 1660), General Monk, who had

taken up his quarters at Whitehall, was invited
to this house by its then owner; and here, in con-
ference with him and the Earl of Manchester, and
other leaders of the nobles and gentry, some of
those measures were concerted which ultimately
led to the restoration of the monarchy in that
year. This is stated by Lord Clarendon.

Horace Walpole tells us one or two other
amusing anecdotes relating to Northumberland
House under the first of the Smithson line. For
instance, he records how in the Wilkes riots of
1768 the mob forced the Duke and Duchess of
Northumberland not only to illuminate, but to
appear at the windows facing the Strand, and to
give them beer. He also speaks of the then
Duchess as a rather " strong-minded " character,
at one time espousing with all a woman's vehe-
mence one side in the famous dispute between
the rival operas in 1771; and at another time
amusing herself with writing witty epigrams at
Lady Miller's house near Bath, and " sitting on
the hustings " at the Westminster elections.

Mr. J. Timbs tells us, in his " Curiosities of
London," that both Hugh the third and Algernon
the fourth Duke of Northumberland, though they
died at Alnwick Castle, were brought to their
town mansion to be buried, and that on each of
these occasions the funeral pageant reached from

Charing Cross down to the gate of Westminster Abbey, in which, as our readers are no doubt aware, the Percies lie in a chapel at its eastern extremity

There is a print by Holler of the mansion at the time when it bore the name of Suffolk House. It was then quadrangular in its plan, and had at each angle a lofty dome-crowned tower, in the Dutch style. There is also a river view of the house at this time in Wilkinson, from a drawing by Hollar in the Pepysian Library at Magdalen College, Cambridge. Canaletti, in the last century, painted the Strand front, and his picture is rendered familiar to antiquaries and biographers by an admirable engraving by T. Bowles, now scarce and valuable.

ECCENTRIC LORD MAYORS.

SIR JOHN BARNARD AND SIR WILLIAM STAINES

AMONG those gentlemen who have filled the
high position of one of the aldermen of
London and its representatives in Parliament,
few deserve to be longer held in memory than Sir
John Barnard, who had paid to him the singular
honour of a statue erected in the Royal Exchange
during his lifetime. He is called, in an old book
of " City Biography " with which I have lately
met, a " distinguished patriot; " and if such an
expression sounds rather hyperbolical in our ears,
let it be mentioned as an excuse for the term that
under the Second George inflexible conduct was
rare, and that he was one of those few M.P.'s
whom even Sir Robert Walpole found it impossible to buy or corrupt, though that Minister held,

as is known, that " every man has, or had, his price." Nor am I venturing to detract from his merits when I say that possibly one good reason for his spotless honesty may be found in the fact that he lived and died immensely rich.

Sir John Barnard came of a respectable family. His parents were of the middle class, of the Quaker persuasion, in which, too, their son was brought up. They were thrifty and careful to a fault, and their son, as he grew up, speedily showed that he was a "chip of the old block." It is true that on reaching manhood he quitted the Society of Friends, probably inspired by a laudable ambition of rising in the world, for all that time the doors of the Houses of Parliament, and of nearly every profession, were closed against Nonconformists of every shade of opinion; but this did not lead him to lay aside the simplicity of his manners or the integrity of his conduct.

In due course of time young Barnard, who had entered a merchant's office when sixteen, and had risen gradually from a clerkship to a partnership in the concern, became a common councilman of his ward; and at length, in 1722, was chosen to represent the City of London in the Lower House of Parliament. He appears to have entered St. Stephen's as a more strictly independent member than most of his compeers, at a time when the government of the country was carried on by party and party only, and the cry was for "men, not measures;" and among other personages who found in him a frequent opponent was the all-powerful Sir Robert Walpole, then Premier. One day the great Minister paid him a high compliment, which is thus told :—

They (Barnard and Walpole) were riding out in two different parties in a narrow lane, near Marylebone, when one of Sir Robert's companions, hearing the voice of Sir John Barnard before he came up to the other party, asked Sir Robert who it was that was approaching. "Oh! don't you know his voice?" was the reply, "for if *you* don't, *I* do, and with good reason, for I have often felt its power in the House of Commons; in fact, I shall not readily forget it." When they met near the end of the lane, Sir Robert stopped his horse, and, saluting Sir John Barnard with that courtesy which he eminently possessed, told him what had happened in a way that set both parties at their ease.

Another story is told of Sir John Barnard, which shows how strenuously he maintained his independence in St. Stephen's :—

When Sir Robert Walpole, then Prime Minister, was one day whispering to the Speaker of the House of Commons, the latter leaning to him over the arm of his chair, while Sir John was "on his legs," he exclaimed, "Mr. Speaker, I address myself to you, Sir, and not to your chair. I will be heard, and I call the right honourable gentleman to order." The Speaker, feeling the rebuke to be not unmerited, turned round, left off chatting with Sir Robert, and begged Sir John Barnard to proceed, as he was "all attention." The story was well known in Parliamentary circles a century ago.

It is said that the high office of Chancellor of the Exchequer was on one occasion offered to the acceptance of Sir John Barnard—I believe in 1746—but was declined by him, as it was offered to and declined by another great London merchant, Mr. Thomas Baring, a century afterwards. Be this story true or false, however, at all events it is certain that during the time when Lord Granville was Secretary of State, if any application was made to the Minister by the merchants and commercial men of the City, he never gave an answer without first asking "what Sir John Barnard had to say on the subject, and what was his candid opinion." Lord Chatham, too—then Mr. Pitt—a man not particularly apt to be lavish of his praise of anyone, gave to Sir John the dignified name of "The Great Commoner"—an appellation which, possibly with greater propriety,

was afterwards retorted upon Pitt by Sir John
Barnard, whose modesty led him by instinct to
repudiate it.

When, by the death of Sir James Thompson,
he came to stand first on the list of aldermen, he
became " the Father of the City ; " and it was
generally thought that the title was never better
deserved. Such, at all events, is the inference
which is naturally drawn from the fact that, if
the records of the time are to be believed, a statue
was not only voted in his honour, but actually set
up during his lifetime in the Royal Exchange—

> " Præsens Divus habebitur
> Augustus."

He could not prevent its erection, or prevail upon
his fellow-aldermen to refrain from establishing
what, if followed largely, might prove an awkward precedent. It is said of him, however, that
from and after that day he never made his appearance in any " walk " within the quadrangle
of the Exchange, but transacted his business in
the street in front of it.

Nor was Sir John Barnard less distinguished
by honourable and consistent conduct in his
capacity as a City magistrate than he was in
in the senate ; in either position he did his duty
without fear or favour, and with the most minute

and scrupulous attention to the requirements of each case brought before him. The following story will serve as an example :—

" A young woman decently dressed was brought to him late one night at the Mansion House by a watchman, having been found alone in the streets at a late hour, and under circumstances which at all events looked suspicious. She requested to be heard in her defence. The facts, however, still seemed against her—indeed, so much that Sir John asked her if she could not produce some person to speak to her character. She said that her relations and friends lived a long way off— indeed, as far as beyond Whitechapel—but that she could produce them if his worship would only wait till they could be sent for. There were no telegraphs or telegrams in those days, not even a hansom cab or a 'growler;' and it would take at least an hour before her friends could be summoned and attend at the Mansion House. But that was no matter to Sir John Barnard. He said that as a magistrate and an alderman he was a servant of the public, and that his time belonged to them, and their convenience was his own, and that therefore he would willingly sit up until her friends could come to him, and, if her story could be shown to be true, save her from being sent off to prison. A messenger was despatched for the girl's friends, who on reaching the City gave her the best of characters, and accounted to the good alderman's satisfaction for her being out so late. Sir John Barnard at once ordered the girl to be dismissed, adding that he had never felt more pleasure in his life than in discharging her." It would be well if such an example were more frequently copied.

It is stated that it was at Sir John Barnard's suggestion that an Act of Parliament was passed restricting the number of play-houses in London, and embodying most of the regulations which fettered till recently, and still to some extent fetter, the freedom of "Her Majesty's servants," the dramatic body.

Sir John Barnard lived well into the reign of George III., and at his death left behind him a handsome fortune, which his son increased by a carefulness and thrift which almost entitled him to the character of a miser, his care for little things extending even to the candle ends at his father's funeral, which he added to his hoardings. Who has not heard of the penurious John Elwes, who at the age of seventy robbed the crows' nests on his estate in order to gain materials for the winter's fire? Who has not heard of Ostervald, who laid the foundation of his large fortune by corks, gathering together all the drawn corks that he could find about the yards of inns and taverns until they produced him ten shillings, with which capital he commenced business on his own account? Who has not heard of the broker, Taylor, who finding on his death-bed that his attendant had not made away with a candle-end for which he had searched in vain, but had carefully put it aside in a cupboard, declared that he could now die contented?

But the foresight and prudence of Mr. Barnard, as he sat in the easy-chair at his residence in Berkeley Square one day towards the close of the last century, calmly providing for his coming death, is a match for any and all of them. It appears that one night he dreamed or fancied that he would die within four days. Now it so happened that he used to have a cup of chocolate every morning, and that at the beginning of every week he used to tell his housekeeper to order the regular quantity. On this occasion, however, he told her to get in only half the supply, and to take only enough for three mornings. Before the fourth morning came round, his dream had proved true, for Mr. Barnard was dead; and the family of Sir John Barnard, we believe, has passed away, so far as concerns the heirs of his name. His riches no doubt soon found other possessors.

The other eccentric Lord Mayor whom I wish

to introduce to my readers, belongs to the next generation.

On September 11th, 1807, died at Clapham, at an advanced age, Sir William Staines, ex-Lord Mayor of London. It was much to the credit of this worthy knight that he was the son of humble parents, and that he himself began life as a labouring bricklayer, and carried a hod upon his back. Judging from the advanced age which he had attained at his death, it is probable that he was born about the year 1730, or a little later. Of his early employment he was so far from being ashamed that, if Hone's *Year-Book* may be trusted, he would often tell the following story after he had filled the civic chair:—

" When quite a young man he happened to be employed upon some repairs at the parsonage house at Uxbridge. As he was going up the ladder one day with his hod and mortar, he was accosted by the parson's wife, who told him that on the previous night she had been visited by an extraordinary dream; for that as she lay asleep she dreamt that he would one day, like Dick Whittington, wear a gold chain as Lord Mayor of London. Taken aback at the story, and astonished at hearing such a prophecy, young Staines could only scratch his head, and thank the lady for telling him of such a promotion awaiting him in the future. But he had neither money nor friends, nor had he received more than the very slightest and poorest education; so he put away the thought of rising in the great City world, and gradually forgot the prophecy."

The clergyman's wife, however, was not easily to be turned from her dream, which had made a great impression upon her, and gradually ripened into something like a settled purpose and design. Her mind was fixed on young Staines, and she was resolved that it should be with him as she had said, and that he should become Lord Mayor. Accordingly she dreamed the same dream again, and again communicated its substance to the young bricklayer, who soon after left Uxbridge, not, however, without very many thanks to the good lady for the flattering notice that she had taken of him.

From a working man he rose—by what steps is not recorded by the muse of history and biography —to be a master-bricklayer and a builder: and by the time he had reached middle life he must have been in possession of a competence, and something more. At all events I find that in 1783 he was elected into the Common Council for the ward of Cripplegate; was appointed a deputy for the ward in 1791, and obtained the aldermanic gown in 1793. He was chosen to serve as sheriff in 1796-97, when he received the honour of knighthood from his Sovereign.

It was not until he had risen to be Sheriff of London and Middlesex that this dream of the good lady came to be made the subject of much notice among his friends, though doubtless it made a much deeper impression on his mind than he would have admitted, and probably acted as an inducement to him to pursue a path of steady perseverance and industry, and so paved the way for its realization and fulfilment. The Uxbridge clergyman lived long enough to become chaplain to Sir William whilst holding the shrievalty.

But this is not the full extent of the wonder connected with the rise of William Staines, for another old lady foretold that he would be Lord Mayor during a period of great scarcity and trouble; that the country should be at war with France during his mayoralty, but that his term of office should also witness the restoration of peace and the return of plenty.

This prophecy was fulfilled in 1801, when Sir William Staines was chosen Lord Mayor, and the peace of Amiens was concluded under the auspices of Mr. Addington, during Sir William's term of office in the City.

As member of the aldermanic body, and as Lord Mayor, Sir William Staines appears to have gained the respect of his fellow-citizens, but little is known in detail of his career.

He survived his mayoralty about six years, dying, as already stated, in 1807, at his house at Clapham. His age is not stated in the obituary notice which briefly records his career in the columns of the *Gentleman's Magazine*, in which he is styled the "venerable alderman of Cripplegate Ward." Sylvanus Urban adds, with a terseness and brevity for which he was not always remarkable, that he "had passed the civic chair with equal reputation to himself and advantage to his fellow-citizens. He had discharged the various civic offices with the utmost integrity; he had raised himself by honest industry to opulence, and always had the good sense to acknowledge his humble origin. In him," adds Sylvanus Urban, "the poor have lost a fatherly protector; his tenants a kind landlord; and his workmen an indulgent and beneficent master."

A volume of "City Biography" published 1801, simply records of Sir William "that he began life as a paviour and stone-mason, made a fortune honourably, and "married his cook-maid." The author adds, "His manners may be judged by the following anecdote. At a City feast when Sheriff, sitting by General Tarleton, he thus addressed him, 'Eat away at the pines, General, for we must pay all the same, eat or not eat.' From this it will be seen to follow that Sir William had not studied carefully the motto of William of Wykeham, 'Manners makyth man.'"

A week after his death, his remains were conveyed from Clapham to Cripplegate, where they were laid to rest in the church-yard, his funeral being attended by the Lord Mayor and most of his brother-aldermen, and by the authorities of the ward and the parish with which he had been so long connected. A flat stone in the churchyard marks his grave. His career may possibly serve as an encouragement to some one of the " working classes " of our own day to go and do likewise.

Hone, in his *Every-Day Book*, records the fact that the cold bath at what we may now call the late Peerless Pool, in the City Road, faced with marble and paved with stone, was executed by Sir William Staines in the days when he worked as a mason. When in after-days he smoked his pipe at the Jacob's Well in Barbican, or at his home at Clapham, he would often boast of this as one of his best works.

A likeness of Sir William Staines, taken after the end of the mayoralty, was published in 1803 by Kirby, of London House Yard, and Scott, of 447, Strand. It represents him dressed in an old-fashioned long coat, rather of the Quaker cut, cocked hat and wig, knee-breeches, and large shoe-buckles, and having a scroll of paper in his hand. He has a very benevolent face. The print, now very scarce, is entitled "Sir William Staines, late worthy Lord Mayor of the City of of London."

ANNALS OF ST. PAUL'S.[*]

THERE is a melancholy history about this book. It was the last work of the late learned and accomplished Dean Milman, whose decease broke off his narrative of the "Annals" of our metropolitan Cathedral at the funeral of the Duke of Wellington. Indeed, he was struck by the hand of death while busy in revising the proof sheets;

> "Atque opere in medio defixa reliquit aratra."

And, accordingly, the work has been finished by his son, who has added the last touches to his father's imperfect manuscript.

It was fitting and proper that such a book

[*] "Annals of St. Paul's Cathedral, by Henry Hart Milman, D.D., late Dean of St. Paul's, 1868.

should have been undertaken by Dean Milman, not only on account of the special interest which he took in the edifice committed to his charge, but as a companion volume to Dean Stanley's corresponding work on " Westminster Abbey." And if, in a strictly architectural and antiquarian point of view, the Dean of St. Paul's has not produced a work quite so interesting as the Dean of Westminster has done, still he has contrived to show us that, viewed in another light, St. Paul's Cathedral, including the former as well as the present structure, has a history of its own in no way inferior to the proud Abbey of St. Peter's.

As might be expected, the Dean throws aside as fables many of the statements which have met with favour from credulous historians as to the early history of the Cathedral. He rejects the story of the great Apostle of the Gentiles having visited " the great Trinobantine city of Geoffrey of Monmouth, the Troy-novant of later romance;" and he is equally sceptical as to the preaching of Joseph of Arimathæa or of the missionaries of King Lucius in this island. In the comparatively lofty site on which St. Paul's stands he reads the very great probability that on that spot once stood a heathen " templum," in the original sense of the word " tuemplum," from *tueor*. This was very possibly a temple of Diana, a supposition confirmed, we may add, by the discovery of an altar to that goddess which was found close to the General Post Office some forty years ago, and of which the Dean gives us a sketch on his title page. In his opinion, this temple flanked the Roman Prætorium or camp, which, as we know, frowned down upon the Thames and the River Fleet; and, when the Christian faith superseded the Pagan deities of the Roman soldiery, no doubt the common practice was followed of turning the heathen temple to the purposes of Christian worship :—

"Considering what capital hunting-grounds must have been the wild and wide forests to the north of London, peopled as they doubtless were with all kinds of game, deer, wild boars, perhaps the urus, or wild bull, it cannot be surprising that the Roman sportsmen, the officers and soldiers of the great Prætorian camp, should have raised altars and images to the Goddess of the Chase."

The fact that the neighbourhood of St. Paul's was used as a burial-place in the earliest times is established by the bones of Romans and Britons which have been dug up around it *in situ* in the various layers of clay, drift, and gravel.

Be this, however, as it may, the Saxon invasion

swept away most traces alike of Roman civilization and of the Christian faith in London. Still, under the Saxons, the city held its place as the capital of the land, and within it the area of St. Paul's would, no doubt, remain a place at once of dignity and of strength. With Mellitus, the companion of Augustine, we get to the *terra firma* of history; and he, no doubt, on fixing his see at London, would take possession of a place already hallowed by the religious feelings if not of Christians, yet, at least, of pagans. No sooner was a diocese assigned to him than Ethelbert, then King of Kent, with the sanction of Sebert, King of the East Angles, here founded and endowed a cathedral, which in that rude age may have been, and probably was, "magnificent," and which he dedicated to St. Paul. After Mellitus, follow periods of alternate light and darkness, till we come to his fourth successor, Erkenwald, " whose legendary life teems with records of his munificence in raising and adorning the Church of St. Paul with a splendour rare in those days." This Erkenwald was also the founder of the noble Abbey of Chertsey; and with the story of his life and death is connected a long series of miracles which we have not leisure to examine or space to recount, and which our readers may safely pass by, as we presume that neither Bishop Tait nor

Bishop Jackson will expect us to believe them implicitly, and as they were never pronounced to be *de fide* by the Mediæval Church.

Dean Milman observes with regret that the other Saxon Bishops of London, with the exception of Dunstan, and also their contemporary deans, have left few traces behind them as Churchmen, or statesmen, or scholars, though the list of Anglo-Saxon saints is countless. But this may not have been their fault. They may have done great things, though we know not the record of them, *carent quia vate sacro.* So we pass on to the Norman era, when the Bishop of London became a baronial noble, the strong castle of Bishop's Stortford, in Hertfordshire—not in Essex, as Dean Milman says—being granted to him by the Conqueror as a country palace. As they resided for many years so far from the metropolis, we may perhaps see in this grant one reason for the fact which the Dean remarks—namely, that the Bishops of London never took much part in the affairs of the City, and that they never gained, or even sought to gain, that " supreme power which was exercised by the bishops in Germany, France, and Italy over many great cathedral cities." Perhaps, too, some part of this result must be ascribed to the antagonistic secular influence of the Mayor and his aldermen, who extorted

charters from their Sovereign, and took the lead
in the cause of freedom through many a long
struggle for the liberties of the realm. Bishop
William, however, obtained great influence in the
City by playing the part of peacemaker between
the King and his new subjects; and, as it was at
his intercession that the Conqueror restored and
confirmed the ancient privileges of the City, it is
no matter of wonder that he was regarded as a
public benefactor, and that for several centuries
the Londoners made an annual procession to the
tomb of their " good Bishop " in the nave of their
cathedral.

We next find Lanfranc sitting in St. Paul's at
the head of an assembly of his clergy, which Dean
Milman calls " the first Convocation of England."
But a few years later the cathedral built by Mellitus was destroyed by fire, and, strange to say,
no record survives from which we can learn anything about its style, size, or ornaments. Wonderful, indeed, that such should be the case, when,
as the Dean remarks, we find no lack of curious
details respecting the sister churches even of
York, Hexham, and Lindisfarn, in the far north,
the growth of which we can almost trace " from
enclosures of wattell and timber to stately buildings of stone."

The new edifice that arose upon the spot, we

are told, was far superior to the Saxon structure which it replaced. William of Malmesbury tells us that " it could contain the utmost conceivable multitude of worshippers." It was built in the heavy Norman style, and " combined, to some extent, the massy strength of a fortress with the aspiring height of a cathedral." It occupied the lives of two successive prelates—some forty years —to complete it; and Richard de Belmeis is said to have devoted the whole of his episcopal income to the work, and to have lived on his own private means while it was in the course of erection. He cleared the area around the church of certain " mean buildings inhabited by laymen," as far as Carter-lane, Creed-lane, and Paternoster-row. The King seems to have contributed but little in the way of money, but to have satisfied his con- science by paying his tithe in kind ; for he handed over to the builders the stone of an old tower which defended the entrance of the River Fleet, between what now is Blackfriars and Printing- house-square. Henry de Blois, the Bishop of Winchester, ordered collections to be made throughout his diocese to forward the building, on the ground that " though St. Paul had planted so many churches, this was the only church dedi- cated to the great Apostle of the Gentiles." Even this kind of aid, however, does not appear to have sufficed; for Foliot, the next who sat in the seat of St. Erkenwald, in order to stimulate the piety of the faithful, was obliged " to offer liberal indulgences to the living and to promise masses for the souls of the dead," before the fabric could be completed.

We have neither time nor space to chronicle here the long and fierce contest between Foliot and Beckett, and their mutual anathemas; the strife between those of the cathedral clergy who espoused and those who reprobated matrimony; the forced closing of the doors of St. Paul's under the interdict of the reign of King John; the convention of the Bishops and other prelates in St. Paul's, which immediately preceded the memorable scene at Runnymede and the extortion of Magna Charta; the ratification of that sad scene which had occurred in the Templars' Church at Dover, when John laid his crown at the feet of Pandulph; the cowering of the Bishop and Archbishop before successive Papal Legates; the gradual introduction and growth of the scandal of the *focariæ* in the houses of the Canons; and the still greater scandal of the murder of a prelate—Walter Stapleton, Bishop of Exeter—who had taken sanctuary at the doors of the church. These and many other matters are narrated at length as they deserve by Dean Milman, who is too honest and conscientious an annalist to throw a cloak over such failings and faults in his predecessors as his duty as an historian compels him to admit to be only too true in fact.

Other scenes, worthy alike of the historian, the poet, and the painter, occurred within the walls of the old Norman Cathedral of St. Paul's. For instance, it was there that Wycliff appeared, at the summons of the Archbishop of Canterbury and the Bishop of London, to make answer for the publication of those " new " opinions which, when they arrived at maturity, were destined to cause a revolution over one half of Europe, and to end in making the Church of England independent of the Western Church. We should like to have been present and beheld the scene, Wycliff standing before that clerical tribunal in the Lady Chapel, accompanied by John of Gaunt and Lord Percy, and a host of other enthusiastic and excited admirers. If the strife of principles, new and old, was afterwards transferred to Oxford, to Lambeth Palace, and to the House of the Gray Friars hard by, that does not detract from the importance of the first scene in the drama, which was acted within the walls of old St. Paul's, when the throne of London was filled by William Courtenay.

Dean Milman also reminds us that " Henry

Bolingbroke, not as yet known as King Henry IV., appeared in St. Paul's to offer his prayers—prayers for the dethronement of his ill-fated cousin—prayers for his own successful usurpation of the throne. Here he paused to shed tears over the grave of his father, for early in that year 'old John of Gaunt, time-honour'd Lancaster,' had been carried to his rest in the Cathedral. Perhaps the last time that John of Gaunt had appeared in St. Paul's was in his armour, and in all his pride, to confront the proud Courtenay. Some years elapsed ; and, after the silent and peaceful pomp of his funeral, he had been laid under the pavement of the church."

Hither, as we are told by the same authority, Richard II. was brought, but not to worship or to weep. His dead body, after the murder at Pontefract Castle, was exposed for three days in the Cathedral before it was interred in Westminster Abbey. Here, too, the first martyr of Wycliffism, William Sawtree, was publicly degraded, his priestly robes, his paten, and his chasuble being taken from him, his alb and maniple torn off, his tonsure wiped out, and a layman's cap put upon his head. Somewhat analogous, in its results, at least, was the following scene, described by Dean Milman :—

" At a somewhat later period appeared before a convocation at St. Paul's one Richard Walker, chaplain in the diocese of Worcester, charged with having in his possession two books of 'images with conjunction of figures,' and of having himself practised these diabolical acts. Walker pleaded guilty to both charges. On another day the said Richard Walker appeared at Paul's Cross, and, after an exhortation from the Bishop of Llandaff, solemnly abjured all magic. The two books were hung, wide open, one on his head, one on his back; and, with a fool's cap on his head, he was made to walk along Cheapside. On his return his books were burnt before his face, and Walker was released from his imprisonment."

" Paul's Cross," mentioned in the above extract, was for a long time, until demolished by Puritan frenzy, from its imposing grandeur and consummate gracefulness, one of the chief ornaments of London. Dean Milman tells us that it stood at the north-east end of the Cathedral between the Close and Cheapside. It is to be seen in Ralph Aggas' Map of London and in other early prints. It was built as far back as the reign of Richard I., and rebuilt by Thomas Kemp, who was Bishop during the reigns of the fourth and fifth Edwards,

and to whom Oxford owns its Divinity School.
The Cross well became its position, and during
two centuries it was the pulpit from which the
preachers of successive generations addressed the
citizens of London, and through them the public
at large, and often also the leading dignitaries in
Church and State. Even Kings did not disdain
to sit there at the feet of the best preachers that
the two Universities could supply, and it served
as the place for all public proclamations, both
religious and secular, including such Papal Bulls
and edicts as the anti-Roman zeal of our forefathers allowed to find their way into the kingdom. Indeed, as preaching came to be more and
more popular, in the 15th and 16th centuries,
" Paul's Cross " became so influential a means of
indoctrinating the public mind on subjects of
general interest that a collection of " Paul's Cross
Sermons " would be almost a history of the Anglican Church during the whole of the Reformation and Tudor periods, and even into the days
of the Stuarts.

Our Oxford High Churchmen of the Ritualistic
school in general are fond of looking back upon
the Church under the Plantagenet Sovereigns as
affording, in many respects, a pleasant contrast
to the Church of the post-Reformation era. To
such we would say that not merely is the history

of St. Paul's during those ages for the most part barren of great events and of saintly personages; and that, for instance, through the long and glorious reign of Edward III. we hear of no splendid thanksgiving even for such signal victories as Cressy and Poitiers; but that, if Dean Milman can be trusted as an historian, the Cathedral clergy showed as strong a tendency to the ordinary vices of such bodies as any Capitular Chapter ever exhibited in the deadest period of the 18th or 19th century. No sooner are broad acres and pleasant manors in Essex, Middlesex, and Bedfordshire assigned by the piety or the qualms of Churchmen to the thirty canonries in St. Paul's, than the thirty occupants of those posts betake them to their country seats, leaving just enough of their body in residence to conduct the services of the church, shirking their own duty, and robbing the Cathedral of half its dignity; then *per contra,* on a sudden, when they find that more frequent and liberal payments for masses for the souls of the dead and the dying begin to fill the pockets of the "residentiaries," they all fly back to its sacred precincts, like vultures or eagles to a carcase, in the hopes of dividing the spoil. As Dean Milman remarks, "There was quite a rush to become residentiaries." It is often thought and said, too, by sentimental writers of the High

Church School that reverence for holy things and holy places is a growth entirely of pre-Reformation times. But what says the Dean?—

" In all times there has been a strife, more or less obstinate, between the worldly and the unworldly for exclusive possession of churches. The place of concourse becomes a place of trade. Bishop Braybroke issued letters denouncing the profanation of St. Paul's by marketing and trading within the church itself. He alleges the example of the Saviour Himself, who cast the buyers and sellers out of the Temple. ' In our Cathedral not men only, but women also, not on common days alone, but especially also on the festivals, expose their wares, as it were, in a public market, and buy and sell without reverence for the holy place.' More than this, the Bishop dwells on yet more filthy abuses. ' Others,' he adds, ' by the instigation of the devil, do not scruple with stones and arrows to bring down the birds, pigeons, and jackdaws which nestle in the walls and crevices of the building; others play at ball and other unseemly games, both within and without the church, breaking the beautiful and costly painted windows, to the amazement of the spectators.' "

In another place the Dean tells us that the

building was largely frequented by thieves and women of doubtful character; and we know from other independent sources that somewhat later "Paul's Walk" was notoriously one of the most favourite haunts of persons of both sexes who desired to make assignations for not the most moral of purposes.

We pass by the Reformation era, and the deaths of Nicholas Ridley and of John Rogers, and the reigns of Mary and Elizabeth, with their alternate persecutions of Protestants and Catholics, and also that of James I., merely remarking that the fabric was severely injured by fire in 1561, the steeple being struck by lightning, and the roof being wholly destroyed. So cold was the national zeal that years passed by before the edifice was thoroughly repaired and refitted for service. Thus, in Aggas' Map of London, the tower of St. Paul's is spireless. Even then it never regained the glories which belonged to its former state. The abuses alluded to above were renewed and redoubled. Shakespeare makes Falstaff " buy" Bardolph in " Paul's,"* and our Elizabethan literature shows that there was no use so vile to which it was not appropriated by the citizens of the day. Here, however, we will not use our own words, but let the Dean speak for himself:—

* Second Part of King Henry IV., Act I., Scene ii.

"If when the old Cathedral was more or less occupied with sacred subjects . . the occupation of the sanctuary by worldly business . . resisted all attempts at suppression, now that the daily service, and that in the choir, had shrunk into mere forms of prayer, at best into a mere 'cathedral service,' carelessly, perhaps, or unimpressively performed (for organs and antiphonal singing were looked on by many with suspicion), when the pulpit and the hearers under the pulpit were all in all, it cannot be wondered at that the world took even still more entire possession of the vacated nave and aisles, and that the reverence which all the splendour and continuity of the old ritual could not maintain, gradually, though slowly, died away altogether, as Puritanism rose in the ascendant, and finally reached its height in the days of Cromwell."

Under Charles I. St. Paul's was subject to a restoration by the hands of Laud and of Inigo Jones, who was wholly ignorant of Gothic architecture, and had studied no form of art but Italian. He added to the west front a portico of the Corinthian order, possibly with the excellent intention of making a "Paul's Walk" outside instead of inside the edifice. But the design was most incongruous, and happily was short-lived. The Great Fire in 1666 made brief work of portico, pillars, architrave, and all; but its destruction was no great loss, by whatever standard we may measure it. Let us hear the opinion of Dean Milman, on whose tolerant ears the very name of Laud appears to fall with a most discordant sound:—

"On the whole, the Cathedral, restored under the auspices of Laud, who seems to bear a singular resemblance to the religion which Laud wished to establish in the Church of England, retaining as much as would stand of the old mediæval building, but putting a new face upon it. It was altogether an inharmonious and confused union of conflicting elements, a compromise between the old and the new, with services timidly approaching to Catholicism—though Laud's more obnoxious innovations do not seem to have been introduced into St. Paul's—but rejecting their vital and obsolete doctrines, and with an episcopal Popedom at Lambeth, not at Rome."

Under Cromwell and the Puritans St. Paul's or, as they called it "Paul's," came to be regarded, as might be expected, as a vast useless pile, the "lair of old superstition and idolatry;"

and accordingly, it was allowed to go rapidly to
decay. At one time, it is said, Cromwell thought
of selling it to the Jews as the site of a syna-
gogue; but the wily Israelites felt that the purchase would be a bad investment, and that
neither the Churchmen nor the Puritans—which-
ever got the upper hand in the long run—would
be likely to allow such a bargain to stand.
Somehow or other it escaped being pulled down;
but at the Restoration, while its Dean, Chapter,
and other members were revived as a corporate
body, the fabric appears to have been in a hopeless state. Sir Christopher Wren was consulted
as to the best means of repairing it, and making
it once more fit for public worship; but, while
King, Bishop, Dean and architect were discuss-
ing the subject, there came in a strange arbiter,
who settled the question in a summary manner.
The plans and estimates had been scarcely commenced a week, when the Great Fire came, and
in three short days laid the fabric in ruins. The
citizens had placed their papers and libraries in
cartloads for safety in the vaults of St. Faith's
which led, as a sort of crypt, under the building;
but the merciless fire seized on these and continued
to burn them for several days, the east wind
scattering their ashes as far, it is said, as Windsor
and Eton.

The rest of the story of St. Paul's may be told briefly, for it is known to most of our readers. The religious feelings of the nation were deeply moved at its destruction; it was resolved to restore the ruin which the fire had made, and the work of rebuilding the metropolitan Cathedral was intrusted to Sir Christopher Wren, one of the most accomplished of philosophers and scholars as well as the most learned man of the age; and who, though he had had little or no experience as an architect, soon showed that in scientific attainments he had few or no superiors. The old Cathedral was not very rich in monuments; and if we except the shrine of St. Erkenwald and the tombs of John of Gaunt and of Bishop William the Norman, there were very few memorials of past greatness which it was impossible to replace. Happily, too, the tombs of Bishop Braybroke, Dean Colet, Dean Nowell, and Dr. Donne, though sadly mutilated, were not hopelessly destroyed; and the same was the case, more or less, with those of Sir Philip Sidney, Sir Nicholas Bacon, Lord Chancellor Hatton, and Sir William Hewett. In November, 1673, letters patent were issued under the Great Seal, in which, after reciting his desire that the new Cathedral Church should surpass the glory of the former, the King appointed a commis-

sion for carrying out the plaus and designs
of his Surveyor-General of Works and Buildings, Sir, Christopher Wren. The cost was to
be defrayed partly by a subscription throughout the kingdom, and partly by a tax to be
levied on the cities of London and Westminster. With this were joined other sums arising
out of forfeitures and "impropriations due to the
King and not yet pardoned." The King himself
promised (though it does not appear that he ever
gave) £1,000 a year out of his privy purse; and
the bishops and wealthier noblemen were liberal
contributors in act as well as in promise to the
fund. A tax on coals also was granted to the
city of London for the purpose of rebuilding St.
Paul's and the other churches which had been
destroyed. Wren himself was speedily appointed
architect in chief, and he had the satisfaction of
living to see his great work completed and
solemnly opened for public worship. That towards the end of his task charges of needless
and not unprofitable delays and other accusations
should have been brought against him is perhaps
nothing more than what men of high merit, in
high positions, must·expect as their fate from the
fickle and unreasoning temper of the multitude;
but that *jam extremo sub fine laborum* the Royal
Commissioners should have joined in the outcry

against their old and faithful servant, have fettered and controlled his better judgment in the paltry, but not unimportant matter of the railings that should surround the edifice, that they should have commissioned Sir James Thornhill, in the teeth of Wren's advice, to paint the interior of the dome, and finally have dismissed the architect himself—this was scarcely to be expected from men in so exalted a position. But such was Wren's fate. It was not his fault (as Dean Milman remarks) that the fine fabric of St. Paul's was not set off to advantage by a broad, wide area round it, cleared of all those buildings which now, soaring to more ambitious heights than the edifices of the seventeeth century, cross, break, and dislocate the exquisite flowing and harmonious lines of the Cathedral. We may add that it was not Wren's fault that our city did not arise again with broad and spacious streets, on every side and with magnificent quays to give order and facility to the commerce of the Thames.

Dean Milman adds some facts which are not generally known, and which deserve a record here. The great man who built St. Paul's never saw St. Peter's at Rome; and he had little or no special education in architecture. It is no small credit, then, that he, a single individual, should have conceived, and have elaborated such a noble edifice; and that, while St. Peter's was the work of twenty Popes, and of half as many architects, St. Paul's is (to use the Dean's own words), "the creation of one mind—one great, harmonious conception;" and "was begun and completed, so far as its exterior at least, during the life of that one man." We cannot well imagine any higher satisfaction or nobler pride than that which the old man must have felt when, at the ripe age of ninety years, he saw the last stone placed upon the sacred edifice which he had created, and that too, by the hand of his son. It must have been then, if ever, that he felt the full meaning of those words that afterwards were written on his tomb—" *Si monumentum quæris, circumspice.*"

For other information relating to our metropolitan Cathedral we really must content ourselves with referring our readers to Dean Milman's work, which they can hardly consult for any purpose unsuccessfully. It is well and systematically put together, and, though showing but little of that high poetic feeling for which the late Dean was so remarkable in early life, it has many of the charms of his later prose works. The information which it contains, too, has the great additional recommendation of a careful and tolerably complete index. Here and there we notice a few trifling errors in the text, which, no doubt, will be corrected in another edition. For instance, the prelate who sat in the chair of London sixty years ago was " Porteus," not " Porteous," and it was Dr. " Cosin," not Dr. " Cosins," who was Bishop of Durham after the Restoration.

There are, however, those who lament that the pointed or Gothic style was not chosen by Wren for the Metropolitan Church of London. Our answer is that it is better to have a good Italian edifice than a bad and bastard Gothic; far better to have St. Paul's than a third-rate copy of Canterbury, or Salisbury, or Winchester. On this subject the Dean observes :—

" At that time . . . Gothic-architecture throughout Christendom was dead. In England, its last refuge, it had expired in what after all were but Collegiate and Royal Chapels—King's at Cambridge, and Henry VII.'s at Westminster. Throughout Europe the terms ' Gothic ' and ' barbarous ' bore the same meaning ; Catholicism had revived under the Jesuit reaction ; but her churches affected the Classical Renaissance style. St. Peter's was the unrivalled pride of the Christian world, the all-acknowledged model of Church architecture. To rival St. Peter's, to approach.

its unapproachable grandeur, was a worthy object of ambition to an English, a Protestant architect. St. Peter's had been built from the religious tribute of the whole Christian world; it might be said at the cost of a revolution which severed half the world from the destinies of Rome. It had been commenced, at least, by payments out of the sins of mankind. It had wrought up the doctrine of indulgences to such a height, to such revolting excess in the hands of Papal fanatics, as to force the awakening world to resistance. If Julius II. had not begun, if Leo had not continued the Church of St. Peter's, Luther would at least have wanted one note of that fierce trumpet-blast with which he woke the world."

But the fact is that it is scarcely fair to Sir Christopher Wren to institute a comparison between the edifice which he raised and St. Peter's at Rome. Let us imagine, or try to imagine, what would be the effect of St. Paul's if it could rise out of an area clear and uncrowded on every side, and bask in the cloudless Italian sunlight, instead of brooding under our lifeless and murky sky. Even as it is, setting aside these adventitious accessories, it may safely challenge comparison even with St. Peter's, not in site, nor in internal decoration, but in the grace and harmony of its exterior form. The Dean asks :—

"What eye trained to all that is perfect in architecture does not recognize the inimitable beauty of its lines, the majestic, yet airy, swelling of its dome, its rich harmonious ornamentation? It is singular that St. Paul's, which by its grandeur of old asserted its uncontested dignity as the crown and glory of London, even now . . . . . still appears at a distance with a grace which absolutely fascinates the eye."

Mr. Fergusson himself, though in his work on architecture he criticizes some of the details of the building, expresses an opinion that "the exterior of St. Paul's surpasses in beauty of design all the other examples of the same class which have been carried out, and, whether seen from a distance or near, is, externally at least, one of the grandest and most beautiful churches in Europe." It is well, indeed, then, that the worthy Dean who has so recently passed from among us should be laid in his grave, side by side with Nelson and Wellington, beneath that dome which he loved so dearly as an artist, and in that sacred building which he laboured so steadily and so successfully to make useful to the inhabitants of this great metropolis.

CURIOSITIES OF LONDON.*,

(1869.)

SUCH is the title under which "honest John Timbs," as he is styled among his literary friends, has collected together notices of nearly all that is or has been rare and remarkable in "Modern Babylon," interweaving with them his own personal reminiscences of half a century. During that time Mr. Timbs has lived a busy life, most of which he has spent "within the sound of Bow bells;" in that time he has seen much, and when he has seen it, like Captain Cuttle, he has "made a note of it." The result of these notes and observations he has very naturally embodied in a book, which appeared some few years ago in a small volume; but, having come to the honours of a second edition, it has now reached the gigan-

* "Curiosities of London." By John Timbs.

tic size of a royal octavo, such as might fairly claim the title of a " Cyclopædia " of London, had not Mr. Charles Knight forestalled the term.

It is usual to say that " a great book is a great evil ;" but we must put in a plea for exemption from this too sweeping assertion on behalf of the *Curiosities of London*. We wish that we could honestly say of it that it is thoroughly and entirely perfect; but it certainly is good, and not bad, as far as it goes ; and in spite of some very obvious defects, and some equally obvious redundancies, it will be found a useful addition to our library shelves as a book of reference. Much more useful, indeed, would it be, if, instead of several classified lists of contents at the end, it contained one general index, in order to facilitate reference ; but this defect can easily be remedied in a future edition.

In a book which treats of not only the present but the past of a city, dating from the times of the Romans, it is difficult to decide where to begin ; such a *dubia cœna* is set before us that we well may be excused if we own ourselves not a little perplexed by it. Shall we look for Exeter Change and its Lions? Shall we hunt up the history of the Charterhouse, and of the Carthusian monastery on the site of which it stands? Shall we make a search for a notice of Marylebone

Gardens of last century, or of the more recent
"Ranelagh" and "Vauxhall?"   Have we been
lately at an Archæological Congress, and are we
interested in such questions as the city crypts,
and Guildhalls, and Roman remains and church
bells, and Bartlemy Fair, and the Tower of
London, and Tyburn Tree?   Do we feel an
interest in the Thames Tunnel and old London
Bridge, and the Lord Mayor's State barge, and
the "Frost Fairs" on the river, and the dolphins
and whales which occasionally have been foolish
enough to swim too high up its bed for their
personal safety?   Does little Tommy ask us
to tell him "all about" the old gingerbread
carriage in which he saw the Lord Mayor
drive along Fleet Street on the 9th of last
November, and the mysteries of the Egyptian
Hall at the Mansion House, and to explain to him
how that building differs from the Egyptian Hall
in Piccadilly, where Messrs. Maskelyne and
Cooke hold sway over the world of spirits?
Does the fair Edith or fairer Julia wish to
know how "Almack's" rose into fame and re-
nown, and what is the history of those Botanic
Gardens and the darling "Zoo," to which we took
them (as befitted our country cousins) on that
sweltering day in the middle of last season, or of
the Chiswick Gardens and the Chiswick fêtes of

which they heard talk when in the school-room ?
Does mamma wish to be informed when and
where tea or coffee were first brought into use in
this great metropolis, and what is the real meaning of that horrible "Blue Stocking Club" about
which she used to hear Aunt Dorothy talk so
much when she was a child in pinafores ? Does
Paterfamilias, wearied with the cares of married
life coupled with a narrow income, desire to be
told what god, demi-god, or hero was the founder
of the club system, and how it has beautified Pall
Mall, and half revolutionized the system of London life by throwing cold water upon matrimony?
Does grandpapa ask for his spectacles, and wish to
compare the London daily newspaper of to-day with
that of the days of his childhood, "when George
the Third was King?" On each and all these
subjects we turn instinctively, and not in vain,
to Mr. Timbs' *Curiosities of London;* for we find,
if not the most perfect technical details about
most of them, at all events, enough of popular
information to meet the exigency. Here and
there, it is true, he is at fault; for on going
through the book to search for answers to the
questions indicated above, we have occasionally,
though not often, looked in vain. We cannot,
indeed, find any account of Cremorne Gardens,
either under their own name, or under "Chelsea,"

or under " Gardens," or " Amusements;" though
" Ranelagh," " Vauxhall," and " Marylebone "
Gardens are duly honoured with a notice. So,
again, when we turn to the article on " Newspapers," we are, unhappily, doomed to meet
with disappointment. We say nothing about
the *Times;* but, with respect to the other daily
papers, either Mr. Timbs's information is extremely scanty, or their proprietors and editors
must be most provokingly and churlishly reticent
about their past and present history. For
instance, all he tells us about the *Daily News*
is that it " dates from 1846 "—ignoring the fact
of Mr. C. Dickens's connexion with it at its birth,
and the social and political questions it was started
to solve. Again, he places on record the leading
facts of the history of the defunct *Morning
Chronicle,* and, though more meagrely, those of
the *Morning Post;* while of the *Herald,* all he
says is that it was " founded in 1780 by Sir
Henry Bate Dudley, who seceded from the *Post,*"
and of the *Advertiser,* that " since 1795 it has
been the organ of the licensed victuallers ;" omit-
ting all mention of the rest of our daily contem-
poraries, except in an incidental paragraph relating
to the average sale of three or four of them. With
respect to the weekly journals his work is equally
or even more defective; the only papers now

extant that he even so much as names being the *Observer, Bell's Weekly Messenger,* the *City Press,* and the *Illustrated News.* Surely Mr. Timbs might have found matter of interest for scores upon scores of readers in the leading facts of the past history of the *Illustrated News,* with which he was himself so long and so honourably connected, and of such papers as the old *Globe* in "Father Prout's" days, and earlier still, and *Bell's Life,* when it stood alone in the world of sports; of the paper once edited by Benjamin Disraeli, in which John Murray, of Albemarle Street, sank half a fortune; of the *Examiner* and Leigh Hunt and Fonblanque; of the *Spectator* and Rintoul; of the *John Bull* and Theodore Hook; to say nothing of the *Press,* the *Leader,* and the *Atlas,* and such successful ventures of our own day as the *Saturday Review* and the *Pall Mall Gazette.*

Again, if the ecclesiastical fit seizes us and tempts us to consult the chapter which Mr. Timbs devotes to the " Churches and Chapels" of London, we shall find among them many " curiosities " but also many sins both of omission and of commission. With respect to the ordinary Dissenting Chapels—such as those of the Wesleyans, Anabaptists, Independents, Presbyterians, and Unitarians—he is generally well informed, and so far as we can judge a competent

and trustworthy guide. These respectable, but
modern sects have not much of a past; and as
Mr. Timbs, like most antiquaries, shows an evident leaning to the bygone rather than the present, the meagreness of his sketches appears due
less to any defect in himself than to the barren-
ness of the subject in hand; indeed, in one
instance—we mean his description of Whitefield's
"Tabernacle" in Tottenham Court Road—he is
copious and really most interesting.

Very few of our readers, doubtless, are aware
that, in spite of its *soubriquet* of "Whitefield's Soul-trap," that chapel was visited during
Whitefield's ministry by the then Prince of
Wales and his brothers and sisters, Lords
Chesterfield, Bolingbroke, and Halifax, Horace
Walpole, David Hume, and David Garrick; and
that it owed its first enlargement to the charity
of Queen Caroline, the consort of George II.,
who seeing a crowd standing outside and unable
to gain admission, kindly sent a sum of money to
the preacher, saying, "it was a pity that so many
good people should have to stand in the cold."
That the Dissenting interest, in spite of its strong
Protestant tendency, can as a body become
"worshippers of relics," would seem to be the
fitting inference from the fact that Whitefield's
pulpit is still religiously kept in Tottenham Court

Road, and that the "true and veritable pulpit" from which John Bunyan preached is still exhibited in Jewin Street, Aldersgate, though, as is the case with many other relics, it has a rival pretender to that honour in the shape of a pulpit removed some years since to a Methodist Chapel in Palace Yard, Lambeth. With respect to the "Catholic and Apostolic Church" in Gordon Square, however, Mr. Timbs does not seem to be aware—at all events, he does not let his readers know—that " the community who takes this title" are nothing more or less than the Irvingites, or followers of Edward Irving, whose name is not even mentioned in connection with this church, one of the most beautiful specimens of modern Gothic architecture in the three kingdoms.

More scanty still and more crude is Mr. Timbs's store of information when he acts as our "guide, philosopher, and friend" in a circuit of the Roman Catholic chapels and the Jewish synagogues. It might have been easily imagined that the edifices of the most ancient faith of all—at all events, of all faiths current in " modern Babylon," would have had a larger measure of space allotted to them than the page and five or six odd lines in which they are comprised. We must own that a good deal of curious matter respecting the history of the Jews in London in the middle ages is to be

found in another part of the volume; but we repeat that their religious buildings are inadequately
treated.   We hope, too, that not only Mr. Disraeli,
but the Rothschilds, Montefiores, Cohens, and
Mocattas appreciate the delicate compliment paid
them by Mr. Timbs in placing them after all the
rest of the Dissenting communities, with the single exception of the Roman Catholics, who, no
doubt, will quote this fact with exquisite logic as
a plain proof that Mr. Timbs is not the man to
give "justice to Ireland."   We leave our author,
however, on this score to make his peace with Dr.
Manning and Sir George Bowyer, and only hope
that they will not procure for his work the reward
of being "put into the Index" at Rome.

Seriously speaking, however, we note great
shortcomings in his description of the various
Ambassadors' chapels—the Spanish, the Sardinian, the Bavarian, and the French, for instance
—about which he neglects to tell us that for a
century and a half, under the cruel and infamous
penal laws, they were the only places where mass
was allowed to be said, and where alone the Roman Catholics could perform their devotions.   It
would have been easy (and appropriate to the
subject) to have prefaced his account of these
chapels with a few lines about the numbers and
status of the Roman Catholic body under the

Tudors and Stuarts and the earlier Hanoverian
Sovereigns, for which Charles Butler's biographical works and the statistics given in the Roman Catholic almanacs would have supplied most
abundant and reliable materials. We believe that
the fathers of many persons now alive well remembered the time when a little band of persecuted
Roman Catholics used to meet for mass in the
upper chamber of a third-rate tavern between
Holborn and Lincoln's Inn Fields, and knelt round
a table with pipes, ale, and tobacco placed upon
it, in case some agitator like Whalley or Murphy,
or even some common informer, should step in at
an awkward moment, bring the criminal law to
bear upon the congregation, and consign the priest
to Newgate to be tried for his life. Such reminiscences as these, we repeat, are no fables or myths,
but sober realities and facts of less than a century
ago ; and we venture to say that our readers will
agree with us in thinking that they are matters
worthy of record in a Cyclopædia of the "Curiosities of London." If Mr. Timbs can devote a
chapter to the Jews in London, why can he not
find equal space for reminiscences of the past history of that religious body which once was a
power and something more in England, and
which, even at the present moment, is by far the
most formidable of all those communities among

us which stand in antagonism to the Established
Church.   Truly, the Church of Anselm and Lanfranc, and Thomas A'Becket, and Stephen Lang-
ton, and Sir Thomas More, and Cardinal Pole—
to say nothing of Dr. Wiseman, Dr. Manning,
and Dr. Newman, is worthy of better treatment at
Mr. Timbs's hands, and in more senses than one.

We hope that we shall not be thought guilty of
accusing Mr Timbs of irreligion, or of even sug-
gesting that he is a

"Parcus deorum cultur et infrequens,"

if we frankly express our opinion that when he
passes from the department of churches and
chapels to that of clubs and club-houses, his
merits as a writer show a sensible improvement.
He advances rapidly as an author as he approaches
Piccadilly; in Pall Mall and St. James's Street he
is quite at home, though perhaps not so thoroughly
familiar as he is with the neighbourhood of Fleet
Street and the Strand.   In "club-land" he is in
all his glory, and he rises with his subject in proportion to the intimacy of his acquaintance with
its annals.   How clubs arose from the simple fact
that, as Addison said, "they are founded on eating and drinking, the chief points in which all
men agree, and in which the learned and illiterate,
the dull and the airy, the philosopher and the

buffoon, can all of them bear a part;" or, as we
are told by the still older apophthegm of Aristotle,
that "man is a social and not merely a gregarious
animal,"—all this, and the early history of the
clubs of which Steele and Addison, and Swift
and Pope, and Goldsmith and Hogarth, Ben
Jonson and Samuel Johnson, and Charles James
Fox, and Horace Walpole, and Wilberforce, and
Byron, and Rogers, were members in their day,
he unfolds with a rich store of information and
a fund of anecdote, which is usually to the point,
though every now and then he spoils a story or a
joke in the telling. Does Cousin Emma want to
know about that strange " Kit Cat " Club of
which she has read in the *Lady's Magazine*, or in
Horace Walpole's *Letters*, or in Spence's *Anecdotes*,
and why that charming portrait that hangs in her
father's study is said to be of a " Kit Cat " size?
Let her turn to Mr. Timbs's *Curiosities*, pages
250-1, and she will find the mystery solved. He
writes of this club :—

" It was a society of thirty-nine noblemen and
gentlemen, all zealously attached to the Protestant
succession in the House of Hanover. It is said
to have originated about 1700, in Shire Lane,
Temple Bar (a street recently demolished in
order to make room for the new Law Courts), at

the house of one Christopher Kat, a pastrycook, where the members dined ; he excelled in making mutton pies, which were always in the bill of fare, and were called after his name, ' Kit Cats,' Jacob Tonson, the bookseller, was secretary. Among its members were the Dukes of Somerset, Richmond, Grafton, Devonshire, and Marlborough, and (after the accession of George I.) the Duke of Newcastle, the Earls of Dorset, Sunderland, Manchester, Wharton, and Kingston; Lords Halifax and Somers, Sir Robert Walpole, Garth, Vanbrugh, Congreve, Granville, Addison, Mainwaring, Stepney, and Walsh. Tonson had his own portrait and that of the other members painted by Sir Godfrey Kneller; each member gave him his own portrait, and in order to suit the room a short canvas was used (viz., 36in. by 28in.), but sufficiently long to admit a hand. This is still known as the ' Kit Cat' size. The pictures, forty-two in number, were removed to Tonson's seat at Barn Elms, in the parish of Barnes, where he built a handsome room for their reception. At his death in 1736, Tonson left them to his great-nephew, also an eminent bookseller, who died in 1767. The pictures were then removed to the house of his brother at Water Oakley, near Windsor; and on his death to the house of Mr. Baker at Hertingfordbury, where they now remain. Walpole speaks of the club, as 'the patriots that saved Britain.'"

This is to the point, and all strictly correct, except the trifling mistake of fixing 1700 as the date of the foundation of the club, assuming it to be true, as Horace Walpole tells us that it " had its beginning about the trial of the seven Bishops, in the reign of James II." Surely, in that case, some ten or twelve years earlier would be a date more strictly accurate, and more suited to the character of a work of reference?

We wish that we had time to travel in Mr. Timbs's pleasant company round the the city walls and gates of London, the Guildhall, the Tower, the Bank of England, the Exchange, Christ's Hospital, the Charter House, the Inns of Court, and the Halls belonging to the several City Companies, which are carefully described and illustrated with pleasant anecdotes of more than a single century. But really to give a list of all that is worth reading in this book would be to copy out the contents of half the volume. For instance, as soon as November comes round, we shall be asking each other once more the old question, " What *is* a London fog, and how is it caused?" Mr. Timbs will give us the prescription, or rather the recipe for the mixture, and tell us moreover how it can easily be mitigated in its effects. Do we want to identify the scene of Chatterton's death? The very garret in which he perished is immortalized, and faithfully portrayed as by a photographer. Does a puzzled foreigner desire to master the past history of "Lester Squarr?" He has only to turn to page 511; and he will find a great deal of information about it though Mr. Timbs is silent as to the litigation which has been pending for years between the Tulk family and the public as to the legal ownership of its once green enclosure.*

But, though we have put the book to some tolerably severe tests, we are bound to say that on the whole, and after making allowance for all shortcomings, it strikes us as fairly executed. We can find, it is true, no chapter devoted to either Somers Town or Camden Town, nor (as we have already said) to Chiswick or Cremorne; but it is quite possible that these subjects may be treated under other headings, and the complicated index gives us no clue to them. "Brompton," for instance, instead of having a separate article, as

---

* In 1873 this litigation was brought to an end by the decision of a Court of Law, that the Tulks had no right to build on the enclosure in the centre of the square, which thereupon was purchased by Mr. Albert Grant, and made over as a present to the public as a recreation ground in the following year.

it deserves, turns up under " Kensington ;" and when we at last find Brompton, after a half-hour's drive about the book, like a bewildered cab-fare, we light upon no account of the celebrated " Oratory," though its name is incidentally mentioned in another part of the volume.

As Mr. Timbs is so great in the past, we are somewhat surprised at finding no mention of the Napoleon Museum, which we remember to have seen at the Egyptian Hall, when we were many years younger than we are now, and which drew great crowds to Piccadilly at the time. We might complain also—at least the ladies might complain—and with justice, that, while " cricket" figures among the " amusements " of London, " croquet " does not; and yet we have seen it played in more than one fashionable square at the West End, and for all that we know it may be played this morning in Finsbury Circus. But Mr. Timbs, as an antiquary, has every right to live in the past, and to ignore the present. So much for his sins of omission. Some sins of commission or superfluity, however, in conclusion, must, we fear, be set down to his account. We cannot, for instance, see any reason why a chapter should be devoted to " Alchemists," any more than to " Spirit-rappers " or " Highwaymen," because in no sense are they the peculiar growth of the metropolis; and we must certainly enter our protest against the principle, whatever it may be, which has led Mr. Timbs, while he passes over Hampstead and Highgate and Clapham in silence, to include the Crystal Palace on Sydenham Hill, among the *Curiosities of London.*

INSIDE TEMPLE BAR.

(1876.)

THE news that, after the many respites which it has obtained, Temple Bar is at last doomed,* and that, ere long it will have to give place to the irresistible progress of city improvements, can scarcely be a matter of surprise to anyone, more especially to those who have noticed the forlorn and hopeless condition of that historical obstruction now that it has passed the bicentenary of its existence. Its ragged northern extremity, where it was joined by the fish-shop and book-stall and hairdresser's shop which were pulled down to make room for the south-east angle of the new Law Courts; its mud-bespattered gates, hanging loosely on their antiquated and rusty hinges, and the woe-begone appearance

* Since this paper was written Temple Bar has been pulled down and removed.

of its windows above the archway—behind which the ancient ledgers of the banking house of Messrs. Child are stored—all seem as if they prophesied that its last days are at hand for Temple Bar.

It is natural enough to feel regret for the approaching disappearance of a relic whose history is associated with bygone events; but this nineteenth century is a busy age; and its exigencies are such that it really cannot afford to allow an unnecessary barrier any longer to "stop the way" in one of the two great thoroughfares of London. The "Bar," therefore, which has been connected for two centuries with the names of Wren, and Goldsmith, and Johnson, and Lord Lovat and the Jacobite rebels, and Lord Mayors innumerable, and for which the late Mr. Peter Cunningham pleaded so earnestly, must consider that its end has arrived. Fleet Street, in spite of the measure of relief to its traffic, so tardily afforded by the Thames Embankment, sadly needs widening at its western *débouchement*. We can only hope that the authorities in whose hands its fate rests will deal tenderly with a gateway which the citizens of London have claimed the traditional right of closing even against royalty itself; and that they will allow it to be re-erected either as a gate at one of the entrances to the

Temple with which its name connects it, or in some other historic spot, where the curious may still behold the arch on which the heads of the rebels were exposed within the memory of the grandfathers of some of our readers.

Antiquaries tell us that from time immemorial a bar or barrier of some kind stood at this spot, like a statue of the God Terminus, to mark the limits of the rival cities of London and Westminster, or possibly, to speak more correctly, the spot where the freedom of the city ends. The boundaries of London and Westminster have varied considerably at different times, and were not definitely fixed at Temple Bar till the time of the Stuarts. Whether the "bar" was originally a mere chain or not, is uncertain ; but for whatever structure stood here during the reigns of our Norman and Plantagenet kings, the citizens of London were probably indebted to the Knights Templars, who were located hard by on the south-east. It is alluded to, however, in a grant dated the twenty-ninth of Edward I., A.D. 1301, and it is subsequently mentioned in petitions to Parliament about fifteen years later. It is probable that it was destroyed in the rebellion of Wat Tyler.

In spite of the strictest search, no allusion to the Bar as a " gate," properly speaking, is to be

found before the sixteenth century; the first entry
in the city records, dated in 1502, relates to the
custody of Temple Bar at a period of popular
excitement, the cause of which is not stated; but
it is clear that the structure at this date was a
building, and not a mere "bar." Thirty years
later we find it on record that Anne Boleyn
passed under Temple Bar on her way from the
Tower to her coronation at Westminster Abbey;
and there is extant an engraving of a picture of
the Bar at this date, which shows it to have been
an important structure. This picture, or rather
series of pictures, giving several views of this
procession, used to adorn the walls of Cowdray
House, Sussex; but it was destroyed in the fire
which laid that mansion level with the dust.
Philip and Mary, we are told, were greeted at
Temple Bar at the time of their marriage with
an oration in Latin. Elizabeth, James, Charles,
Oliver Cromwell, and Charles II. each and all had
its gates opened at their approach and passed
under it in turn. To use the words of its biographers :—" Whether Temple Bar suffered any
damage at the time of the Civil War, when the
chains and posts without the walls were removed
in 1648, we are not informed; but we are told
that Cromwell, Fairfax, Bradshaw, Monk, and
Charles II. all in turn halted at the gate, in the

time of their prosperity, and that beneath its shade were enacted those scenes of political excitement of one of which Hogarth has given us a curious picture, with the still more curious circumstance that in his plate he represents the present Bar as standing some dozen years before its time."

The old " Bar " itself, as shown in Hollar's map of London, exhibits a gateway with a centre arch and two side arches, as at present. With the exception of the carving of the Royal Arms over the carriage-way, and those of the City over the posterns for foot-passengers, and some foliage on the pediment and architrave, the old Bar was architecturally as plain as possible. The roof of the building was slanting, with gables; and between the three openings for traffic stood two columns with plain pedestals, and there was another column at each end. An engraving of this structure will be found in the *Illustrated London News*, for March 28th, 1863.

Three years, however, had scarcely passed after the coronation of Charles II. ere the fate of old Temple Bar was sealed. It was agreed between the magnates of " East and West London " that it was desirable that the Bar, which had so narrowly escaped from the Great Fire, should be pulled down and rebuilt on a somewhat more convenient scale. King Charles himself took great interest in the plan, as is clear from several documents still extant in the Record Office, among others the following, which is addressed by His Majesty to the Lord Mayor and Aldermen of London :—

"And finding great inconvenience for want of yᵉ opening of Temple Barr and yᵉ passage and gatehouse of Cheapside into St. Paul's Churchyard, both which are mentioned in yᵉ Act and have been divers times recommended by us, we desire you would forthwith cause yᵉ same to bee putt in execution, according to such contracts as are already or shall be made with you. And although wee recommend this now particularly to your care, wee do hereby promise you to make it our expressly concerne by *aiding and encouraging* yᵉ effectuall execution of it from time to time since wee have made this our city yᵉ place of our royall residence and doe continue to receive from it such marks of loyalty."

Here was a promise of financial aid from the King. How far it was subsequently redeemed may be easily guessed from his conduct in other more important matters—the building of St. Paul's, to wit. Architects, however, were consulted in order to carry out the royal will, and, among others, Inigo Jones, though the matter went in his case no further than the production of a design which, had it been accepted, would have given to London a triumphal arch really worthy of the name. The original design is still extant in an engraving, and also a description of it is to be found in the manuscripts in the British Museum. Had Jones's plan been carried out, there would have been statues at the summit of each corner, and over the centre, upon a pedestal, a fine equestrian statue—of the King, we suppose —with other carvings and medallions on the face of the buildings.

It was on the 27th of June, 1669, that it was finally determined between the Court and the City that the Bar should be pulled down and rebuilt, and a month later Sir Christopher Wren was called into council on the matter. The cost of the new building, to the extent of £1,005, was to be defrayed out of certain funds arising from the then recent introduction of hackney coaches.

The first stone of the new Bar, it would appear, must have been laid in 1670. In two years the plan of Sir Christopher Wren was fully carried out, and the present Bar was the result. It is not a little singular that in the Chronicle of the great architect's life, a work in the handwriting of his son, in the British Museum, there is no mention of the Bar, except the mere date of its erection. Sir Christopher Wren's own Ledger, in the Bodleian Library at Oxford, is equally meagre. The documents in the Record Office are silent; and it is only in a folio volume of expenses of public buildings after the Great Fire, now in the Library at Guildhall, that, under the date of 1671, we read of "Porta urbis, vulgo dicta Temple Bar." On folio 30 of this volume, under the heading of "Temple Barr," with a note attached, "Cash out of the Chamber," we find an account of the payments made during the time of its erection. These range over a period of nearly three years, from August 14, 1669, to March 10, 1672-3, and amount in all to the modest sum of £1,397 10s., including the four effigies, which cost £480. The sculptor of these was a certain John Bushnell. The statues themselves, which have suffered sadly from the weather or from rough treatment, or from both, represent James I. and his Queen, Anne of Denmark, on the City side, and Charles I. and Charles II. on the Westminster side. The present dirty and dingy gates were put up new at the time of Nelson's funeral; they are of oak, panelled, and surmounted by festoons of flowers and fruit. Many persons now alive remember them when they looked bright and even elegant;

but, if it be true that, five years ago, nearly 12,000 vehicles passed under the archway in twelve hours, who can wonder that the gates are splashed with venerable mud? It may be desirable to add here that the present structure is of the Corinthian order, and is built of Portland stone. Each façade has four Corinthian pilasters, an entablature, and an arched pediment. Over the keystone of the arch were formerly a pair of large coats of arms in stone, those of the City on the east side, and those of the King on the west. The former, however, fell down in 1828 ; and the Royal Arms were removed in 1852, to make room for the funeral decorations in honour of the Duke of Wellington, and neither the one nor the other has since been restored.

If the stones of Temple Bar could speak, they would, no doubt, be able to tell us many a tale of street brawls, Mohawk riots, and drunken frolics, as well as of more serious disturbances of a party character. They must have witnessed many a Pope burnt in effigy, and the " Gordon Riots " of 1780, as well as the more recent political outbreaks of the present century, to which we need not allude.

It is a curious fact that, just as Blackfriars Bridge stood for a century, and then was sentenced to come down, Temple Bar had no sooner

celebrated its centenary than it found its existence
to be to some extent doomed. But "doomed persons live long;" and for a hundred years the cry
for its demolition has been raised at intervals, but
without effect. But in 1766, John Gwynn, in
his "London and Westminster Improved," suggested not only the widening of the Strand and
Fleet Street, and the formation of a quay on both
sides of the river, but also the removal of Temple
Bar as the "greatest nuisance" to the City. In
1789, however, the Bar really had a very narrow
escape. A year or two previously, Alderman
Pickett had petitioned the Court of Common Council for the removal of certain obstructions to the
City traffic, and he followed up this petition by
introducing a resolution to the effect that Temple
Bar should be taken down and the materials sold.
This motion was lost by a majority of one. The
alderman, however, was not a man to be easily
beaten; he brought forward resolution upon resolution year after year, and sent round to all the
members of the court a printed letter, urging the
necessity of widening the Strand and Fleet Street,
and pulling down the gateway. At last, in 1789,
he published, in quarto, a pamphlet in which he
vehemently denounced the personal character of
the poor Bar as not only a "great nuisance," but
a "screen for filth," a "shelter and protection for

thieves and pick-pockets," and above all, as " preventing a free circulation of air."   In its place, he proposed to erect " a noble and ornamental pilaster on each side of the street, with chains agreeable to the ancient Bars," which, he hoped, would answer every purpose for preserving the City rights intact.   And what was more, as he saw that the fear of expense kept the Common Council from giving its consent to the project, he offered to head a subscription for the removal of the Bar with £100 out of his own pocket.

At last he got a committee appointed to report upon his plans. It was then found that the purchase of the freeholders' interests, and the removal of the houses in order to widen the street on each side, and the pulling down of the Bar, would cost something over £120,000. An Act, however, was obtained, which allowed the Corporation of London seven years to purchase the buildings, and ten to complete the improvements. The notorious " Butchers' Row," accordingly, was removed, and the Strand was widened from St. Clement's Church to the Bar ; but there the matter ended. A batch of new houses erected on the north side—now swept away to make room for the new Law Courts—turned out a failure ; the alderman died ; and the subject was tacitly allowed to drop, the attention of the Parliament and Government being directed too closely to the outburst of the French Revolution and subsequently to the movements of the great Napoleon, to allow them to bestow a thought on such a commonplace matter as a social improvement in London.

Having had this all but miraculous escape from destruction, the Bar was destined to witness a succession of important events. In 1802, it was gaily hung with oil-lamps (gas then being an unknown luxury) in honour of the Peace of Amiens. In 1806, it received the body of Nelson on its triumphal car on its way from Trafalgar to St. Paul's. In 1814, it was again illuminated in honour of the visit of the Allied Sovereigns, who passed through it on their way to dine at Guildhall, accompanied by the Duke of Wellington. In 1820, Queen Caroline passed under it on her way to St. Paul's to give thanks for, we fear, a very small instalment of mercies ; and a year later her corpse was carried through it on its way to Harwich *en route* for its last resting-place at Brandenburg. In 1830, the Bar looked down as in grim derision upon a Reform riot, in consequence of the unpopularity of the Duke of Wellington and the new police, and the postponement of the expected visit of the King and Queen to the City. On Lord Mayor's Day, 1837, the Bar was once more illuminated on the occasion of Her Majesty's

first state visit to the City to dine with the Lord
Mayor at Guildhall ; and again, in 1844, Queen
Victoria passed beneath it in state when she went
to re-open the Royal Exchange. And to come to
more recent times, in 1858, the Princess Royal
and her husband, the Prince of Germany, in a
storm of snow, passed through its open gates on
their way to Berlin. And, in 1863, who of us
can fail to remember how magnificently decorated
was the City Gate when the citizens of London
offered their loud greetings of " welcome" to the
Princess Alexandra of Denmark on landing upon
our shores as the bride of our own Prince of Wales ?
More recently still, there have passed through it
the King of the Belgians, the Viceroy of Egypt,
and the Sultan of Turkey. In February, 1872,
the Bar was for the last time washed, cleaned,
and decorated in order that the Queen and the
Prince of Wales might pass under it on their
way to St. Paul's to attend the Thanksgiving service which followed on the Prince's recovery from
an illness which was well-nigh fatal.

In 1853 the cry for the removal of the Bar was
renewed in the papers ; but it quietly died away,
and nothing was done. In 1858 the Metropolitan
Board of Works politely reminded the Corporation
that " Temple Bar presents an obstruction to the
traffic of the Strand and Fleet Street ;" but again

with the same result, for nothing was done: in 1861 the Court of Common Council tried to turn the tables on the Board by resolving that the Bar was really no obstruction at all, and they actually passed a resolution " discharging" all further reference to the subject, although only a few years previously the citizens of London had refused to spend even the modest sum of £1500 in order to put it in repair. From that day to this, however, owing to the mooting of the question of our new Law Courts, and the necessity of a new bridge connecting them with the Temple, the Bar has lived a doomed life, and is now practically sentenced to death, although a variety of circumstances may conspire to prolong its reprieve. In 1868 the cry was raised that the structure was unsafe, and, if not repaired, would soon tumble about our ears ; but the alarm subsided speedily.

The following description of an ancient custom, which henceforth must, of necessity, die away, we may be pardoned for transferring to our pages from those of *Belgravia* :—

" Here, on those rare occasions when Royalty visits the City, the gates are closed in order that a curious and old custom may be performed with becoming dignity. The royal procession having arrived at the gate which is the entrance to the civic domain, the herald sounds a trumpet and knocks thrice upon the closed doors, which are immediately thrown open, and the Lord Mayor, for the time being, makes over his Sword of State to the Sovereign, who is graciously pleased to return it. Such is the custom of the present day, and such it has been for many centuries.

"When the Spanish Armada was driven from our shores, and good Queen Bess proceeded to St. Paul's to give public thanks for so great a deliverance, the same ceremony was enacted; and Cromwell some years later, when he and his Parliament dined in state in the City, allowed the old custom to be carried out, but with this difference, that the Sword was delivered up to the Speaker instead of to the Head of the State. After Marlborough had humbled France at Oudenarde, Blenheim, Malplaquet, and Ramillies, Queen Anne went through the same ceremony, when she, too, proceeded to give thanks at St. Paul's."

The same writer observes on another page:—

"In the dirt-begrimed niches, two on either side of the archway, are statues representing James I., his Queen, Charles I., and Charles II.; and on the gate above, in more recent times, were put up ornaments of another description. Here, for the edification of His Majesty's liege subjects the mangled remains of Thomas Armstrong, one of the Rye House Plot conspirators, were displayed. And here, too, might be seen, a little later, dangling in the wind, the quarters of Sir John Friend and Sir William Perkins, who attempted the life of William III. The last mementos of this usage appeared in the year 1745, when the heads of Lord Lovat and several others of the unfortunate followers of the so-called 'Pretender' were placed upon the Bar—a grim and unedifying spectacle, one would fancy, for business men; but people in those days thought otherwise, for Walpole, in a letter to Montague, says: 'I have been this morning to the Tower, and passed under the new heads at Temple Bar, where people make a trade of letting spying-glasses at a half-penny a look.' It was here, too, that Dr. Johnson, a true Jacobite at heart, stood with Goldsmith, and, pointing to the heads that still disfigured the gateway, exclaimed, with some hidden humour, 'Forsitan et nostrum nomen miscebitur istis!'"

But an account of Temple Bar would be quite incomplete if we were to dwell merely on its outside features and did not stop to say a word or two about its interior, and about the banking-house of Messrs. Child, of which that interior forms a part.

It is well known that it was only gradually that

the goldsmiths and silversmiths of London changed their especial trade for that of " bankers " in the modern sense of the term ; and all readers of the "Fortunes of Nigel" will remember that Fleet Street and Whitefriars were the head-quarters of those worthies.   As a proof of this assertion, we may here quote an entry from what may be called the earliest known " London Post Office Directory," which was reprinted a few years ago by the enterprising Mr. J. C. Hotten, of Piccadilly.   In a list of "all the Goldsmiths that keep running cashes" in London, we find the names of "Messrs. Richard Blanchard and Child, at the Marygold, in Fleet Street."   The only other now existing banking firm that is mentioned is that of " Messrs. Hoare (or, as the name is there spelt, 'Hore), at the Golden Bottle, in Cheapside."

But it is time to enter in ; so, passing through Messrs. Child's bank, where the Marygold still greets us on the inside wall of what is still known as " the shop," we go upstairs to the first floor, and are shown into a small parlour in which hang Sir T. Lawrence's portrait of the late Lady Jersey as she shone a " Court Beauty " at the coronation of George IV., and also another picture, to which we shall presently allude at greater length.   Cut in, or rather through, the old City wall, of which the Bar itself is but a continua-

tion; there are some steps to be mounted, like
the entry to a church belfry ; and our way lies on
through a crooked passage, over which might be
written, as well as over the doorway of a Cathedral, the couplet—

> " See that ye make the western portals low;
>   Let none here enter who disdain to bow."

When we have cleared this passage, we are inside the chamber of Temple Bar itself. It is
panelled in the style of the period at which it
was built, and lined from top to bottom with the
ledgers and journals of Messrs. Child, which have
accumulated for the last two hundred years.

On our right hand and our left are windows
looking down into Fleet Street and the Strand
respectively. Their frames are scarely water-
proof, and they look as if they had not been
dusted or cleaned for years. This, however, is
the room which has been always used for the ac-
commodation of the Lord Mayor and Aldermen as
often as they have come to the Bar in state in
order to receive royalty, or for other purposes, as
for example on the occasion of the funeral of the
Duke of Wellington.   For the use of this chamber
Messrs. Child pay the City a rent of £25 a
year.

We gaze in awe and wonder at these mute

memorials of the "accounts" of customers—who have all long since gone to their own last account; and, passing on into an inner chamber still more dusty and grimy than the outer one, we are confronted by an almost perpendicular ladder, having climbed which we are in the "attic." Here the dust is venerable and positively solid; the ledgers and journals are still older, many of them belonging to the seventeenth century. Among the other treasures of the bank which are kept here, are to be seen piles on piles of the bank-notes issued by the firm in the early part of the last century, before the right of issuing such paper money was restricted by law to the Bank of England. There are hundreds upon hundreds of these, rotting with age and covered with dust and dirt in this upper story; and each of them bears in dexter upper corner an engraving of the Bar as it then appeared. It is singular that the house of Messrs. Child should have allowed this venerable "trade mark" to fall into disuse.

The books of the banking firm, its ledgers and journals, which line the walls of the house and of the room over the archway, fill about seventy or eighty shelves; and the large amounts with which the earliest volumes deal, leave no room to doubt that the transactions of Messrs.

Child extend back to a still more remote date.

The list of the customers of the bank two centuries ago, as revealed to us by a casual glance at the headings of the banking accounts in Messrs. Child's ledgers, is a very distingnished one. In 1687 we find not only those of "the King's and Queen's Majesties," but of the Dukes of Newcastle, Bolton, Leeds, Buckingham, and Albemarle, the Marquises of Winchester and Carmarthen, Lords Danby, Halifax, Mulgrave, Rivers, Crewe, Thanet, Exeter, and Torrington, of the "Tellers of the Exchequer," of Lady Anne Walpole, of Horace Walpole, Esq., and his lady, and of such families as the Coke, Proby, Brook Bridges, Vyner, Palmer and Jenyns—very many of whose heads and representatives still continue as customers to the present time. Some of these accounts, to judge from a single page, must have been very large. For instance, there appears standing to the credit of the then Duke of Newcastle £12,670, while on the opposite page his Grace's drafts appear as only £412. Monk, Duke of Albemarle, in like manner is credited a few days further on with £40,743; but against this he appears to have drawn two cheques within a few days of each other to the tune of £15,000 a-piece. The Duke of Bolton's account, on the other hand, stands only at £197, and this sum he seems to have drawn out in driblets almost as soon as it was paid in.

In one of these ledgers we were shown the banking account of Nell Gwynn. It is headed "the honourable Madame Gwinn, Cr." There are only three or four entries on this page; but it appears that Messrs. Child had advanced to her on the security of plate no less than £4,600, and that after her death she owed the bank, on a debtor and creditor account, £808 14s 3d. Among her assets, however, were 14,443 ounces of plate, which realised £2,300; and the statement of account between the bank and her representatives, the Duke of St. Albans, and other well known personages, bears the signatures of the Earls of Rochester and Pembroke, H. Sydney, and R. Sawyer. The account is dated, "1687, January ye seventh."

It appears that at this time, and even to a very much later date, no such machinery as that of "Pass Books" was known, but that customers were in the habit of calling occasionally when they came to town in order to see how they stood with their bankers, and that when they were satisfied they wrote in the ledgers, "I allow this account," adding their signatures and the date; when this was done, the balance was carried forward as the commencement of a fresh account. It was a female customer of this house, Lady Cartaret, to whose suggestion the first introduction of "Pass Books" is due.

Messrs. Child, however, appear to have done also a little business as jewellers; for in the private account of "the King's and Queen's Majesties," under date 1687, May 17, we find the following entries on the debtor side: "For loan of jewels for the coronation to the Queen, £222;" "for diamond earrings for the Queen, £300;" "for a ring for his Majesty's own hand, £215." On the same page and on the following are similar entries for rings given by James to the Ambassadors from France, Savoy, and other countries. It may be added that Messrs. Child still hold some fine pieces of family plate deposited as security for loans as far back as the days of the Stuarts.

In the room through which alone you can gain access to the interior of Temple Bar, hangs a curious picture of the structure, apparently about a hundred and twenty years old. It is very much in the style of Hogarth; it gives the western front; and through the arch up the vista of Fleet Street you see the church of St. Dunstan with its figures of Gog and Magog, which stood there till our own days, when Lord Hertford removed them to his villa in the Regent's Park. On your right as you look at the picture is Messrs. Child's bank, and wonderfully little has it altered in outward appearance. The shop on the north side, in which half a century or more ago John Crockford, the founder of "Crockford's Club" made his fortune, was then apparently a confectioner's, if we may judge from the glasses in the windows, which look as if they were full of sugar plums. It is May-day, and a " Jack in the Green " is being carried, or, led near the pavement on the south, much to the amusement of the little *gamins*, whose ragged and tattered clothes bespeak the " gutter children." On the north side is a young " swell " of the period, neatly and fashionably dressed, with sword, wig, and wig-box all *en règle*; he is chatting with a cit on the weather ·or some passing topic, and a sweep comes behind him and prints the marks of his five dirty fingers on the back of his pale-coloured coat. The drayman who is passing enjoys the fun, as also does the driver of a vehicle under the archway, which looks for all the world like one of those huge-wheeled cabs where the driver sat aloft, and which were so common in London about forty years ago, before " Hansoms " were invented.

The heads, or rather sculls, of the " rebel Lords "—Lovat and Derwentwater—which are seen on high poles at the top of the picture, help us at all events to fix the date of the painting at about 1750-60, and remind us of the horrors of a civil war even when waged on a small scale. It is a tradition in Messrs. Child's bank that the head of Lord Lovat, when taken down from the pole, was kept for some years in the upper story of Temple Bar, and eventually given up to the Frasers, of whose clan Lord Lovat was the chief. It is stated by Mr. Noble in his antiquarian work on Temple Bar, that the painter of this picture was a Mr. Michael Angelo Rooker, one of the earliest Associates of the Royal Academy, who died in 1801, and lies buried in the cemetery of St. Giles'-in-the-Fields. Mr. Noble adds that the picture was painted in 1772; but as the last of the skulls fell down in 1770, it is clear that if his date is correct, in that case the artist has been purposely guilty of an anachronism, though perhaps a pardonable one.

The back portion of the premises of Messrs. Child's bank are part and parcel of the once celebrated "Devil Tavern,"—originally the "Devil and St. Dunstan,"—a place of resort as old certainly as the reign of James 1. Here the celebrated "Apollo" club used to meet; here Ben Jonson composed some of his plays, more particularly "The Devill is an Asse." Here also

Dean Swift, Steele, and Addison dined in 1710 in Garth's company and at his cost; and here for several years, about 1746-1750, the Royal Society held its dinners. The sign-board of the "Devil" is shown by Hogarth in his "Burning of the Rumps;" but, curiously enough, he places it on the wrong side of the street. On the wall of one of the rooms in which Steele wrote, and which still remains in much the same state as a century and a half ago, and on the wainscot over the fire-place are painted the following convivial lines, which date back probably as far as the year 1600, and are ascribed to Ben Jonson himself. As they have never been published in full, we give them at length, the more willingly as we understand that together with Temple Bar itself this old house too is doomed to come down, and probably will soon have passed away :—

> Welcome all who lead to follow
> To the orácle of Apollo.
> Here he speaks out of his pottle,
> Or the Tripos, his Tower-Bottle.
> All his answers are divine ;
> Truth itself does flow in wine.
> 'Hang up all the poor hop-drinkers'
> Cries old Sym, the King of Skinkers,
> He that half of life abuses,
> That sits watering with the Muses,
> Those dull girls, no harm can mean us ;
> Wine it is the milk of Venus,

> And the poet's horse accounted,
> Ply it, and you all are mounted.
> 'Tis the true Phæbian (*sio*) liquor,
> Cheers the brain, makes wit the quicker;
> Pays all debts, cures all diseases,
> And at once three senses pleases.
> Welcome all who lead or follow
> To the orácle of Apollo.
>   O! RARE BEN JONSON!

It only remains to add that Temple Bar was pulled down in the winter of 1877-8, and that Messrs. Child's bank is now (April, 1879) in course of demolition and re-construction. The houses on the south side of Fleet Street being thrown back a few feet, so as to widen the thoroughfare.

AT FABYAN'S TOMB.

IT is probably unknown, and quite unsuspected, by all the hundred thousand persons who daily pass up and down the pavement of Cornhill, that hard by, within the walls of St. Michael's Church, there reposes a civic celebrity of the olden time, who was at once an alderman, a chronicler, and a poet. I will not say that he ever rose into the foremost rank among the servants of the Muses; but he affords, nevertheless, a rare instance of a citizen and merchant of London, who in the dark ages of the fifteenth century devoted himself to the pleasures of literature.

The person to whom I refer was one Robert Fabian, or Fabyan, who appears to have been a man born and bred " within the sound of Bow Bells," and who, after holding sundry less distinguished offices, was chosen one of the Sheriffs of London in 1493, and died, as was recorded on his tomb, in the year 1511, two years after the accession of Henry VIII. Strype, who gives a copy of his epitaph, says that his monument was no longer extant in 1603. According to Bayle, Fabian died on the 28th of February, 1512. He is better known as an historian, or rather an annalist, than as a poet; for English writers often refer to, and quote with advantage, his two large volumes of *Chronicles*, which give us accounts of the leading events of the history of this kingdom—the first, " from the landing of Brutus, or Brute, down to the death of King Henry II.," and the other, " from the first year of King Richard I., to the death of King Henry VII." Yet even in these books of most unquestioned prose and prosiness, the poetic element crops up continually under the author's hand; for prefixed to each of his chronicles are introductory verses, some of which are exceedingly droll and quaint.

Fabian was, according to Winstanley, who quotes from a still earlier biographer, a man " of a very merry disposition," and one who " used to entertain his guests with good victuals as with good discourse," He adds that " he bent his mind much to the study of poetry, which, according to those times, passed for current." It is just probable that the good dinners which

he gave to his friends at his house in his ward,
—for at that time all the aldermen resided
within the city walls,—may have had something
to do with making the Londoners tolerate and
perhaps even admire his poems, which, like many
other poems of that day, consist of little more
than " doggrel " verses, as he himself repeatedly
styles them with genuine or affected modesty.

Sir John Suckling, in his *Contest of the Poets*
of his time, it may be remembered, makes Apollo
adjudge the laurel crown to an Alderman for the
reason assigned above :—

> " He openly declared that it was the best sign
>   Of good store of wit to have good store of wine ;
>   And without a syllable more or less said,
>   He put down the laurel on th' alderman's head.

But in " the days of the witty Suckling," as
Charles Knight observes in his `Table Talk`,
" there were good poets, and no alderman who
was a verse-maker.   Indeed, Fabian was
unique.   There never was another."   Had Mr.
Charles Knight lived till now, however, he
would not have made so rash an assertion, for
he would have remembered that Mr. Alderman
Cotton was, and is, a devoted slave to the muse
of poetry.

I may, perhaps, be pardoned for quoting here
in extenso Fabian's encomium on London. It is

certainly whimsical and curious enough to justify
repeating in these pages, preserving the original
spelling and pointing :—

> Now woulde I fayne
> In wordes playne
> Some honour sayne
>   And brynge to mynde
> Of that auncyent cytye
> That so goodly is to se
> And full trewe euer hath be
>   And also full kynde.
>
> To Prince and Kynge
> That hath borne just rulynge
> Syn the fyrste winnynge
>   Of this Iland of Brute
> So that in great honour
> By passynge of many a showre
> It hath ever borne the flowre
>   And laudable bruit.
>
> Of euery cytye and towne
> To serche the world rowne
> Neuer yet caste downe
>   As other many have be :
> As Rome and Carthage
> Hierusalem the sage,
> With many other of age
>   In storye as ye may see.
>
> Thys so oldely founded
> Is so surely grounded
> That no man may confounde yt
>   It is so sure a stone
> That yt is upon sette

For though some have it thrette
With Manasses grym and greate
   Yet hurte had yt none.

Cryste is the uery stone
That the cytye is sette upon
Whyche from all hys foon*
   Hath euer preserved yt.
By meane of dyvyne seruyce
That in contynuall wyse
Is kept in devout guyse
   Wythin the mure† of yt

As Houses of Relygyon
In diuerse places of thys towne
Whyche in great devocyon
   Ben euer occupyed :
When one hath done, another begyn
So that of prayr they neuer flyn‡
Such order is these houses wythin,
   Wyth all vertue allyed.

The Paryshe churches to reken
Of which nomber I shall speken,
Wherein speke many preste and deken
   And Cryste dayly they serve.
By meane of whych sacryfyce
I trust that he in al wyse
This Cryste for her servyce
   Doth euer more preserve

This Cytye, I meene ye Troynouaunt,
Where honour and worschipp doth haunt,
Wyth vertue and ryches accordaunt,
   No Cytye to yt lyke.

---

* Foes.   † Wall.   ‡ Fail.

To speke of euery commodity
Fleshe and fishe and alle dentye
Clothe and sylke wyth wyne plenty
　　That ye for hole and syke

Brede and ale wyth spyces fyne
With houses faire to soup and dyne
Nothynge lackynke that ys condygne
　　For man that ys on molde.
With riuers freshe and holesome ayre
Wyth women that be good and fayre
And to this Cytye done repayre
　　Of straungers many folde

The vytayle that herein is spente
In the householdes dayly tent
Betweene Rome and ryche Kent
　　Are none may theym compare
As to the Mayre and Shriues* twayne
What myght I of justyce sayne,
Kept wythyn this Cytye playne
　　It were long to declare.

For though I should all day tell
Or that wyth my ryme dogerell
Myght I not yet halfe do spell
　　This towne's great honour
Therefore shortly, as I began,
Pray for yt, both chyld and man
That yt may continue, and
　　To bere of all the floure.

I venture also to give a specimen of another

* Sheriffs.

of the short poems with which the worthy
Alderman interspersed his *Chronicles.* It is
headed, " To his Reader of these Rymes :"—

> " Who so hym lyketh these verses to rede
> Wyth favour, I pray he will theym spell,
> Let not the rudeness of theym hym lede
> For to desprave thys ryme dogerell,
> Some part of the honour it doth you tell
> Of this olde Cytye Troynouant
> But not thereof the halfe dell
> Connyng in the maker is so adaunt.
> But though he hadde the eloquence
> Of Tully and the moralytye
> Of Senek, and the influence
> Of the sweyte-sugred Armony
> Or that fayre Ladye Caliope,
> Yet hadde he not connynge perfght
> This Cytye to prayse in eche degre
> As yt shuld duely aske by ryght."

The author appears to have set great store on
his productions, and especially on his Chronicles,
which he styles, *The Concordaunce of Historyes.*
The work itself is divided, like an epic poem, into
seven parts, of which the first to the sixth
inclusive carry the annals of England down to
the Norman Conquest, whilst the seventh is
devoted to the history of our Norman and Plantagenet sovereigns. In this last portion of the
Chronicle we have the results of the author's
personal observations interspersed with the text.

A copy of verses such as those given above is added as a sort of epilogue to each part, and they are severally named after "The Seven Joys of the Blessed Virgin."

There have been no less than five editions of the *Chronicle;* the first was printed by Pynson in 1516, the second appeared in 1533, the third in 1542, and the fourth in 1559. The work was reprinted in 1811, in quarto, with a biographical obituary preface by the late Sir Henry Ellis, of the British Museum.

Bishop Nicolson, in his *English Historical Library*, bears a strong testimony to the value of *Fabyan's Researches.* He writes:—"The first post in the sixteenth century is due to Robert Fabian, an eminent merchant, and some time sheriff of London. Both Bale and Pits subdivide his historical writings into a great many several treatises, but I presume what they call his *Historarum Concordantiæ* is the sum of all. . . He is very particular in the affairs of London, many good things being noted by him which concern the government of ' that great city, hardly to be had elsewhere."

Warton also, in his *History of English Poetry*, passes on Fabian the following criticism: "Our author's transitions from verse to prose, in the course of a prolix narrative, seem to be made with much ease; and, when he begins to versify, the historian disappears only by the addition of rhyme and stanza. . . As an historian, our author is the dullest of compilers. He is equally attentive to the succession of the mayors of London and of the monarchs of England; and seems to have thought the dinners at Guildhall, and the pageantries of the City Companies, more interesting transactions than our victories in France, and our struggles for public liberty at home."

The epitaph in " doggrel" rhyme, once inscribed on the tomb of Fabian, though destroyed in the Great Fire of London, is happily preserved in Weaver's Funeral Monuments; it ran as follows:—

" Here lyeth Robert Fabian, Alderman and Sheriff of London, who composed a laborious chronicle of England and France, with the monuments and succession of the Lord Maiors of London, and died Anno Domini 1511; for whom this monument was made.

> " Like as the day his course doth consume,
>   And the new morrow springeth againe as fast,
>   So man and woman by Nature's custome
>   This life to pass at last in earth are cast.
>   In joy and sorrow, which here their time doth wast.
>   Neuer in one state, but in course transitorie,
>   So full of change is of this world the glory."

This epitaph is " bad enough," as Charles

Knight wittily observes, " to have been written by Fabian himself."   The quaint and honest old Fuller remarks in his " Worthies," if I remember aright, that " none have on their monuments worse poetry than poets themselves;" and it is some comfort to those who like to see poetical justice observed; for, whatever Robert Fabian may have deserved as a giver of dinners, and as an Alderman of the City, he at all events did not merit a better epitaph as a poet.

GORE HOUSE AND LADY BLESSINGTON.

ANOTHER relic of our age is gone, so rapidly does the present become the past to us all. Gore House, at Kensington Gore, so long the abode of Lady Blessington, and the house where she ruled among an admiring and fashionable throng as a Queen of Society, is levelled with the dust, and another and prouder mansion is rising to the skies in the garden close behind it. But the new Gore House, however lofty and splendid it may be, will never rival that which, thirty years ago, used to call Lady Blessington its mistress. And why? Because it will not be easy again to find a woman, however fair, rich, and titled, who will be able to play in the *salons* of London as cleverly as did Marguerite, Countess of Blessington, the *rôle* which Madame de Staël played with such success in those of

Paris. It was vacated by her in the spring of 1849, and in the May of that year its costly effects were sold by auction on the premises. Lady Blessington's death ensued in the following month, her heart being broken by the loss of all her earthly treasures.

In the course of its existence—probably less than a hundred years from first to last—Gore House saw several vicissitudes. In the last century, when it was little more than a cottage, it was tenanted by a stingy, money-scraping Government contractor, who would not lay out a penny even to keep his gardens in order. The mammon-worshipper who meditated in those neglected grounds was succeeded, about the year 1800, by the " Saint," William Wilberforce, who thus mentions them in his Diary :—

" We are just one mile from the turnpike gate at Hyde Park Corner, . . . having about three acres of pleasure ground around my house, or rather behind it, and several trees, of walnut and mulberry, of thick foliage. . . . I can sit and read under their shade, which I delight in doing, with as much admiration of the beauties of nature (remembering at the same time the words of my favourite poet, ' Nature is but a name for an effect whose cause is God,') as if I were two hundred miles from the great city."

After an interval of some fifteen years, a new meditator, but not so much on the beauties of nature as on those of art and literature—one who was more *spirituelle* in *salons* than " spiritual " in Wilberforce's sense of the term—the " gorgeous " Lady Blessington became in turn the proprietor of Gore House. Illustrated " Annuals " and fashionable novels were the results of her ladyship's meditations in those pleasure grounds which had served Mr. Wilberforce for solitude and for pondering on sacred things.

Gore House was low and unpretending, its external beauty, if it had any, belonging to its southern or garden side. Along with its neighbour, it was faced with white stucco, and, standing close to the road side, looked as if meant originally for the lodge of some great mansion which had never actually been built; the row of which it formed a part, as Leigh Hunt so comically observes in " The Old Court Suburb," might easily lead one to imagine that it had been divided into apartments for the retainers of the Court, and that either a supernumerary set of maids of honour had lived there, or that some four or five younger brothers of lords of the bedchamber had been the occupants, all being bachelors, and expecting places in reversion. " The two houses," adds the writer, " seem to be nothing but one large drawing-room; they possess, however, parlours and second stories at the back, and they have good gardens; so that, what with their flowers behind them, the park in front, and their own neatness and elegance, the miniature aristocracy of their appearance is not ill borne out."

It was from and after the year 1836 that Gore House became a centre of attraction to the world of letters, for, besides giving such dinners as Dr. Johnson would have thought " worth being asked to," Lady Blessington prided herself on her success in " bringing people together," in order to please and be pleased in turn. " In this benevolent project," says Leigh Hunt, " she was assisted by Count d'Orsay; and here, according with somewhat of an excess on the side of universality, were to be seen poets and prose writers, both Whig and Tory, distinguished journalists, Edinburgh and Quarterly reviewers, actors, artists, travellers, exiles, Landor and ' Tommy ' Moore being the leaders amongst the poet tribe, and 'Prince' Louis Napoleon at the head of the exiles." Every celebrated novelist, in particular, naturally made one of a circle over which presided the charming woman, who was herself a novelist. We do not hear of many ladies among the visitors, though the Countess herself appears to have had cordial female friends; but this was to be accounted for by

the fact that English ladies viewed with some
suspicion the residence under the same roof of a
pretty widow of five-and-forty with a man ten
years her junior and separated from his wife—an
arrangement more in accordance with French habits than with English ideas of propriety.   Still,
there were several of our countrywomen of un-
blemished reputation who despised and defied
" Mrs Grundy," and were glad and proud to find
themselves included in the invitations to the "At
Homes " of Lady Blessington ; and really there
would seem to have been about the fair hostess of
Gore House a charm which defies description.

" About the beginning of Her Majesty's reign,"
writes Mr. R. R. Madden in his " Life and Correspondence of the Countess of Blessington," " there
were three circles of fashionable society in London, wherein the intellectual celebrities of the
time did chiefly congregate.   Over these presided
three very remarkable women—Lady Holland, the
Countess of Charleville, and Lady Blessington.
The qualities, both mental and moral, of the ladies
differed very much, but their tastes concurred in
one particular.   Each of them sought to make
society in her house as agreeable as possible, to
bring together as much of ability, wit, and intel-
lect as could be assembled and associated with

advantage; to elicit any kind or any amount, however small, of talent that any individual admitted into that society might possess; and to endeavour to make men of letters, art, or science, previously unacquainted or estranged, or disposed to stand aloof from each other, or to isolate themselves in society, think kindly and favourably of one another. I am not quite sure, however, that a very kindly feeling towards each other prevailed among the rival queens of London literary society.

"The power and influence of Lady Blessington's intellectual qualities consisted chiefly in her conversational talents. It would be difficult to point out any particular excellence, or to say that any one constituted the sole or peculiar charm of her conversation. It was something of frankness and archness, without the least mixture of ill-nature, in everything she said, of *enjouement* in every thought she uttered, of full confidence in the out-speaking of her sentiments, and the apparent absence of every *arrière pensée* from her mind, while she laughed out unpremeditated ideas and *bon-mots* spontaneously elicited, in such joyous tones that it might be said she seldom talked without a smile, at least, on her lips. It was a felicity in her mode of expression, and its freedom from all reserve, superadded to the effect produced by singular loveliness of face, expressiveness of look and gesture, and gracefulness of form and carriage, that constituted the peculiar charm of Lady Blessington's talk."

"It would be idle," writes one who knew her well, "to compare the conversational talents of Lady Blessington with those of Sidney Smith or Sir James Mackintosh in any respect but one, and that was her power of making light matters appear of moment and dull things brilliant in society, and bright thoughts, uttered even in sport, contribute to the purposes of good humour, thus tending to enliven, amuse, and exhilarate people's minds when in search of amusement and relaxation."

The end of the affair can be easily imagined. The contents of Gore House were sold by auction on the premises, by Mr. Phillips; in whose catalogue they are thus described:—

"Costly and magnificent effects, comprising all the magnificent furniture, rare porcelain, sculpture in marble, bronzes, and an assemblage of objects of art and decoration; a casket of valuable jewellery and *bijouterie*, services of rich chased silver and silver gilt plate, a superbly-fitted silver dressing-case; a collection of ancient and modern pictures, including many portraits of distinguished persons, valuable original drawings and fine engravings, framed and in portfolios; the extensive and interesting library of books, comprising upwards of 5,000 volumes; expensive table services of china and rich cut glass, and an infinity of useful and valuable effects. All the property of the Right Hon. the Countess of Blessington, retiring to the Continent."

It may be interesting to know that the gross amount of the sale was £13,385, and the net sum realised £11,985. The sale at Gore House is thus described by an eye-witness who had often been admitted within the house as an ever-welcome guest :—

"On the 10th of May I visited Gore House for the last time. The auction was going on; there was a large assemblage of people of fashion. Every room was thronged; the well-known library salon in which Lady Blessington's *conversaziones* took place was crowded, but not with guests. The arm-chair in which the lady of the mansion was wont to sit was occupied by a stout coarse gentleman of the Jewish persuasion, busily engaged in examining a marble hand extended on a book, the fingers of which were

modelled from a cast of those of the absent
mistress of the establishment.   People as they
passed through the room poked the furniture and
pulled about the precious objects of art and ornaments of various kinds that lay on the table; and
some made jests and ribald jokes on the scene
they witnessed.   It was a relief to leave that room.
I went into another, the dining room, where I had
often enjoyed in goodly company the elegant
hospitality of one who was indeed a most kind
hostess.   I saw there among the crowd of gazers
an individual who looked thoughtful and even
sad.   I remembered his features; I had dined
more than once with that gentleman in that very
room.   He was a humorist, a facetious man, one
of the editors of *Punch*, but he had a heart, with
all his drollery and his *penchant* for fun and
raillery.   I accosted him and said, 'We have met
here I think, but under different circumstances.'
He made some observations which showed that
he felt as I did.   I took my leave of Mr. Albert
Smith, thinking far better than I ever did before
of the class of facetious persons who are expected
to amuse society on set occasions, and to make
sport for the public."

According to a letter addressed to Lady
Blessington after all was over by her faithful

French valet, there was at all events one other ancient guest of the house who left it on that sad day with tears in his eyes, and who seemed far more truly pained than anyone besides, and that was William Makepeace Thackeray.

As to the details of the sale, the portrait of Lady Blessington, by Sir T. Lawrence, which had cost only £80, was knocked down to Lord Hertford for £336; the companion portrait of Lord Blessington, by the same, being purchased by Mr. Fuller for £68 5s. Lord Hertford purchased also the portrait of the Duke of Wellington, by Count d'Orsay—his *chef-d'œuvre*, and the only portrait which the Duke himself thoroughly liked—for £189; Sir E. Landseer's picture of a spaniel fetched £150, and that of Miss Power £37 10s.; while Sir T. Lawrence's picture of Mrs. Inchbald was knocked down for £48.

Lady Blessington and her two nieces, the Misses Power, had left Gore House for Paris just one month previously, being preceded by a fortnight by Count d'Orsay, who had long been confined to the house and grounds in fear of the sheriff's officers, and had been glad to make his escape to a land where he could not be arrested for his debts in London, and where he trusted that his old friend Louis Napoleon, then Prince President, would not forget him.

And the sadness of the scene must have been bitterly increased to Lady Blessington if at that last moment she remembered what she had written in her very first book, which had made its appearance from her pen about a quarter of a century before. We allude to her " Sketches and Scenes in the Metropolis," which begins with an account of the ruin of a large and fashionable establishment at the West End, and of an auction in the house of its late proprietor, a " person of quality " —the sale of all his furniture and effects, his costly ornaments, his precious *objets d'art*, and valuable family pictures. Strange to say, as if with a foresight of her own case, she mentions the name of the ruined gentleman whose " household gods " were thus departing from him as " B——," and portrays with graphic power the very scenes which twenty-seven years afterwards were destined to be enacted in her own drawing-room, even anticipating the heartless and unfeeling remarks of the brokers, the dealers in *bijouterie*, the starched exquisites, the simpering damsels, and the sour elderly ladies, who harangued each other on the faults, follies, errors, and extragavancies of " poor Mr. B——." " And this," adds her ladyship, at the end of her sketch "and this is an auction. A scene that has so often been the resort of the young, the grave, and the gay, is now one where those who have partaken of the hospitality of the once opulent owner of the mansion now come to witness his downfall, regardless of his misfortune, or perhaps even to rejoice in their own contrasted prosperity."

This sketch would, indeed, have answered *verbatim et literatim*, and with a bitter because unconscious irony, for the auction scene at Gore House, in May, 1849. And so passed away the glories of Gore House.

"For nineteen years (says Mr. Madden), Lady Blessington had maintained, at first in Seamore Place, and afterwards at Kensington, a position almost queen-like in the world of intellectual distinction, in fashionable literary society, reigning over the best circles of London celebrities, and reckoning among her admiring friends and the frequenters of her *salons* the most eminent men of England in every walk of literature, art and science, in statesmanship, in the military profession, and in every learned pursuit. For nineteen years she had maintained in London establishments seldom equalled, and still more rarely surpassed, in all the appliances of a state of society brilliant in the highest degree; but alas! it must be acknowledged at the same time, a state of splendid misery for a great portion of that time to the mistress of those elegant and luxurious establishments. And now, at the end of that time, we find her forced to abandon that position, to leave all the elegancies and refine- ments of her home to become the property of strangers, and in fact to make a departure from the scene of all her former triumphs, with a privacy which must have been most painful and humiliating."

The exile of Madame de Staël from Paris was looked upon by her, as we know from her life, not only as an evil, but a cause of suffering, past all endurance, almost as bad as death itself. And Lady Blessington's love for London and its celebrities was of the same all-absorbing nature.

Count d'Orsay, as is well known to all who in former years had the *entrée* to Lady Blessington's *salon*, painted a large garden view of the house, with portraits of the Duke of Wellington, Lords Chesterfield, Douro, and Brougham, Sir E. Landseer, the Miss Powers, and other members of the fashionable circle that gathered there. "In the foreground, to the right," says a description of the picture, " are the great Duke and Lady Blessington in the centre, Sir E. Landseer seated in the act of sketching a fine cow with a calf by her side; Count d'Orsay himself, with two favourite dogs, is seen on the right of the group, and Lord Chesterfield on the left; nearer the house are the two Miss Powers (nieces of Lady Blessington), reading a letter; a gentleman walking behind. Further to the left are Lord Brougham, Lord Douro, &c., seated under a tree, engaged in conversation." The picture was 3 feet 8 inches, by 3 feet 2 inches, in a gilt frame, and was purchased at the Gore House sale by Mr. T. Walesby, of Waterloo Place.

Mr. Madden, in his book already quoted, gives us anecdotes of, or letters from, most of the visitors at Gore House when it was in its prime. Thomas Moore, who sang so touchingly as to unlock the fount of tears in the drawing-room, was often there; so were Horace and James Smith, the authors of the " Rejected Addresses;" so were Sir Henry Lytton Bulwer and his brother, the late Lord Lytton. Walter Savage Landor would repair thither, with his stern eyebrows and kindly heart; and Albert Smith and Thackeray, Charles Dickens and William Jerdan, the future Emperor, Louis Napoleon—an intimate friend of Count d'Orsay in his years of exile

—Mr. Monckton Milnes, Mr. A. Baillie Cochrane, Mr. N. P. Willis, the Countess Guiccioli (Byron's *chère amie*), Lord Brougham, Lyndhurst, Chesterfield, and all the other celebrities who being added up together in one sum, made up what Joseph Hume would have styled the "tottle of the whole" of the Gore House circle. Mr. N. P. Willis thus records an incident during an evening at Gore House: "We all sat round the piano, and, after two or three songs of Lady Blessington's choosing, Moore rambled over the keys awhile, and then sang "When first I met thee," with a pathos that beggars description. When the last word had faltered out, he rose and took Lady Blessington's hand, said good night, and was gone before a word could be uttered. . . . I have heard of women fainting at a song of Moore's; and if the burden of it answered by chance to a secret in the bosom of the listener, I should think, from its comparative effect upon so old a stager as myself, that the heart would break with it."

Of Holland House, and of its charming mistress and queen, Lady Holland, we have a portrait from life drawn by the pen of Macaulay in the *Edinburgh Review*. Lady Charleville's receptions in Cavendish Square, and those of Lady Cork in Burlington Street, though at one time almost as brilliant, are now forgotten, *carent quia vate sacro;* and it is only Mr. Madden who attempts to give us any general picture of society at Gore House.

It is often said that "books which make one think" are most highly valued by persons of a high order of intelligence; but "conversation which makes one think" was not the kind of discourse which told most in the salons of Gore House, even when it was most frequented by eminent literary men, artists, or statesmen. "Conversation which makes one laugh, which tickles the imagination, which drives rapidly, lightly, and pleasantly over the mind, and makes no impression on the roads of the understanding, which produces oblivion of passing cares, and amuses for the time being"—this, according to Mr. Madden, is the real enjoyment that is sought in what is called the brilliant circle of literature and art *à la mode.* Fox used to say that he learned more from conversation than from all the books that he had ever read; but this remark would refer more truly to Holland House than to its eastern rival, where we fear that politicians and statesmen came only to be amused, after having made their mental dinner off more substantial fare at Holland House.

Poor Lady Blessington, who joined to all her

frivolity a kind and generous heart, when she launched out into her magnificent and expensive establishments, at first in Seamore Place, and latterly at Kensington, had little idea of the difficulty of making both ends meet as a "queen of society" on a jointure of £2,000 a year, even when supplemented by her own literary earnings. Besides this, troubles came upon her thick and heavy in the last decade of her life. First came the loss of her plate—£1,000 at least—by robbers, and then a few years later other losses, owing to the potato blight in Ireland and the sudden diminution of an income up to the full amount of which she had been living. Then came the failure of Charles Heath, the engraver, on whom her "Annuals" mainly depended, which may be put down at £700 more. To these must be added the embarrassments of her son-in-law, Count d'Orsay, who had for many years made a common purse with her, and lived in her house. In 1847 and the following year things went on from bad to worse, and in the midst of her splendid *salons* she lived a prisoner in her own house, afraid to admit a stranger inside her doors lest he should turn out to be a sheriff's officer. " Early in April, 1849," says Mr. Madden, " the clamours and importunate demands of Lady Blessington's creditors made it evident that an inevitable crash

was coming. She had given bills to her bankers,
and her bond likewise, for various advances in
anticipation of her jointure to an amount approaching £1,500. She was obliged to renew
bills frequently as they became due, and on the
24th of the month of which we speak it was
necessary for her to renew one for a very large
amount, which would fall due on the 30th of May,
only four days before the great debt of all debts
was to be paid by her, as it turned out."

Before the April was over, the "end of all
things" came, and the long threatened break up
of the Gore House establishment took place. A
swarm of creditors, money-lenders, bill-dis-
counters, jewellers, lace-vendors, tax-collectors,
gas company's agents, all persons having claims
to urge upon her —pressed them simultaneously.
An execution for a debt of £4,000 was at length
put in by a firm largely engaged in the silk, lace,
India shawl, and fancy jewellery trade. Some
arrangements were made, a life insurance being
effected ; but it became necessary to agree to a
sale for the benefit of the rest of the creditors.
Several friends offered pecuniary assistance,
which it was hoped would have prevented the
break up of the establishment. But she declined
all offers of the kind. The fact was that she
was fairly worn out with cares and anxieties, and

that she was prepared to meet the worst. For two years at the least she had been sick of life— sick to the heart's core, even while she wore a smile upon her face in her gilded *salon*—sick of her splendid position apparently, but really of a life of wretched slavery.

After the "wreck of all things," as she called it, the house of Lady Blessington was vacant until it found a new tenant in M. Soyer, of culinary fame. Another species of composition was carried on at Gore House, whose chief glories now were its sauces and condiments. The culinary line had displaced all literary attractions; and everyone, during the first great Exhibition of 1851, had the *entrée* of those *salons* —at least everyone who had a few shillings to expend on a dinner *à la mode*.

But the glory of Soyer, his soups and his sauces, was not to last for ever; it perished and passed away in a few months, and Gore House was turned into a temporary crowded receptacle of ornamental cabinet work and studies for the School of Art.

As all our readers know, a new destination is henceforth to be given to the well-wooded gardens and pleasure grounds of Gore House, for they are absorbed into the grounds of the new buildings of the Government at South Kensington.

A WALK ROUND ST. CLEMENT DANES.

———

THE clean sweep which has been made during the last few years a little to the north-west of Temple Bar, whereby about a fifth part of an ancient parish has been laid desolate, in order to form a site for the erection of our long-contemplated "Palace of Justice," offers, at all events, a good excuse to Mr. Diprose, or any other public-spirited individual, for sitting down and preparing a "History of St. Clement Danes." But he has the great additional advantage of treating about a parish which is eminently rich in historical associations; one within the bounds of which there have figured in their day the representatives of Royalty, of nobility, of art, of literature, of genius, of unblushing and flaunting vice, and of open and notorious crime; a parish which witnessed such diverse scenes as the plague raging in its fury and carrying off its scores of victims daily, the escape of " Jack Shepherd" from the Bow-street runners, and the canvass of Georgiana, Duchess of Devonshire, who, in the cause of " Fox and Liberty," did not disdain to kiss its honest but somewhat susceptible voters; a parish within which Dr. Johnson used to go constantly to church in the morning, and dine in the afternoon with the learned wits of the day; a parish where the " Kit Cat" Club used to hold its meetings; a parish which holds—or rather held—the graves of " honest" Joe Miller as well as of hundreds of the Danes of an earlier age; a parish, which, at the " Crown and Anchor," witnessed struggles for popular freedom little inferior to those enacted further to the west at Covent Garden or at Westminster; in a word, a parish which contained in it what two centuries and a half ago was the Bond Street of London, where Pope would exhibit his decrepit little body and satiric face to crowds of intellectual admirers, and Bolingbroke his noble presence, and Steele would display on fitting occasions his gaudiest attire.

Such reminiscences, belonging to a parish lying close to our city walls, could not fail to invest the parish of St. Clement Danes with an interest superior to that which attaches to almost any parish of London or Westminster; and they de-

serve to be recorded at a time when the hand of
the sanitary and architectural reformer is working
in its outward appearance such changes as those
which we have seen, and shall shortly see, carried
into effect. A history of such a parish, written
with accuracy and with spirit, too, which should
enliven the dulness of mere topography with personal anecdote and call up the dry bones of the
past into a new state of existence, was a desideratum in the historic literature of London,
and one which ought to have been attempted.

We are far from saying either that Mr. Diprose
has not succeeded, to some extent, in producing
such a book, or that he has really succeeded to
our satisfaction in his effort. From the best
means which occur to us for forming a judgment,
we should say that he is an accurate and pains-
taking compiler, that he has made good use of the
parochial registers and other local documents
which he has been able to consult, and that he
has contrived to extract from them a mass of very
curious and interesting materials. But still,
owing to his want of method and plan in his
arrangement—in a word, of literary and artistic
skill—he has given us a volume which partakes
very much of the character of materials only, but
is scarcely to be called a finished book. In a
single word it lacks unity; it is *rudis indigestaque*

moles—rather more of a chaos than such a book ought to be, if it is to become popular beyond the narrow circle of mere local and parochial readers. Mr. Diprose himself, however, appears to be in some measure conscious of this defect, for he modestly tells us that he " cannot presume to offer it to the public as a history in the usual sense of the word ' history,' but chooses rather to submit it to the public as *Some Account of the Parish of St. Clement Danes.*"   Let us then, come to his rescue with words of comfort: it *is* a " history" in the original sense of the term : the sense in which Herodotus claims to be the writer of an " Historia," while Thucydides is the " Syngrapheus." It is eminently a book of " Researches," though little more.

We will own, with Mr. Diprose, that as Tarsus of old was " no mean city," so St. Clement Danes is " no mean parish."   Within its bounds, as we have said already, " have been enacted some of the most noteworthy events in the history of our country ; and in it many great and worthy men, authors, actors, statesmen, and lawyers, have been born, flourished, and died."   On the other hand, time has unravelled within the parish many a plot against the Throne and the people ; and it is not a little curious to find that on the very spot which has been the scene of many a crime and deed of infamy will soon be erected one of the most magnificent buildings ever dedicated to the great cause of justice, and, consequently, of order and of peace. "*Solitudinem faciunt :*" We trust that we may soon finish the quotation, and add, "*Pacem appellabunt.*"

It appears that the original parish church, which stood a little to the north-east of the present structure, was dedicated to St. Clement, the disciple of St. Peter, and one of his successors in the See of Rome. The word "Danes" was probably added on account of a Danish colony who settled here in the time of Canute—like the Irish colony of our own days about Drury Lane—and were buried within and around the church's walls, among whom no less a personage than Harold, the son and successor of that King, is said to have found here his last resting-place. The present edifice is the work of Sir Christopher Wren, all but the tower, which was added by an architect of the name of Gibbs early in the last century. The parish of old contained no less than four small and crowded graveyards; and it is almost within our own remembrance that the contents of three out of these have been removed to a suburban cemetery, while the fourth, that which surrounds the church itself, has been closed. It is well known that it was in the neighbourhood of St. Clement's, near the top of Drury Lane, that the Great Plague first appeared in this district in 1664-5 ; and we happen to know that the death-rate in the parish at that time was very heavy, as shown by the registers, which we have ourselves inspected. But we do not see that Mr. Diprose has given us any record of these matters; neither does he mention the fact that among the distinguished persons who lie buried in the churchyard is one, and possibly more than one, of the foreign bishops who administered the affairs of the Roman Catholic Church in England when its members were groaning under the weight of the infamous Penal Laws. Perhaps the author, who asks to have his information supplemented, will make a note of these facts for the next edition of his book. We will turn, however, to points in which Mr. Diprose has succeeded more completely.

It would be impossible to mention within the limits of this article one tithe of the distinguished persons who at some portion or other of their lives have been connected with the parish of St. Clement Danes. We have mentioned that Samuel Johnson used to worship within the walls of its parish church ; and there, in the last year of his life, according to our author, he publicly returned thanks to God for his recovery from a long illness. In the same church, too, was solemnized,

some century or more ago, the marriage of Sir
Thomas Grosvenor to Miss Davies, the heiress of
Ebury Manor, an union which brought the Pimlico
property into the family of the Duke of Westminster. Here, too, the profligate Sir Charles
Sedley was baptised. In the days of the Stuarts,
Boswell Court was the home of what was called
"the Quality." There lived the widow of Sir
Walter Raleigh; Gilbert Talbot, son of the Earl
of Shrewsbury: Sir Edward Littleton, Lord Chief
Justice in the reign of Charles I.; Sir Richard
and Lady Fanshawe; and Sir John Trevor, twice
Speaker of the House of Commons. Not far off,
on the site of what now forms the close-packed
and poverty-stricken region of Clare Market, stood
the proud mansion of Holles, Earl of Clare, the
names of whose family connexions still survive,
sprinkled about the adjoining streets, much as
those of the Cavendishes, and Bentincks, and
Portmans, and Russells a little further westwards. To the south of the Strand stood the
town residence of the unfortunate Essex, who
inherited it from his father-in-law, the Earl of
Leicester, and who has bequeathed his name to
Essex Street and Essex Stairs, where Royalty
before this has often embarked and landed. On
the same side of the Strand, towards Somerset
House, was the house of Thomas Howard, Earl of

Arundel, and afterwards of the Dukes of Norfolk, men whose family names are as lastingly imprinted on this parish as they are on the pages of English History. In Wych Street stood Craven House, a mansion associated not only with the Lord Craven of two hundred years ago, but also with Monk, Duke of Albemarle, who stayed here during the pestilence, in order to set an example of self-possession, and to maintain order among his panic-stricken neighbours. In Clement's Lane, too, at one time of his career lived Oliver Cromwell, though the exact house which he tenanted cannot now be identified. Peter the Great was the temporary tenant of a house in Norfolk Street; and the Cecils of more than a single generation resided at a house called after them, and the site of which is still to be identified in the yet living name of "Cecil Court."

A change, however, came over these once courtly abodes; and where the noble ladies of the Stuart days walked delicately abroad, displaying their costly robes and flowing trains, under the Hanoverian dynasty squalid poverty, vice, and crime took up their abode, and that which was once the abode of wit, talent, and fashion was converted by the lapse of time into a huge overcrowded den, where rags, gin, and penury, and stinted industry were heaped and huddled together in strange confusion. We venture to think that in spite of all that has been written about the cruelty of dislodging our London poor, few greater boons could have been conferred upon them as a body than the dismantling of the nest and rookery of dark and narrow courts and filthy dens which has been made to give place to our intended courts of law. Strange, indeed, that the term " court" should be applied to buildings so wide apart in plan and design. Mr. Diprose gives the names of between thirty and forty of such courts thus swept away; these contained about three hundred and fifty houses; and in these, according to his estimate, lived some nine hundred families—in other words, probably upwards of four thousand souls; one tenement in Plough-court, used as a low lodging-house, having had as many as eighteen families residing within its walls. Where such was the case, we hold that a radical reform is an act of positive mercy, and that the only right course to be followed is to make a clean sweep of the existing state of things. In this dreary region lived, among others, a colony of the poorest Irish, attracted to it, no doubt, by its nearness to the Sardinian Chapel at the corner of Lincoln's Inn Fields; but these, though quite as dirty in their habits and as drunken as the tenants of the neighbouring courts, perhaps even a trifle more troublesome too, were never absorbed by their English neighbours. To the last they remained; *ipsis Hibernis Hiberniores.* They have probably migrated to join their Celtic brethren in the purlieus of Drury-lane, whence, in the course of time, they will again be driven forth, when the sanitary reformer commences his operations there.

Turning to what may be called the low life of St. Clement's we find in Mr. Diprose's pages an account of the "Black Horse," in Old Boswell Court, one of the most frequented and convivial of low concert-rooms before the rise of the modern music-hall. Mr. Diprose writes:—

"Many of the public celebrities of thirty years ago were wont to gather round mine host of the ' Black Horse,' and as the French say, ' assist' at his nightly ' sing-song ;' to hear Dowson, Harry Perry, J. Bruton, Toplis, Mrs. Paul, and the celebrated Miss James in her favourite character of the Dashing White Sergeant; and such was the attraction of this fascinating vocalist that she drew to this concert-room nightly a number of the fast men of the day. . . . Occasionally the room would be visited by some sparkling, rollicking, sporting men about town, on whose entry additional devilry and ' life' would be thrown upon the scene. The singers might then be seen

seated next to a marquis or lord, who were never
particular about the ' one bottle more.' . . . In
fact, all fast London life here assembled to make a
night of it.' "

But enough of these " Waterfordiana." We
pass over also Mr. Diprose's amusing reminiscences of the " Thieves' Clubs," and " Cross
Gents," and " Charlies," and of " Bow Street
Runners," who seem to have found plenty of employment around Newcastle Court, Plough Court,
and Shire Lane, and, indeed through all the slums
which till but yesterday lay immediately to the
north-west of Temple Bar. We learn that some
of the houses here were built with double entrances, in order that the cadgers and thieves
might secure an exit into the Strand, if their front
door was entered by the " Robin Redbreasts" from
Bow Street. Mr. Diprose tells us that, owing to
their vicinity to the Temple and the other Inns
of Court, these lanes often became the scenes of
nightly rows, in which young gentlemen bore no
very creditable part. As a single instance in
point, we may mention that Sir John Denham,
when a student of Lincoln's Inn, after a frolic at
the ' Griffin,' in Shire Lane, went out at night with
a pot of ink and a plasterer's brush and blotted
out all the signboards in the neighbourhood—a

freak for which the poet and his companions, we hope and trust, were brought before the " beak " and duly punished.

In Ship Yard, too, was a colony of professed thieves, such proficients in their trade that Mr. Diprose tells us that when wholesale executions occurred at Newgate for robbery, it was rare for this locality not to have a representative among those who paid the last penalty of the law. Our author writes :—

" At the back of this yard stood formerly a block of houses from four to five stories in height, which were let out to vagrants, thieves, sharpers, smashers,   and   other   abandoned   characters. Throughout   the   vaults   of   this   rookery   there existed   a   continuous   communication,   so   that easy   access   could   be   obtained   from   one   to   the other, facilitating concealment or escape in event of pursuit, which, from the nature of the nefarious traffic in practice, very often occurred. The end house of this block of buildings was selected for   the   manufactory   of   counterfeit   coin,   and passed by the name of the 'Smashing Lumber.' The ingenuity employed in the construction of its apartments may be mentioned here. In the first place, every room had its secret trap or panel, so that a free entrance or exit might be effected quickly from one place to the other; and from the upper story, which was used as a workshop or factory, there was constructed a shaft or well in direct communication with the cellar before noticed. The whole of the coining apparatus, and the *employés* too, could be conveyed away as by a touch of magic, being lowered in a basket by means of a pulley, like the ' lift ' in one of our large clubs or hotels. For many years this secret mint had a most prosperous run; its master amassed a large fortune, and wisely disappeared just at the right time, for not long after the formation of the new police force and the appointment of detectives this den was discovered and abolished."

It is not a little singular that such misdeeds in the way of a base and spurious coinage should have been going on only a few yards to the north of Temple Bar, while just across the street, on the south side, the great banking-house of Messrs. Child was busily engaged in coining money in a very different sense of the term.

Mr. Diprose commemorates in his pages the names of several other banking firms which have been, and still are, connected with the parish of St. Clement's Danes. Among the former must be mentioned the house of Messrs. Strahan, Paul, and Bates, whose melancholy end is fresh in the memory of our readers. Among the latter, the large establishment long and honourably conducted by Messrs. Twining, a family whose name is so largely known in connexion with the mercantile world, and with the charities, not only of the parish but of the metropolis, besides producing one of the most accomplished of our Aristotelian editors and commentators—a fact which is far less known.

The ancient house immediately adjoining Temple Bar on the north-west, lately occupied by Messrs. Reeves and Turner, and which has been pulled down only very recently, was noteworthy as having been the abode of Crockford, who died a millionaire some quarter of a century ago. It was then a shell-fish shop; and it was remarkable as one of the last genuine specimens of an old-fashioned lathe and plaster penthouse, with projecting upper story and ornamented eaves, which decked our leading thoroughfare between the City and the West End.

Gone now are the Sedan chairs and coaches that once had in St. Clement's their favourite and, it is said, their earliest stands; gone, too are the Thames watermen, whom our fathers and grandfathers so well remember, resplendent in their scarlet coats and badges, who have been fairly driven to "other retreats" by those penny steam-boats which demolished their trade and spoilt their monopoly. Gone, too, are the "smashers" and the "Charleys" the very last of whose old boxes, long disused, stood till within a short time ago in Boswell Court, a relic of other days now all but antediluvian; gone is old Lyons' Inn, that haunt of men about town, honest and rogues, clever and swinish, gamblers and swindlers; gone, too, is the little court to the north of St. Clement's Church, of which Winter says,—

"So we met behind St. Clement's, Mr. Catesby, Mr. Percy, Mr. Wright, Mr. Guy Fawkes, and myself, and having upon a primer given each other the oath of secrecy in a chamber where no other body was, we went after into the next room and heard mass, and received the blessed Sacrament upon the same."

Gone, too, is Strahan's Bank; gone are the once fair gardens of Essex House and Norfolk House; gone are the wild beasts that once had their *habitat* in Holywell Street; gone, to a large extent at least, are the sirens of Wych Street; gone is the last of the stocks which once awed the roguish apprentices and the young roughs of St. Clement's parish; gone is the "Denzel Street Gang" and the "Alphabet" publichouse, once so well known to the lower members of the theatrical profession; gone is the "Black Jack" Tavern in Portsmouth Street, where the Cato Street conspirators held their nightly meetings; gone is the Norfolk Giant, who kept the "Craven Head" in Drury Lane; gone also is "Joe Miller," and gone are his jests.   But within the bounds of the ancient parish of St. Clement Danes there still stand one or two obstructions of which we may as well be rid, so as to make the approaches to our new "Palace of Justice" as available and imposing as possible.   We allude, of course, firstly, to that dingy and dilapidated structure known as "Temple Bar," which has but little of antiquity or historic interest to recommend it, and might easily be removed and rebuilt as an entrance to the Temple itself*; and, secondly, to that long block of houses between St. Clement's and St. Mary's Churches, which narrows the otherwise noble thoroughfare of the Strand, and which, if suffered to remain, will prove the greatest possible of standing eyesores to what, we trust, will prove the finest of our public edifices. Alderman Prickett, a generation or two ago, succeeded, by his own individual efforts, in removing "Butchers' Row,"

* The Bar was removed in 1877-8, see above, p. 167.

and so widening the thoroughfare from St. Clement's Church eastwards to Temple Bar. It is but recently that Middle Row was carted bodily away out of Holborn, after being doomed to death for a century; and now the greatest possible improvement to the parish of whose history we have been treating would be the removal of that unsightly impediment, which impedes the traffic of the Strand between the two churches, and which must be clean swept away if the grand edifice which has been intrusted to Mr. Street's hands to rear is to have approaches worthy of itself. Should Mr. Diprose's book lead only in a very remote degree to such a consummation, it will not have been written in vain.

THE OLD ROMAN BATH IN THE STRAND.

OF all the many hundreds and thousands of passengers, on foot or on horse, in cabs or in omnibuses, who daily make the journey into the City *viâ* the Strand and Fleet Street, we wonder how many fancy or imagine, as they pass the eastern end of Somerset House, that they are within some fifty or sixty feet of one of the oldest structures of London, one of its few real and genuine remains which date from the era of the Romans in England, and possibly even as far back as the reign of Titus or Vespasian.

But so it is. Let the pedestrian, when he reaches the east end of St. Mary's Church in the Strand—that church before which the maypole used to be set up in the days when England was

" Merrie England,"—dive under a low archway between the shops, and follow a rather winding and rapidly-descending path; and on his left hand, just before reaching a flight of steps, he will see a somewhat rural cottage, on the front of which hangs a card engraved with the words, " The Old Roman Bath." The outside of the cottage is not very attractive, or at all events it does not present any very striking features, or bears the least mark.

The lane in which this bath is situated is classic ground. It used to lead down to a pier or jetty called the Strand Bridge, which was once a place where the gallants of the day took boat, or landed on their return from Lambeth, Chelsea, and Putney; and allusions to it under the above name are frequent in books of gossip in the last century.

Thus, for instance, Addison, in his pleasant and chatty way tells us in the Spectator (No. 454), how he landed there one fine summer morning, on his way to Covent Garden. " Nothing remarkable happened on our voyage ; but I landed with ten sail of apricot boats, at Strand Bridge, after having put in at Nine Elms, and taken in melons, consigned by Mr. Cuffe of that place, to Sarah Sewell and Company, at their stall in Covent Garden. We arrived at Strand Bridge at six of the clock, and were unloading, when the hackney coachmen of the foregoing night took their leave of each other at the Dark House to go to bed before the day was too far spent. Chimney-sweepers passed by as we made up to the market, and some raillery happened between one of the fruit-wenches and those black men about the Devil and Eve, with allusions to their several professions." The stairs are long since gone; but a few coal barges were still moored at the bottom of the lane till the formation of the Embankment gave them " notice to quit." We fear that the steamboat piers at Waterloo Bridge and at the Temple have had their full influence upon the traffic of Strand Lane or Passage, and that for more than half a century Addison's landing-pier has been thrown into the shade of oblivion. It is thought by antiquaries that the Lane, which is somewhat tortuous, follows pretty nearly the line of a little brook or rivulet which carried off the water from the higher grounds about Catharine Street and Drury Lane, and passed under the thoroughfare of the Strand, which, as honest John Stow tells us, was carried over it by a bridge.

We cannot better describe " the Roman Spring Bath " itself than in the words of Mr. Charles Knight's " London," where he tells us of a visit which he paid to it a few years ago.

" Descending several steps, we found ourselves in a lofty vaulty passage, evidently ancient; and its antiquity became still more apparent on walking to the end of the passage, where the ceiling of the opposite or terminal wall exhibits half of a great circular arch, the upper portion of the other half being occupied by a descending piece of masonry, supported by a beam, which appears to be at least two or three centuries old, possibly much more. The age of this beam speaks significantly as to the age of the arch, which it and the accompanying masonry have mutilated. On the left of the passage is a door leading into a vaulted chamber, measuring, we should suppose, about twenty feet in length, the same in height, and in breadth about nine feet. In the massive wall, between the chamber and the passage, is a recess, passing which, and standing at the farther end of the room, we have before us the view seen in our engraving. The Bath itself is about thirteen feet long, six broad, and four feet six inches deep. The spring is said to be connected with the neighbouring holy well, which gives name to Holywell Street, and their respective positions make the statement probable. Through the beautifully clear water, which is also as delighful to the taste as refreshing to the eye, appear the sides and bottom of the Bath, exhibiting, we are told,

the undoubted evidences of the high origin ascribed
to it. Minutely, as the height and peculiar cold-
ness of the water would permit, did we and the
artist of our drawing examine the structure of
these supposed Roman walls and pavement. The
former consisted, we found, of layers of brick of
that peculiar flat and neat-looking aspect which
certainly seemed to imply the impress of Roman
hands, divided only by thin layers of stucco; and
the latter of a layer of similar brick, covered with
stucco, and resting upon a mass of stucco and
rubble. The construction of the pavement is made
visible by a deep hole at the end near the window,
where the spring is continually flowing up; and,
in pursuing our inquiries among those persons
best calculated to satisfy them, we were told by a
gentleman connected with the management of the
estate, who had had a portion of the pavement
purposely removed, that the rubble was of that
peculiar character well known among architects as
Roman. The bricks are nine inches and a half
long, four inches and a half broad, and an inch
and three quarters thick."

It should be added that these tiles lie on a bed
of mortar, under which again is rubble, extending
to a considerable depth. At the further end of
the Bath is a small projecting strip or ledge of
white marble, and beneath it a hollow in the wall

slanting down to one corner. These are, beyond
a doubt, the remains of a flight of steps which
once led down into the water.

Mr. Charles Knight adds :—"Immediately opposite the steps, we learn from the authority of the
gentleman before referred to, was a door connected
with a vaulted passage, still existing below and
towards the back of three houses in Surrey Street,
and continuing from thence upwards in the direction of the Strand. These vaults have some remarkable features. Among others, there is a low
arch of a very peculiar form, the rounded top projecting gradually forward beyond the line of its
sides in the house immediately behind the Bath."

But the history of the Bath—is there nothing
known of it ? All we can say in reply is that the
property can be traced back into the possession of
a very ancient family, the Danvers (or D'Anvers)
of Switbland, in Leicestershire, whose mansion
stood on the spot ; that, although the existence of
the Bath was evidently unknown to Stow, Maitland, Pennant, and Malcolm, and the later historians of London, from the absence of any mention of it in their pages, yet from time immemorial
in the neighbourhood the fact of its being a Roman
Bath has been received with implicit credence ;
and, lastly, that a kind of dim tradition seems to
exist that it had been closed up for some long

period and then re-discovered. It will not be thought we have spent too much of our attention on this matter, when it is considered how great an interest has always been felt on the subject of any remaining traces of the residence of the former masters of the world in our own island, and particularly in London, and that among those remains, consisting chiefly of fragments of walls, mosaic pavements, and articles of use or ornament, a bath, presenting to-day, probably, the precisely same aspect that it presented sixteen or seventeen centuries ago, when the Roman descended into its beautiful waters, must hold no mean place. The proprietors, we are happy to say, rightly estimate its value, and have long ago caused another bath to be built and supplied from it, and it is in the latter alone that persons are allowed to bathe.

Mr. Timbs, in his "Curiosities of London," speaks of this Bath as the most ancient in the metropolis, and also observes that it was evidently unknown to Stow, who says nothing about its existence, although he mentions the locality as "a lane or way down to the landing place on the banks of the Thames." The water is beautifully clear and extremely cold, and it is said to be supplied by the spring at the rate of ten tons a day.

If, indeed, the place that we have thus described

be in reality a Roman bath, of which fact no antiquary entertains a doubt, it is probable that it
marks the extreme westerly point of Roman London, and there is only one known duplicate of it
existing in the metropolis, namely, under the Coal
Exchange in Upper Thames Street, where are, or
were lately, to be seen some similar remains, in a
very dilapidated condition, though showing still
traces of the *débris* of a furnace and pillars of
bricks, which once, no doubt, supported a suspen-
sory pavement, and seats for the sitters, plastered
in the usual manner.

Mr. Thomas Wright, in his interesting and in-
structive work, "The Celts, Romans, and Saxons,"
remarks that among the Romans almost every
town had its public baths, or thermæ, and that
the latter were very often placed near the Basilica,
or Court House, or the head-quarters of the general
in command of the legions. Although the remains
of thermæ are so scanty in London, yet there are
several fine specimens, in tolerable preservation,
scattered up and down the country, as, for instance,
at Chester, under the " Plume of Feathers " Inn,
in Bridge Street; at Wroxeter, the ancient Uri-
conium, recently brought to light ; at Caerwent,
in Monmouthshire ; at Witcomb, at Cirencester,
at Crickley Hill and Woodchester, in Gloucester-
shire ; at Brecon, in South Wales ; at Bignor, near

Petworth, Sussex; at North Wraxall and Pitmead, Wiltshire; at York, the old Eboracum; at Hartlip, in Kent; at Waterby, in Lincolnshire; and at North Leigh, in Oxfordshire.

Looking at the gloomy little apartment in Strand Lane—for clear and sweet as flows the spring, the room *is* gloomy and prison-like—it is rather difficult to conjure up in one's fancy what these thermæ were in the days of Gordian or of Constantine. But a comparison of the thermal remains of Herculaneum and Pompeii, and others in the Lipari Islands, and at Wroxeter and Bignor, warrants us in drawing a picture of what were the appendages and decorations of such a structure as this some fifteen or sixteen centuries ago; and the writings of the Roman architect Vitruvius, read by the light of existing specimens, make everything as clear as the daylight.

So prevalent was the worship of the goddess Hygieia, or Health, and so great the fondness of the Romans under the Empire for every bodily luxury, that we can hardly be surprised at finding historians and satirists, and writers like Petronius Arbiter, using somewhat grandiloquent language in describing them. The finest and most perfect specimens consisted of some twelve or thirteen apartments, all or most of which were decorated with tesselated marbles, both on the pavements and on the walls, representing, in gorgeous colours, the national mythology, the Roman games, and the battles of the Gods, while heroes, birds, beasts, fishes, and monsters of every kind, griffins, sealions, sea-demons, and other imaginary beings were portrayed in mosaics. Thus Gibbon remarks, in his " Decline and Fall":—

" The walls of the lofty apartment were covered with curious mosaics that imitated the art of the pencil in the elegance of their design and the beauty of their colours. It was the ambition of the Roman emperors to construct these superb thermæ either to conciliate the people or to exhibit their own power and riches. They were the common luxury of all classes, and in them the people found their chief amusements—music and dancing, gymnastics and gladiatorial exhibitions, often accompanied the recreations of the Sudatory and Piscina."

Dr. Wollaston also, in a recent work on "Thermæ Romano-Britannicæ," gives a full description of the various apartments of a Roman bath, from which we condense a large portion of the following remarks:—

The thermæ were usually approached through an " atrium," or entrance-hall, which served for the purpose of promenading before and after bathing. It was large, and generally decorated with

busts and statues of Æsculapius and Hippocrates,
and of Hygieia, and other deities. Next came the
" Frigidarium," or grand hall, which was kept at
the natural temperature. This was often as much
as 120 feet in length, and surmounted by a lofty
dome, and adorned with elaborate mosaics on the
floor, walls, and cornices, with busts, statues, &c.
From this place a door led into the " Tepidarium,"
or warm room, which was intended to bring the
bather into a partial state of perspiration, and to
enable him, by a graduated process, to bear the
greater heat of the " Sudatorium," the heat of
which was so raised as to make the bather's perspiration burst forth profusely. This done, he was
shampooed and rubbed by an attendant and
scraped with a " strigil," a kind of curry-comb,
which carried off all scurf and impurities. The
" strigil " was an instrument used invariably in
the bath at Rome, as every scholar knows ; and it
may be asserted that wherever a " strigil " has
been found, there are good reasons for believing
that a Roman bath was not far off. The instrument was made of ivory, bone, copper, bronze,
iron, silver, or even gold : its form was curvili-
near, something like a sickle, but rather less
curved, and occasionally a small groove ran round
the outer edge, to collect the fluids which were
scraped off by the thin edge which was applied to

the skin, It required some skill in its use, as otherwise the skin would have been torn or scratched; and the Roman slaves were taught to use it with care and art. Specimens of the "strigil" have been frequently found at Rome and Pompeii; and also in England. One discovered in London, under the Coal Exchange, is now in the Guildhall; one found at Reculver, Kent, is in the library of Trinity College, Cambridge; one found at Caerleon-on-Usk is in the local museum. Besides these, other specimens have been found in the Bartlow Hills, near Saffron Walden, Essex, and at Wroxeter. Every scholar will remember a host of allusions to the "strigil" in Horace, Juvenal, and the other classic satirists.

The patient was sent next into the "Lavatorium," a semicircular recess at the end of the "Sudatorium," and sometimes constituting a separate apartment, where he was washed from head to foot with copious ablutions of warm and then hot water. In this room was the "Loutron," a large receptacle of marble, porphyry, granite, or tiles, for entire immersion, in tepid water. According to Dr. Wollaston, it was generally seven or eight feet long, and about three feet deep and three wide. Contiguous to this was the cold plunge-bath, or "Piscina," where the more vigorous used to brace their skin and muscles after the relaxation of the "Loutron." Its dimensions varied extremely; but the smallest must have been nearly identical with the bath which we are describing.

The "Hypocaust," or fire-place, which heated the chambers, was placed on the ground, under the flooring, or "suspensura," of the warm and hot rooms. It was like a cellar, the roof of which was supported by pillars of stone or brick tiles, between which the fuel was placed.

Close to the "Frigidarium" were two or three other smaller chambers which ministered to the luxuries of the Roman "prætextati." In one the hair was combed and arranged, as it is now-a-days by Mr. Truefitt; in another, the superfluous hairs were removed by the aid of depilatory powders; in another, slaves applied fragrant odours to the bather's body, and smeared him with costly ointments of delicious scents. Add to these chambers a "Sphæristerium," for games, and exercises—answering to our own billiardrooms; a "Capsarium," for the bather's clothes; the "Exedra," for poets to recite and philosophers to discourse; and a "Crypto-Porticus," or covered cloister round the outside of the baths, for walking exercise; and the reader has a general view of what the Roman thermæ were, though of course they ranged from edifices of great magnificence down to a very humble and unpretending style.

It is needless to add that the " Piscina " is all that remains of the bath in the Strand.

Rightly, then, is Glaucus made by Bulwer to exclaim, in " The Last Days of Pompeii," " Let us to the baths ; blessed be he who invented baths ;" and, in answer to Diomed, to reply :

"Imagine all Pompeii converted into baths, and you will form some notion of the size of the imperial thermæ of Rome, but a notion of the size only. Imagine every entertainment for mind and body, enumerate all the gymnastic games that our fathers have invented, repeat all the books that Italy and Greece have produced : suppose places for all these games, admirers for all these works ; add to these baths of the vastest size and the most complicated construction ; intersperse the whole with gardens, theatres, porticos, and schools ; suppose, in one word, the City of the Gods, composed out of palaces and public edifices, and you may form some faint idea of the glories of the great thermæ of Imperial Rome."

No doubt it is to the Greeks that the Romans owed their knowledge of the hot-air bath as a therapeutic agent, just as the Greeks derived their knowledge from the East. Even in the earliest times, in India, Phœnicia, and Egypt, we find the bath, under various modifications, employed as a remedial agent, as well as a means of cleansing the body, and dedicated to the Goddess of Health. The restorative virtues of the hot-air bath were constantly put into exercise by the combatants in the Olympic games, after the struggles of the chariot race, the cestus, or the palæstra. Its balmy influence soothed the wearied muscles and calmed the excitement of the brain. From Phœnicia the knowledge of this remedy travelled to Carthage, where the baths formed a prominent ornament, as described by Dr. Davis in his work on that city. But the full development of the thermæ was reserved for the Augustan and succeeding ages of imperial luxury; as if to prove the boast of Augustus, that he had found Rome of brick and had left it of marble. The magnificent thermæ, of which the present Pantheon forms a part, and which were built in his reign by the Consul Agrippa, and dedicated by the Emperor to the Roman people, form no small portion of the work on which that boast was founded. And Dr. Wollaston remarks with respect to the thermæ at Rome of more recent date, that they were built by Titus,

Hadrian, Caracalla, Diocletian, and Constantine, those very emperors who had once trodden with their victorious legions the soil of Britain. This fact may tend to explain the otherwise singular circumstance that the Roman and Anglo-Roman thermæ are more closely identical in structure and embellishment than those of any other two countries, so far as antiquaries have investigated their remains.

From what we have said above, our readers will already have concluded that what is now so generally known as the Turkish bath is, in reality, but a revival of the ancient Roman bath ; and when Captain B.—— and Colonel C.—— are enjoying the luxuries of Mr. D. Urquhart in Jermyn Street, or the Euston Road, they are undergoing the same process which 1,500 or 1,600 years ago, Captain Balbus, or Flavius, or Claudius, of the —th Roman legion, was enjoying in the Strand. But so it is! It is not a little singular, as Dr. Wollaston remarks, that " a practice so ancient as that of the Roman bath, which was in common use for many hundred years in all the most civilised countries of Europe, and still extensively practised by all Mahometan nations, has been almost entirely abandoned by Western Europe." The Turks and other Oriental nations still adhere to the customs of their forefathers, bequeathed to them by the descendants of the Greeks and Romans: no small legacy to bequeath; and no small boon to the people which had the good sense to adopt, almost as national, so valuable an inheritance.

" Among the Turks," as Dr. Wollaston adds, " the bath has been the great means of cleanliness, and of cultivating the enjoyments of social life, and almost answered the purposes of hospitals.

" Unquestionably the frequent use of the bath, whether hot-air or vapour, has been long practised by the Sclavonian races, by the Russians, Hungarians, Poles, Swedes and Germans; and it is strange, and not readily explicable, that the English and French, the Italians and the Spaniards, have almost entirely discarded the ancient luxury—perhaps because they have invented other means of enjoyment and of personal cleanliness, and substituted the domestic hot-water bath, instead of resorting to the public thermæ. But in a medical or therapeutical point of view, the hot-air bath claims an attention which is being slowly recognised by the profession and the public, and possesses medicinal and sanitary properties far beyond the ordinary bath of warm water. During the Crimean war frequent opportunities occurred of visiting the baths in Constantinople, which are held in popular reputation, not only as a luxury, but as a simple means of curing diseases; and no doubt the bath has superseded to a great extent the necessity of building dispensaries and hospitals: for the habits of daily life among the Turks are comparatively simple—they drink no intoxicating liquors, and are an abstemious people; the ordinary classes of diseases to which they are subjected, are much under control by the frequent use of the bath. The bath is as essential to the welfare and happiness of the Turks as the enjoyment of their chibouk; under the soothing delights of coffee, tobacco, and the bath, they are a temperate, peaceable, industrious, and cleanly people; their minds as well as their bodies are free from the excitement, the fever, and perturbation which disturb other European people; and so far as physical agencies influence the moral and intellectual condition of the Turks, it might almost be said that their calm, grave, and dignified demeanour is the result of their national adoption of coffee, tobacco, and the Bath."

And the ancient Roman bath, thanks to Mr. Urquhart, still survives in the Turkish Bath, formerly called " Hamaum," or " Hummum." Under the latter title, their name is still retained in the signs of the two hotels in Covent Garden, known to every reader as "The Old and New Hummums." Mr. Wright, in his "History of Domestic Manners of England," says, "Among the customs introduced from Italy was the hot sweating-bath, which, under the name of the 'Hot-house,' became widely known in England for a considerable time." Sweating in these hot-houses is spoken of by Ben Jonson, and in the old play of "The Puritan," a character, speaking of some laborious undertaking, says, "Marry, it will take me much sweat; 't were better to go to sixteen hot-houses." These Hummums, however, when established in London, seem to have been mostly frequented by women, and they became, as in the East, favourite rendezvous for gossip and company of not the most moral kind. They soon came to be used for the purposes of intrigue, and this circumstance gradually led to their suppression.

Dr. Wollaston tells us that there is in the British Museum a copy of an extremely rare print (a broadside of the reign of James I., but evidently copied from a French etching in the Print Department of the Imperial Library at Paris), entitled "Tittle-tattle, or the several branches of Gossiping," which represents in its different compartments the manner in which the women of London at that time idled away their time in these hot-

houses. In one division they are represented as
in bathing-tubs; in another as regaling themselves
with an abundance of very substantial dainties;
and in a third as busily engaged in picking each
other's and their neighbours' characters to pieces.
In Paris, where the same customs prevailed, the
ladies seem to have added to it the attractions
of a *pique-nique*, or *pic-nic*, if we may believe
the French etching above mentioned.

RALPH AGGAS' MAP OF OLD LONDON.

IT is not a little singular, considering the
antiquity of our metropolis, and its importance in the days of the Plantagenets, that,
with the single exception of a view of London
and Southwark drawn by a foreigner, Anthony
Van den Wyngrede, in 1543, and to be seen in
the Bodleian Library at Oxford, we have no
earlier map or plan of our metropolis than that
of Ralph Aggas, entitled " Civitas Londinum,"
and which would seem from internal evidence to
have belonged to the later years of Elizabeth's
reign. But so it is. No doubt earlier plans were
made, struck off, and sold by enterprising drafts-
men. But few have been kept. From the very
nature of things such plans would soon pass into
a ragged and tattered condition if much used;
and if unused would lie and rot in cellars or

garrets. Even the plan of Van den Wyngrede is rather a view than a map, and clearly deals with London in its poetical and picturesque aspects by far too much to be thoroughly trustworthy.

But it is different with the map of Ralph Aggas, or Agas, as he writes his name. Only two copies of this map are known to exist; the one in the Guildhall Library, and the other in the library bequeathed by Samuel Pepys to Magdalene College, at Cambridge. The former of these two copies has lately been photographed and reproduced in facsimile by Mr Francis, accompanied by an essay on its history and a memoir of its author by Mr. W. H. Overall, the City librarian; and a few stray notes upon it may not be void of interest to our readers. The map is a little over six feet in length; and, as it extends from Rotherhithe and Ratcliffe in the far east to Westminster and Lambeth in the west, it is evident that it must embrace not merely the London of Agas' time, but nearly all the space covered by the " inner circle " of London in the reign of Victoria.

The old Roman walls of the City here are still standing almost perfect; in fact we see them nearly as they must have stood in the days of the earlier Cæsars; and the gates of the City are

given—Ludgate, Newgate, Aldersgate, Cripplegate, Moorgate, and Aldgate—the first-named
facing the Fleet River and Bridge, and the last
standing a little north of the Tower.   The
Tower rises here in all its completeness and
strength, standing sentinel on guard, and frown-
ing down upon and dominating the river approach.
A little to the west of it is a small building, "the
Custom House;" and then comes "Byllyngsgate,"
close to the Middlesex end of old London Bridge.
This appears crowned and surmounted from end
to end with houses of brick and timber, of a most
picturesque appearance, and with fortifications at
either end, especially at the south, near the church
of St. Mary Overie.   Southwark, if we except a
few houses on either side of the High Street and
near the palace of the Bishop of Winchester and
the "Bolle-baiting" and "Bear-baiting" circuses,
consists for the most part of open fields and
pleausance; and dapper young citizens are stroll-
ing leisurely with their lady-loves along Bankside
as far to the West as "Parrys (Paris) Garden."
We trace back our way over the bridge (with our
eyes), and bearing westwards find ourselves at
Queenhithe.   Here are some animals in the river,
knee-deep in the water, and apparently enjoying
their bath; but a closer inspection reveals the
fact that here (as also at Tower Stairs) they are

horses, not oxen, and that they carry each a pair
of leathern panniers. These, we find, are being
filled by the attendants and slung across their
backs; for the drivers are not amateurs, but
members of the honourable and worthy society
of Water-bearers, who once formed an important
City Company, and one of the sources whence the
water was supplied for the washhouses of the
citizens and their wives. The streets and
thoroughfares, as was the case with Roman
cities, run mostly at right angles, and converge
at the western and eastern ends of Cheapside
respectively; the former being then, as now,
the ecclesiastical, and the latter the commercial
centre of London. Old St. Paul's appears in
all its mediæval glory, with the exception of
its lofty spire, which has recently fallen down,
having been struck by lightning, and has not
been rebuilt.

As a proof that at this time the Thames
was the "silent highway," it may be added
that in mid-stream, off Baynard's Castle, is
to be seen the Royal barge, on which are displayed the arms of Queen Elizabeth. It is towed
by another boat with six or eight oars. We see
the Round Tower of the Temple Church, the
church of St. Bride (or St. Bridget) in Fleet
Street, the architecture of Baynard's Castle, and

the gardens of Lambeth Palace, all carefully and minutely given.

It may be of interest to note that the map of Aggas, in the Guildhall Library was purchased at a sale at Messrs. Leigh and Sotheby's, in 1841, for £26, and that its estimated value at the present moment is between £500 and £1,000. A copy of it, but with several inaccuracies, was made by one Vertue, for the Society of Antiquaries, and published at their cost in 1738. There is reason to suspect Mr. Vertue "took in" the antiquaries with his copy, which deserves to be regarded as a "fabrication" rather than as a "facsimile," in Mr. Overall's opinion. For example, in Vertue's copy, the animals on the Thames are plainly cows, not horses; and they are engaged in drinking water on their own account, not in drawing it for the use of the citizens. It is to be feared that it is this spurious edition of Aggas' map, and not a real facsimile, which Messrs. Cassell and Co. have given to the public with the last volume of their "Old and New London." It is an extremely interesting and valuable illustration, however, with all its defects; but it has one fault, namely, that it is not "the genuine article;" and in these critical and fastidious days that is every-thing.

In the lower corner of Aggas' map—near where St. Thomas's Hospital and the Tabard Inn once stood—is a shield containing some curious verses, which runs as follows :—

" New Troy my name; when first my fame begun
　　By Trojan Brute; who then me placed here,
　On fruitfull soyle. where pleasant Thames doth run,
　　Sith Lud, my lord, my king, and lover dear,
　Encreast my bounds; and London (far that rings
　　Through regions large) he called then my name.
　How famous since (and stately seat of kings)
　　Have flourish'd, aye, let others that proclaim ;
　And let me joy, thus happy still to see
　This virtuous Peer my sovereign King to be."

These lines do not appear in Vertue's reproduction. It would appear, from evidence brought forward by Mr. Overall, and extracted from the " proceedings of the Society of Antiquaries," that the map from which Vertue made his copy was formerly in the possession of Sir Hans Sloane. But, somehow or other, it never seems to have found its way into the treasures of the British Museum, of which Sloane was the founder.

As to Ralph Aggas himself very little is known, except that he was a native of Stoke-by-Nayland, a Suffolk village near the Essex border; that he was a land-surveyor of great experience, having practised in London for forty years—as he says in a sort of advertisement touting for pupils; that, as such, he was consulted on various occasions by Lord Burleigh, the "Virgin" Queen's Lord High Treasurer; that he married a widow with some store of money, and carried on sundry legal suits against her relations; that he lived in Holborn, near the top of Fetter Lane, at or close to the sign of the "Helmet," and that he died at an advanced age in 1621. Besides his survey of London, he produced and engraved also an elaborate map of Oxford, of which only one copy is known to exist, in the Bodleian Library. It so happens that on this map of the University are some doggerel lines which, as they help to fix the date of the survey now before us, we may be pardoned for quoting here:—

" Neare tenn yeares paste the Author made a doubt
Whether to printe or laie this work aside,
Untill he quite had London plotted out,
Which still he craves, although he be denied.
He thinkes the Citie now in hiest pride,
And would make showe how it was beste beseene
The thirtieth yeare of our moste noble Queene."

There can be little or no doubt that these lines are intended to convey to the public the author's desire to portray London as it was in the thirtieth of Elizabeth; in other words, in 1588. Does not this, therefore, seem to fix the date of the map conclusively? It certainly appears to us to do so; and the more we examine the survey in detail, the more closely it will be found to correspond to the London of that date. For instance, the Royal Exchange appears in the map; and that building, as we know, was not open till more than ten years after the earlier and most usual date assigned to Aggas' map, namely, 1561. Be the date, however, what it may, one thing is certain, namely, that an hour employed in its study will give the inquirer a better idea of Tudor London than a week spent in poring over honest John Stow and the learned tomes of Speed and Maitland.

THE NEW LIGHTS OF LONDON.

MOST of us who chance to have been born and bred in the country, can recollect with glee our first sight of " the lights of London," when as children we approached the great metropolis, assuming that we entered it after nightfall. And who does not remember Don Juan's first view of these lights, whether of gas or only of oil, as he journeys down Shooter's Hill to Blackheath, and gradually enters the southern suburbs of London by way of the Kent Road and classic Newington Butts—

> " Here the lamplighter's infusion
> Slowly distilled into the glimmering glass—
> For in those days we had not got to gas."

But they are not the " lights" of Byron's days that we refer to here ; nor are we about to speak of the recent experiments with Mr. Edison's electric lights, that bid fair to supersede the gas with which we have been so long content, and which was once regarded as a magnificent triumph over the oil which preceded it. We purpose going back to the "Lights of London" nearly two centuries ago—the first infantine attempts which were made to conquer the "darkness visible" in which our forefathers of the Stuart days were content to live and have their being," though hardly to "move;" for to move about after sunset in London at that period, except on moonlight nights, must have been simply a physical impossibility.

It appears then, from the second edition of an old work called "Angliæ Metropolis, or the Present State of London," published in 1690, that up to about six years before that date—in other words, to the end of the reign of Charles II.—the worthy citizens of London were content to spend their evenings within doors, if they wished to avoid "accidents and casualties by falls, &c., which a man is liable to by walking in the dark, and abundance of tumults, affronts, and sometimes murther itself, which some dissolute and profligate persons, under covert of a dark night, would be ready to commit." But in 1684 came a change; oil lamps were introduced;

"When nature's night astonished rolled away
  Before the flood of artificial day."

These lamps are here grandly styled "the new lights," and an entire chapter is devoted to their description. The writer, indeed, goes almost into ecstasies on the subject, and compares the new invention with the work of Archimedes, who, "in imitation of the superior world, contrived the celestial spheres in a very small compass, which mathematically did turn and compleat their courses in twenty-four hours' space." And he asks, with an air of triumph, "If Archimedes deserved from the poets such hyperbole of praises, what deserveth the inventor of so useful luminaries that turn the nocturnal shades into noonday?"

What was the contrivance which had this wonderful effect on the social condition of London, and wrought a change which, in the words of Macaulay, "had added as much to the happiness of the great body of the people as revolutions of much greater fame?" And who was the author and founder of it? The work to which we have referred shall tell us. It appears from its pages that the innovator and benefactor was one "Edmund Heming, of London, gentleman," to whom and his partners King Charles the Second, of blessed memory, granted letters-patent for the enjoyment of the profits arising, or likely to arise from his invention. It further appears that Mr. Heming, on the part of himself and his partners, " sealed leases to persons upon very moderate and reasonable terms," namely " to pay five shillings down, and five shillings a quarter for five years, in two quarterly payments, due at Christmas and at Lady Day," in return for which he undertook (or, as the book says, " obliged himself") to "light the front of each house every night, from Michaelmas to Lady Day, from six to twelve p.m., beginning the third night after every full moon, and ending the sixth night after every new moon; in all, one hundred and twenty nights." It would appear from this that the " new lights" were entirely dispensed with in the summer mouths.

This curious little book, passing into the present tense, tells us that generally " there is one of these lights before the front of every tenth house on each side of the way, if the street be broad," quaintly adding, " by the rectangular position whereof there is such a mutual reflection that they all seem to be but one great solar light." It is clear that in the opinion of the writer, the introduction of these " new lights" was a real and solid contribution to the cause of order and social prosperity; for " this," he remarks, " is a security in great measure to one's goods and estate, and to one's person too, which is nearer than either;" and he enumerates among its special benefits, the prevention not merely of accidents, but also of "fires, robberies and housebreakings"—all of which things are fostered by the dark and chased away by the light. Like every other reform, the scheme of Edward Heming was loudly applauded by one party and as furiously attacked by another. His friends voted him the first of civic benefactors; his enemies wrote him down an ass. As Macaulay says: "In spite of these eloquent eulogies, the cause of darkness was not left undefended. There were in that age fools who opposed the introduction of what was called the new light, as strenuously as fools in our age have opposed the introduction of vaccination and railroads," and it is clear from Seymour's "History of London," that many years after the date of Heming's patent, there were extensive districts in which no lamp was to be seen.

These oil-lamps continued to be the sole means in use for lighting the streets of London for nearly a century and a quarter; though, as time went on, their brilliancy, or rather their effect, was heightened by being hung on ropes across the highways, instead of on the fronts of houses, as shown in contemporary prints.

It was not till five years of the present century

had passed away that London saw the first introduction of that artificial means of lighting which
was destined to supersede oil. We refer, of
course, to the first experiments in gas, which, in
its turn, came to be called "the new light," just
as oil had been in its time. We learn from a note
in Murray's edition of Byron, that the year 1812
may be taken as the date at which the adoption
of gas became general in the metropolis, both in
the City and also at the "West-end." And hence
there is no doubt that Lord Byron is really describing what he saw with his own eyes, when he
writes-in "Don Juan"—

> "The line of lights, too, up to Charing-cross,
>   Pall Mall, and so forth, have a coruscation
> Like gold as in comparison to dross,
>   Match'd with the Continent's illumination,
> Whose cities Night by no means deigns to gloss ;
>   The French were not yet a lamp-loving nation ;
> And when they grew so—on their new found lantern
> Instead of wicks they made a wicked man turn.

> "But London's so well lit that if Diogenes
>   Could recommence to hunt his honest man,
> And found him not amidst the various progenies
>   Of this enormous city's spreading spawn,
> T'were not from want of lamps to aid his dodging his
>   Yet undiscover'd treasure."

But those new lights—the gas-lamps—have had
their day of fashion and supremacy, and now, like

everything else that is mortal, they seemed doomed to pass away, and to be superseded by something better and brighter. Mr. Planché—who still survives, happily, amongst us, an honoured octogenarian and something more—tells us in his amusing "Recollections," that one of the reminiscences of his boyhood was that of being taken to see the first experiments made in lighting the London streets with gas. It was in the year 1805 or 1806, and the spot that part of Pall Mall which fronted Carlton House—as nearly as possible where Waterloo Place now stands—that the trial took place. In spite of the experiment being pronounced a "success" by competent judges and the unprejudiced part of society, and in spite of the brilliancy of the new favourite, throwing the dull oil-lamps quite into the shade, it was six years, as already stated, before gas was universally adopted; and it is a fact that Her Majesty had sat upon the throne for several years before the residents of Grosvenor Square had consented to allow the introduction of gas-lamps into that aristocratic region. It only remains to add that Mr. Planché, who saw the introduction of gas, has lived to see it receive a serious blow at the hand of Mr. Edison's electric light, which will speedily, we imagine, be entitled to usurp the name of "The New Light of London."

THE CRACE COLLECTION OF LONDON PRINTS.

IF any of our readers wish to spend a leisure morning profitably, and to amuse and instruct themselves at the same time, by all means let them take an omnibus or a railway to the Museum at South Kensington. A gallery, consisting of two long rooms and a staircase corridor, has been set apart at the north-west angle of this building, near the Queen's Gate entrance, for an exhibition of the magnificent collection of maps, plans, and illustrations of " Old London," made by the late Mr. Crace, and continued by his son and successor, Mr. J. G. Crace, of Wigmore Street and Dulwich. There can be no doubt that such an extensive and valuable collection illustrative of the antiquities of our metropolis has never been brought together in public before, and that being unique and as nearly perfect as possible, it ought to be, and must be, secured, sooner or later. for the British Museum—which is sadly deficient in its topographical print department—or else for the Royal Library at Windsor, or for some public institution, such as the City Library at Guildhall.

··At present there is but one drawback to mar the pleasure and utility of this exhibition, and that is the absence of a catalogue. It is true that the prints are well and carefully arranged, first geographically, and afterwards. as far as may be chronologically; and that on most of them are small labels giving their respective names. But this is an awkward arrangement, and at all events prevents the visitor from carrying away with him a list of subjects for subsequent consideration and comparison. Those therefore who visit the col lection at present must be pleased to bring with them the very best of memories if they wish to reap advantage from their trouble. On entering from the Scientific Department of the building, the first room is almost entirely devoted to maps and plans and general views of London as distinct from its several parts. Here Mr. Crace's collection is unique, for there is scarcely an ancient map or plan of real value of which he has not a copy. The arrangement here is chronological.

First and foremost are two ground-plans of
Roman London, presenting us with a view of
" Augusta," as the Romans styled the City
seventeen hundred years ago. One of these plans
is by the antiquary Stukely, and the other by
Britton. They both agree in the outline of the
old Roman walls which once surrounded the City
on the east, north, and west, forming an irregular
parallelogram which included the Tower (then
known as Arx Palatina) at the far east, and ending
on the eastern bank of the mouth of the river
Fleet. In these maps, which of course have no
pretence to a cotemporary date, but are worked
out from historical sources, the site of what is
now St Paul's is marked as " Dianæ Templum,"
and the " Mercatus," or mart of the merchants,
coincides pretty nearly with the Bank and Exchange. The residence of the bishop stands,
according to these maps, a little further to the
east, between St. Michael's, Cornhill, and Gracechurch Street. Inside the walls there are
apparently only four churches, St. Paul's; St.
Helen's, Bishopsgate; St. Mary de Arcubus
(Bow Church); and St. Mary Woolnoth's. The
line of walls runs exactly as it does down to our
own day. On the north stands out a projecting
horn called " The Barbican;" and outside of it are
the Moor Fields, the Clerk's or Clerken Well, and

the Smith's Field; and on the west is St. Bride's Well. The City itself is as nearly as possibly bisected from north to south by a rivulet, which rises apparently out of two springs in the moorland district to the north, becomes the "Wall Brook" from passing under the City wall, and finds its way into the Thames, which as yet is innocent of a bridge.

The next plan of London is one which professes to be that of Ralph Aggas, which has been lately republished in fac-simile in Messrs. Cassell, Petter, and Galpin's capital work on *Old and New London*, but which in reality is a fac-simile of Vertue's reprint.* The copy of this map in Mr. Crace's collection bears date 1560, and shows the walls corresponding with the above mentioned Roman maps, but filled up within by streets mainly following the modern lines of thoroughfare from east to west, cut here and there by others at right angles. Here all the routes converge to one or other end of Cheapside, west or east, the central points of attraction being religious and commercial respectively. The Tower of London stands here in all its completeness "dominating" the river approach; and London Bridge figures as a structure of massy arches, and crowned at its

* See above, p. 263, where the real date of Aggas' map is given.

southern extremity with towers. In the river, near the watering place of Queenhithe, are sundry cows and oxen quietly lapping up the water, and a few small boats are being rowed up and down the " silent highway."

Next comes a rather more ornate and detailed plan, bearing date 1572, and taken from the *Civitates Orbis Terrarum.* It is entitled, "Londonium, Feracissimi Angliæ Regni Metropolis," and, as compared with its predecessor, it shows sundry additions in the extra-mural district. For instance, not only the " Black Freres" have a local habitation and a name, but Parry's (Paris) Garden is conspicuously marked on the Surrey side, not far from where now stands the Waterloo Railway Station; and the north bank of the Thames towards Westminster is dotted with large isolated houses of "the quality." The parts about Southwark form a sort of foreground to the print, and here two gentlemen and two ladies, dressed in the court costume of the period, are standing in a posture which implies a wish that we should step in and look more closely into the show which they are anxious to exhibit.

A plan of the City, by Rythes, printed at Amsterdam, in 1604, follows next. Here the same lines are followed, but they are gradually filled up as the population of London continues to expand itself. Still nearly all of London is "within the walls." Here we have all the gates noted and named, the Ald or Auld Gate, the Moor Gate, the Cripple Gate, the Ealders' or Aldermen's Gate, the New Gate, and Lud Gate—names which need no explanation or comment, to our readers at least. Near the London Stone we have "Conning" Street, where is now Cannon Street, and the name suggests a derivation from "King," the old "Cöning." Here Fleet Street is represented as widened on both sides at the entrance of Shoe Lane, and with a conduit in its centre; and the southern side of the Thames is fringed with a single row of houses nearly from Lambeth to Bankside and Redriff (Rotherhithe).

The fifth plan to which we would direct the attention of our readers is curious, as being divided into a sort of upper and a lower story, the former giving us a view of London as it appeared in the latter part of the reign of Queen Elizabeth, whilst below is a view of the City after the Great Fire. The two parts of the plan, or rather view, correspond very nearly in the places which do not appear touched with the fire; and the engraving is adorned with several quaint views showing the elevation of some ancient houses in Fleet Street, Baynard's Castle, near Blackfriars, Cheapside, with its old cross, the Royal Exchange, and the west front of Old St. Paul's. Here we note, for the first time, the names of "Pell Mell" and "Piccadilly" recorded. This curious print is "sold by J. Bowles," but its exact date is not given. In all probability, however, it was published at the end of 1666, or early in the following year.

Next in order we have Norden's two maps of Westminster and London as those two cities appeared in or about 1550 and 1660 respectively, and a map taken from Norden's "Speculum Britanniæ" in 1653. Cotemporary with the last-named is a "Mapp of London and Westminster" as it was during the Commonwealth, "published and sold by Robert Walton at the 'Rose and Crown,' at the west end of St. Paul's Churchyard." This very scarce and valuable print is from the Stowe collection, and is probably unique. It professes to be a "ready help to direct country-men" who may happen to come up to see the great city from country parts, and is on a scale sufficiently large to realize that profession. Although the title of the map has the "St." prefixed to the metropolitan cathedral, yet in the centre we see the Puritanism of the times reflected in "Paul's Churchyard." Eastward, too, we have "St. Mary's Acts," instead of St. Mary Axe; and there are other blunders arising from an imperfect acquaintance with established and venerable sanctities. At the extreme west end of the map are shown "Piccadilly" and "The Gaming House," the latter occupying the south side of New Coventry Street from the top of the Haymarket eastwards.

This is followed by Fairthorne's well-known large map of London in 1658, and another of about the same date, in which are shown London, Westminster, and Southwark, with four rather artistic views on the river from Greenwich to Gravesend.

Next we have two copies, the one executed in London and the other abroad, of Hollar's "View of London," dated 1664, and valuable as showing the exact state of the City immediately before the Great Plague and Fire. These are "dedicated to Sir Robert Vyner, alderman, knight, and baronet." To this succeed Doorinck's map and view of London at the Fire. This would seem to have been rather a favourite subject for the map and printsellers, for by its side we have another view of London in flames by "R. P.," and "sold by Robert Pricke, in Whitecross Street, near Cripplegate Church;" another similar engraving by John Leeke and others; and two more bearing the name of Hollar. In all of these it is clear that the authors have drawn a little upon their imagination ; at all events, they have taken some poetical licences in arranging them; for they are nearly all taken from imaginary high grounds about half a mile to the south of the Thames, whence the spectator is taught to look down upon a harvest field of flames, which are licking up the spires of the City in one huge mass, over the top of which rises the lofty tower of St. Paul's. A group of large sporting dogs are sitting in the foreground, apparently enjoying the strange sight amazingly.

In the next map, which is from the Stowe Collection, and bears at the top the profiles of King William and his consort Mary, we see Westminster, Clerkenwell, and the parts about Old Street, all being brought into contact with the actual City by the gradual advance of bricks and mortar; and a still greater progress in the same directions is visible in " An Actual Survey of London," dedicated to the Lord Mayor in the eventful year of 1688, the work of two enterprising foreigners whose names have long since been forgotten.

Then we have, in succession, maps of London and its growing suburbs by Jacobsen de la Feuille, published at Amsterdam in 1690; by Morden, of the same date, the latter exhibiting and naming the squares, so far as they had been then finished; a map by Chiswell and others, dated in 1707; one in 1720, " printed and sold by Thomas Taylor at the Golden Lane, in Fleet Street;" one in 1731, where Marylebone is shown as fairly joined on to London as far westward as Marylebone Lane, beyond which lies an unknown region marked as " The Tyburn Road;" and a succession of other plans between the latter date and the end of the last century, a comparison of which will enable the visitor, without any difficulty, to read, as in so many pictures, the history of the gradual and steady increase of Modern Babylon down to a period within the memory of our own immediate predecessors. In these we notice the outskirts of Clerkenwell, St. Pancras, Marylebone, Lambeth, and Southwark, one by one being absorbed by the metropolis, and being gradually consolidated and welded into one coherent mass of bricks and mortar.

We must not, however, forget to draw attention to a large case which occupies more than half one side of this first room, and which comprises three large maps entitled " London Actually Surveyed." These are of three different dates, the first being by William Morgan, his Majesty's chorographer, *tempore* Charles II.; the next by John Ogilby, who held the same post in 1677; and the third and last by Robert Morden and Philip Lee, in the reign of William and Mary.

We have not described thus far one-half of the interesting plans and prints which adorn the walls even of the first of the three rooms devoted to the Crace exhibition; but we must pass on to the two remaining apartments, which are devoted to the various parts of London, such as the City proper and each of its wards, the Strand, Whitehall, Westminster, Piccadilly, the Parks, Marylebone, Kensington, Clerkenwell, Islington, Finsbury, Southwark, and Lambeth, to each of which separate portions of the walls or of the screened recesses between them are devoted.

Continuing our inspection of Mr. Crace's splendid collection of prints, sketches, and drawings of London, we will visit the two inner rooms at South Kensington in which they are being exhibited, and view them more in detail.

It will be apparent at once, on a most casual glance, that no part of the collection is richer in drawings of bygone objects than the City proper. Old London Bridge, old St. Paul's, the original Exchange, the old Custom House, grim Baynard's Castle, the City gates, the Cross and Conduit in Cheapside, each and all of these are gone, but they figure here. The Tower, the Temple Church, St. John's Gateway, and St. Bartholomew's the Great, are almost the only relics of Mediæval London to be found now to the east of Temple Bar. And these all stood just outside the ancient City walls. Inside the area of these walls the lapse of time, the hand of the improver, and the Great Fire of 1666 have conspired to make a clean sweep of the venerable remains of antiquity.

It is here that Mr. Crace steps in, rescuing the London of the Edwardian era from utter oblivion by the treasures which he has spread upon the walls. Here are no less than twenty views of Old London Bridge, as it was with its crown of houses, its subterranean, or rather subaqueous, chapel, and its fortified approaches; here we can see it as it must have been when William Shakespeare used to cross it in order to reach Bankside, and as it stood a century or more later, when Pope walked on it to call in upon his friend the bookseller. And then again we see it as in our childhood, from the vantage ground of the new bridge, in the course of demolition, full justice being done to its colouring. Several views exhibit the old bridge in its latter days, and also its successor (the present structure) a few yards westward of it. Among these etchings and engravings we are shown the rise and progress of the new bridge from its earliest stages till its opening by William IV., in August, 1831. Of this ceremony several illustrations are preserved in Mr. Crace's collection, one of the most interesting being a view of the west front of the new bridge, showing the old bridge in the distance through the arches.

Of Old St. Paul's, we have before us no less than between fifteen and twenty representations. The earliest exhibits to us the cathedral as it appeared towards the close of the fifteenth century, when its elegant Gothic spire rose, like that of Salisbury, on high over the City. Then we have it rather more than a century later, showing the appearance of the " churchyard" at the time of the " Execution of the Gunpowder Plot conspirators," in 1606, when it has already lost its tall and graceful spire; and, again later, when it has had its Gothic beauty spoiled by the classic front stuck on its western end. Four or five etchings by Hollar, published about this time, convey to us a tolerably fair impression of the architectural details of the cathedral as it then stood, and also of its appearance during the " Great Fire" of 1666. And then we are presented with the " Paul's" of the days of the Puritans, when in March, 1639, as we learn from the pages of " Old and New London," a paper was found in the yard of the deanery, before

Laud's house, inscribed, "Laud, look to thyself! Be assured that thy life is sought, as thou art the fountain of all wickedness."   "In October, 1640," as the author of the above-mentioned work tell us, "the High Commission sitting at St. Paul's, nearly 2,000 Puritans made a tumult, tore down the benches in the consistory, and shouted, 'We will have no bishops and no High Commission.' "

The Parliament made short work of St. Paul's, of Laud's projects, and of Inigo Jones' classicalisms.   The choir was converted into a cavalry barracks, the portico was let out to sempsters and hucksters, who lodged in rooms above, while the pulpit and cross—commonly known as Paul's Cross—were entirely destroyed.   All this we can read before our eyes on the walls at South Kensington.

And what shall we say of Paul's Cross itself, that mighty engine of the Reformation days, and the spot whence Anglican and Puritan divines agreed in denouncing Rome, but also occasionally uttered thunders against each other?   It lives once more before our eyes in a rare old engraving, in which we are shown a representation of the pulpit-like building, "with Dr. Shaw preaching, about 1483;" and also, in another engraving, "after an ancient painting in the possession of the Society of Antiquaries," which presents us with a bird's-eye view of the north-east front of the cathedral, with "Dr. John King preaching at Paul's Cross before King James I., March 26th, 1620."

Our readers will find a subject of especial interest in Mr. Crace's pictures of the Old Exchange, which stood at first in Broad Street, till removed to its present position on Cornhill. There we see a plain and rather low quadrangle, Flemish in character, the buildings being surmounted by high-pitched roofs. A bell-tower, crowned by a gigantic grasshopper, the cognizance of the Greshams, appears on one side of the chief entrance, whilst each corner of the building and the peak of every dormer window is surmounted by a similar ornament. The "first brick" of the edifice was laid by Sir Thomas Gresham in June, 1566, and the building was finished by the end of the following year. It was publicly inaugurated by Queen Elizabeth in January, 1570, when Her Majesty bestowed upon it the name of the "Royal Exchange." Heutzner, a German traveller who visited England at the close of the sixteenth century, particularly mentions the stateliness of the building, the assemblage of different nations, and the quantities of merchandise which here changed hands. Three or four views of the first Royal

Exchange, by Hollar, are here preserved, one of which shows us the inner-court and the tower above mentioned. Of the second Royal Exchange, that destroyed by fire in 1838, we find several interesting illustrations, whilst its sucessor is likewise worthily represented.

Mr. Crace's sketches of Smithfield in the olden time, between thirty and forty in number, will also form an agreeable study, bringing before us as they do many of the quaint old houses in and about Long Lane, Hosier Lane and other thoroughfares surrounding St. Bartholomew's Church and Hospital, most of which have now been swept away. Here we see illustrations of its splendid jousts and tournaments, its martyr-fires, its shows and fairs, and lastly its horse and cattle markets, which have, each in turn, contributed to make Smithfield one of the best remembered places in London. These together form quite a study of the various phases of human life, which could not easily be surpassed. Here we find a view showing " the manner of burning Anne Askew, John Lacels, John Adams, and Nicholas Belenian, with certane of ye counsell sitting in Smithfield," July 16th, 1546. Then we have several fine engravings of the Church of St. Bartholomew the Great and of St. Bartholomew's Hospital.

Ely Palace and its chapel, still standing and

now in the course of careful and loving restoration, with the strawberry-gardens on the banks of the Fleet River, figure here in some five or six spirited etchings executed in the middle of the last century.

Here too we can read, as in a book, the history and adventures of Temple Bar from the day when, the borders of the City being driven westwards from " Lud's Gate," the first chains were set up to mark off the jurisdiction of the City of London from that of Westminster, down to the demolition of the gateway just a twelvemonth ago.

Mr. Crace shows us a view of the old Bar erected in the reign of James I., and several of its successors, as it appeared during the last and present centuries. In some of these we find the structure surmounted by the heads and legs of malefactors who have suffered at the hands of the executioners as traitors. Amongst these the skulls of the Scottish rebels mounted on poles upon its top (the last of which fell down just a century ago) remind some of us of sundry witticisms of Dr. Johnson, and may teach others how dangerous a thing it is for enthusiasts to fight in the cause of dethroned dynasties.

St. John's Gateway at Clerkenwell comes in here for due honours. The old gateway, together with the priory to which it belonged, is represented in half-a-dozen or more views, some of them dating as far back as the sixteenth century, long before the place became tenanted by Edward Cave, the enterprising bookseller, and founder of the *Gentleman's Magazine*, who set up his printing presses within its walls, and was there honoured with the friendship and company of Dr. Johnson, Garrick, and Oliver Goldsmith.

Although Hicks's Hall, Bishop Burnet's house, and other historic buildings which stood in the vicinity of St. John's Square, Clerkenwell, have been swept away, the remembrance of them is still preserved in Mr. Crace's valuable collection.

Nor is the Charterhouse quite forgotten, though it could have been wished that a larger selection had been made of drawings illustrative of that admirable hospital, and of the Carthusian Monastery which it superseded; and that the collection embraced one or more portraits of "Good Thomas Sutton," the founder of the school.

Mr. Crace is particularly rich, it may be here remarked, in his drawings of the halls of City companies. Here we may especially notice the views of old Fishmonger's Hall, which gave place to the present building in 1832; the old Goldsmith's Hall, as it appeared in the last century; the old Grocer's Hall in the Poultry (formerly the Bank of England), as it appeared in 1668, and which was pulled down just eighty years ago; the Haberdasher's Hall, in Maiden Lane; and the Girdler's, in Basinghall Street; the old building of Merchant Taylors' Hall, which was demolished in 1848; the old Leathersellers' Hall, in St. Helen's Place, Bishopsgate, taken down in 1799; the Pewterers' Hall, a building of the seventeenth century, as it appeared in 1851; old Salters' Hall, in St. Swithin's Lane, and Surgeons' Hall, in the Old Bailey, both now numbered with the past; and lastly, the old Watermen's Hall, in Upper Thames Street, as it appeared before the Great Fire of London.

In his delineations of the Strand, Somerset House, and Charing Cross Mr. Crace is very fortunate. He has preserved in his collection some two hundred views of buildings standing between the cities of London and Westminster, most of which have long been removed and have passed away out of remembrance. We may enumerate, as of particular interest, old Durham House, the "Thatched House," said to have been Nell Gwynne's dairy, near the Adelphi; Beaufort House, Exeter Change, old Somerset House, the Prison and Chapel of the Savoy, Hollar's views of Arundel House; "the Strand and its neighbourhood in 1700, looking from Arundel House northwards, with the Maypole and Garland," aud

Canaletti's front of Northumberland House—the very last of the many historic mansions of our noble families to pass away. The statue of Charles I. at Charing Cross is also made the subject of half-dozen or more prints and etchings, some of which are remarkably curious, particularly that in which is shown " the notorious cheat, Stroud, being whipped at the cart's tail to Whitehall," a print published in 1731.

Westminster Abbey, as might be expected, comes in for more than an average share of illustration. Here we see the venerable pile before the removal of the miserable houses which at one time closely hemmed it in on the north and west sides, and also as it appeared at the time of the coronations of William and Mary, George IV. and William IV. In others it is shown as it was before the two western towers were added by Sir Christopher Wren.

Of the old Sanctuary, Judge Jeffrey's house, Caxton's house, Thieving Lane, and other noted places in Westminster, the very sites of which are now almost forgotten, we have here several representations, as also of old Palace Yard and the buildings connected with Westminster Hall and the Houses of Parliament. The views of Whitehall, by Vertue, J. T. Smith, T. H. Shepherd, and others, are upwards of one hundred in

number, and of the highest interest, particularly
those in which we are carried back a couple of
centuries, and see the place as it appeared on the
day of the execution of Charles I. In some of
these views, notably in that of Vertue, we see
Holbein's Gateway standing athwart the road
between Charing Cross and Westminster Palace,
as if it would forbid all intercourse between the
Court and the people.

Passing on to the suburbs, we observe that here
Mr. Crace, though not so wealthy in subjects as in
the two cities proper, affords us life-like sketches
of very many well-known scenes and places now
more or less altered and "improved." Perhaps in
none of our suburban parishes is Mr. Crace more
rich than in those of Iseldon (Islington) and St.
Pancras. No less than twenty views are devoted
to the illustration of old Sadler's Wells Theatre
and its surroundings; whilst several others bring
before us the old "Angel" Tavern, the "Three
Old Hats," the "Thatched House" Inn, the "Red
Lion," the "Rosemary Branch," the "Queen's
Head," and other favourite rendezvous of the
pleasure-seekers of "old London," when they
wished to indulge in a quiet stroll to "merrie
Islington," in order to inhale for awhile the fresh
country air, and quit for a time the narrow pent-
up streets of the City.

The " silent highway " of the Thames also meets with its fair share of attention in this magnificent collection. Here we see the noble river and its banks on either side under various aspects, both in summer and winter, and also in the past and present. Of the remarkable frosts on the Thames there are several admirable illustrations. " Blanket Fair," as the proceedings which took place on the ice off the Temple in 1683 were called, is represented in two or three spirited engravings published at the time. One of these shows us an ox being roasted whole off Somerset House, and all the adjuncts of a " fair " upon the ice are vividly reproduced. The state processions of the City companies' barges going to Westminster on Lord Mayor's Day are here again reproduced before our eyes; and in a copy of one of Turner's pictures we see the solemn procession of boats accompanying the remains of Nelson to Whitehall Stairs, prior to his interment in St. Paul's Cathedral.

In many of the views of the Thames the lowlands of Lambeth naturally form the foreground. These are generally raised by a poetic, or rather an artistic, licence into elevated ridges, on which setters and pointers recline, and dapper gentlemen are represented as walking along Bankside with their lady-loves, just as nowadays they may be seen in Hyde Park and Kensington Gardens.

Mr. Crace has printed a catalogue *raisonné* of his entire collection, select portions only of which are before us; but the work is printed in a costly style, and as a *livre de luxe*, and "for private circulation only." Extracts from this catalogue are affixed to the prints and plans on view, so as to explain those which require an interpreter; but, in the absence of a regular catalogue in the hand of the visitor himself, it is not easy to ascertain what treasures are here, and what are "conspicuous by their absence." In making this remark we have no selfish motive, for, thanks to the courtesy of Mr. Crace, the use of a copy of his beautiful book had been placed at our disposal.

COUNT RUMFORD AT BROMPTON.

IN the days of our grandfathers and grand-mothers few names were better known in London, among the upper and the middle classes alike, than that of Count Rumford, the inventor of "Rumford stoves" and of other appliances of domestic comfort, and the founder not only of the Rumford medal bestowed by the Royal Society, but also of the Royal Institution in Albemarle Street. But, in spite of his practical philanthropy, his memory, like that of many another man "in advance of his age," has been short-lived; and the American Academy of Arts and Sciences have lately done good service to the cause of applied science by resolving to publish his life, and also a collective edition of his works.*   On this bio-

* "Life and Works of Count Rumford."

graphy I shall draw largely for the materials for this sketch of the Count's career.

Benjamin Thompson, afterwards Sir Benjamin Thompson, and eventually Count Rumford, though of English extraction, was born on American soil, having first seen the light of day in Massachusetts in 1753. He was consequently a young man when the War of Independence broke out. In it he took the side of the "Loyalist" and "Royalist" party. Finding himself suspected, whilst in the command of a troop, of favouring the cause of " the old country," he came over to England, leaving behind him his young wife and an unborn child. It so chanced that on arriving here he was introduced to Lord George Germaine, then Secretary of State for War, who took him under his wing and made him his deputy, finding his knowledge of American localities of great use to him in his office routine. Just before the end of the war, when his services in this capacity were no longer required by his patron, he was presented with a commission as lieutenant-colonel, and placed on half pay. Obtaining leave from the King to travel on the Continent at the close of the war, he went to Vienna, and thence to Munich, where his practical genius developed itself in the organization of military and other reforms, which we have not space to describe here, but the effect of which was, in the emphatic language of one of his friends, " to banish beggary from Bavaria."

Having spent some years at Munich, and having been created Count Rumford in reward for his services to the State, he now returned to England, and settled in London, taking a house in Brompton Row, Knightsbridge, on account of " the healthiness and rurality of the neighbourhood." Here he took up his abode, fitting the house with all sorts of ingenious appliances for the purpose of warming it, and ventilating it as well ; and so successful was he in the execution of his experiments that his friends called it his " Paradise " and " Elysium." The house still stands, though the green patch of garden ground and the trees in front of it have been absorbed into the roadway. It was then numbered 45, Brompton Row ; and it is to be identified with what now is known as 168, Brompton Road.

The house, as it was at the beginning of the present century, when owned by Count Rumford, is minutely described by one of his guests, M. Pictet, who bears testimony to the pleasant life led by the privileged inmates of this " agreeable and ingenious structure." After describing its situation, " about a mile from London, on the great road which conducts to the bridges of Fulham and Battersea," he writes : " The win-

dows have a double glazing; the exterior makes
a three-sided projection, in which are placed vases
of flowers and odorous shrubs, which you may
have either within or outside of the apartment,
according as you open or close the inner sash.
The table on which these vases stand is per-
forated, in order to furnish the plants of a hot-
house character with the air necessary for
vegetation, and the side sashes of the exterior
windows open or shut as they are needed.

"The house has five stories, including the
offices, which are set under the level of the earth.
The arrangement is the same on each floor—two
apartments and a staircase. On the ground floor
is the parlour, where morning visitors are received,
and the dining room. On the first flight is a bedchamber and a saloon for company; on the second,
again the same arrangement; on the third, a bedchamber and a work-room for the occupant of the
dwelling himself. In this room, which has a view
of the country, the light comes in through a set of
adjoining windows arranged in an arc of a circle,
and through which, even in the middle of the
apartment, you may see a quarter of the horizon.
The sills are arrayed with flowers and shrubs;
and the eye, looking over the trees and the neighbouring fields, and seeing nothing intervening,
the illusion is complete." And then he describes

in equal detail the stables, coach-house, chemical laboratory, and servants' rooms at the back of the house—separated from it by a small garden, but connected with it by a covered gallery, which was warmed in winter by pipes of hot air.

It must be owned that the Count showed much practical talent in combining in his house the agreeable and the useful. Every arrangement for the utilization of heat, whether for personal comfort or for culinary purposes, was carried here to the highest pitch of perfection. "The mantelpiece in the room," writes M. Pictet, "makes no projection, and being masqued in summer by a border of painted canvas, you confound it with one of the panels of the wainscoting. These panels at the right and left of the fireplace are hung on sunken hinges, and you raise either one or other of these, in the style of a table, when you wish to read or write near the fire. The same arrangement is adapted to the piers which separate the windows. You can at will produce either a table or a single panel when you allow it to fall back again." Again, the wainscoting was so combined as to furnish secret closets, in which books, clothes, &c., could be kept out of sight, but free from damp and dust.

The bed-rooms appear to have been similarly arranged. "The bed," writes M. Pictet, "is concealed under the form of an elegant sofa, the seat of which is formed by one of the mattresses, the other being so constructed as to fold up as if with a hinge through the length of the back part, and then contracts the bed by its doubled thickness to the size of an ordinary ottoman. The space under the sofa bed is utilized for drawers, hidden by a fringed valance. In a few minutes the sofa is converted into an excellent bed, and in the morning again becomes a piece of ornamental furniture."

Then, as to the dining-room, it would appear to have been arranged with equal ingenuity. "Its area," writes M. Pictet, "is changeable by means of a partition made of window-sashes, with large panes, forming a very large double door, which opens on the side of the casement for sunlight, and by which the heat also escapes in the winter. When the folding doors are open at right angles, they correspond with the windows, and the room is enlarged to that extent; the same doors then form two side recesses, which serve as sideboards —communicating both within and outside the room, by which the service of the table is performed without the servants having to come in. If you wish to contract the room and to preserve its warmth by the effective agency of the window, you can close the folding doors, and without depriving yourself of the light or of the charming view of the shrubbery with which the windows are decked, you are completely protected from all chills."

Other visitors bear testimony to the elegant simplicity which mixed with the owner's taste in the furniture of the several apartments. " Even in the choice of his colours, the taste of the Count," observes a friend, " has been regulated by those natural rules for the blending of tints which always harmonize for the eye when they are respectively the complement of the colours which the whole prismatic spectrum presents." Thus we see that the discoveries of a Newton can be applied to the choice of a ribbon as well as to a Cosmos.

Certain it is that the Count's house was equipped throughout with perfect order and simplicity, and that its ingenious and tasteful arrangements made it, for many years after it was abandoned by Count Rumford, one of the most attractive objects for various sightseers. He liked visitors to examine it from top to bottom, and he allowed, in a truly cosmopolitan spirit, all classes who cared to inspect it. One of the novel contrivances of the house, however, would appear to have escaped the eye of Mr. Pictet; at all events, the latter says not a word about it. I allude to a "concealed kitchen" in the housekeeper's room, "fitted up (to use the Count's own words) in order to show that all the different processes of cooking may be carried on in a room which, on entering it, nobody would suspect of being a kitchen." This kitchen is described by the Count very minutely in one of his published " Essays" on domestic improvements. It may interest my readers to learn that, although now cut up into apartments, its different floors being occupied by different tenants—one being an artist's studio, and another a servants' registry office—the house was but little altered till the summer of 1876, when the passage connecting it with the offices in the rear was removed. In the upper rooms, the panels by the side of the fire-place still are lifted up as flaps and serve for reading-stands; and though the Rumford stoves for the most part are gone, the cupboards in the several rooms still remain to attest the ingenuity of its former owner, whose name is to be revived, I hear, on the outside, by a board with " Rumford House" painted on it in large letters.

The Count, however, devoted his attention to other branches of his subject, especially to the mechanical improvement of the apparatus then in use connected with fire-places and chimney-flues. When first he published his " Essay on Chimney

Fire Places, with Proposals for Improving them, so as to Save Fuel, to Render Dwelling Houses more Comfortable and Salubrious, and Effectually to Prevent Chimneys from Smoking," he was able to boast—so great was his popularity in London as a social reformer—that he " had not less than five hundred smokey chimneys under his hands." In this respect he was so zealous and unwearied, and so fond of his subject, that he never refused his services either to a palace or a prison, a poor-house or a cottage. It may be interesting to note the fact that his first experiment of the kind in London was tried on Lord Palmerston's house in Hanover Square. Then he took in hand the chimneys of the house where the Board of Agriculture held its meetings, and which, being frequented by persons from all parts of the kingdom, he doubtless regarded as more or less of an advertisement. But his fame grew so rapidly that he had no need to advertise himself. He did the same for the chimneys of Devonshire House in Piccadilly, and for the houses of Sir Joseph Banks in Soho, of the Earl of Bessborough, of the Countess Spencer, of Marlborough House, of Melbourne House, of Lady Templeton, of Lord Sudley, of Lord Salisbury, and of the learned and accomplished Mrs. Montagu, in Portman Square, the head-quarters of the " Blue Stocking Club." Nor

was this all. He gratuitously instructed a class of
bricklayers and builders in his method, so as to
give them constant employment. He found that
the saving of fuel which he effected amounted to
a half, or even to two-thirds, without diminishing
the warmth secured. He further made use of a
room which he occupied in the Royal Hotel, in
Pall Mall, for experiments in the construction of
chimney flues; and he enlisted the services of
master potters and ironmongers, to their own advantage, in carrying out his designs. Mr. C. R.
Weld, the historian of the Royal Society, to
which he was Assistant-Secretary and Librarian,
writes : " One of the earliest of Rumford's stoves
or fire-places is that set up under that gentleman's own superintendence in my office in the
Royal Society's rooms. This is by far the best
fire-place that I have seen."

The stoves and kitchen ranges put up by the
Count were nick-named "Rumford Roasters;"
but they soon came to be very popular, and were
brought into such extensive use that, if there had
been in his days such things as Great International
Exhibitions, they would have been universally
recognised, and have become a permanent institution. The " Roaster," if not the first in point
of time, was the most scientific, ingenious, and
effective apparatus of its kind known in the last

century; by its arrangement for conveying hot air around the food in the oven, and by the economization of fuel, it allowed several articles to be prepared at once at one fire, and greatly facilitated the labours, whilst adding to the comfort of the cook. The families who practised a generous hospitality found it a most welcome addition to their culinary arrangements, and for a time the enthusiasm in its favour was almost an epidemic. But the Count spent the latter part of his life abroad, and died before he was an old man. His "Roasters," therefore, had no one here to protect, much less to "push," his interests as an inventor; and they consequently died out in name, though the best parts of the Count's invention were adapted and adopted by those who followed after him. He wrote and published essays on "Fuel," on "The Preparation of Food," and on " The Extravagant Use of Fuel in Cooking Operations," some of which are reprinted in a Memoir of Count Rumford, by Frederick Edwards.

One point which connects, or ought to connect, the name of Count Rumford with that of this great metropolis is the war which he constantly proclaimed, though he never lived to wage it, against the London smoke. In his frequent journeys into the suburbs and back again, whilst engaged in superintending the introduction of his contrivances in private houses or public buildings, his attention was drawn to the thick clouds of smoke which always hung over the City and covered its spires and the dome of St. Paul's with a dusty and sooty mantle. "In that unutilized smoke he saw the unused material which was burned not only to waste, but to a means of annoyance and unhealthiness. He said playfully, but in all the sincerity of a true economical philosopher, that he would bind himself, if the opportunity were given him, to prove to the citizens of London that from the heat, and the material of heat, which were thus wasted, he would cook all the food used throughout the City, warm every apartment, and perform all the mechanical operations which are carried on by the agency of fire."

There have been from that day to this many skilful experiments made in this "fumifugium," and many scientific papers have been written, printed, and published on the pecuniary loss and the positive nuisance which is represented by the smoky atmospheric pall which hangs over London. But, probably, whoever hereafter shall "hit the mark" in this direction will own that he gathered his first hints from the man who first turned the attention of the Londoners to the philosophy of light and heat, and tried to make them more available for the service of man.

In Count Rumford's various operations for the cure of smoky chimneys, and for the warming of apartments, he steadily refused to protect his own selfish interests by taking out a patent, but preferred to leave his inventions wholly free to the public. It must be owned, however—though this does not militate against merits or value—that his innovation was very simple indeed. In the course of instruction which (as already mentioned) he would give to his ironmonger's workmen upon working out the philosophical principles of combustion, ventilation, and draught, he drew out carefully-adjusted diagrams to show the proper measure and arrangements of all the various parts of fire-places and flues. The cure of smoky chimneys and the economy of heat he found to be dependent upon much the same rules as those which he had applied to the construction of fire-places. In most of those which he was called upon to examine, he found that the heat radiated by them into the apartments which they were intended to warm was scarcely a fifth part of that generated by the fuel—all the rest passing away up the chimney, and being lost. He fixed upon an angle of 135 degrees as that which ought to be formed by the sides of a fire-place with its back, and he also laid it down that the back should be just one-third of the front opening, and should be carried up perpendicularly till it joins the breast, and that the throat of the chimney should be left only four inches wide. It is a pity that some enterprising builder does not seize upon the idea, and use it in building his next Victoria Row or Alma Cottages.

I have said that Count Rumford banished beggary from Bavaria; but as to the means by which he accomplished that task I must refer my readers to the work from which I have drawn so largely, merely remarking that I know of nothing except our intense and obstinate conservatism, and the love which our middle classes feel for "vested interests," that should make his plans unsuited for England, or should render that impossible in London which he proved to be possible at Munich. Indeed, it seems to me that his essays on pauperism alone, and his plans for its relief and prevention, followed up by his conduct in Bavaria, where he actually suppressed it, most justly entitle him to the name of a philanthropist. At Munich a noble statue in the public park commemorates his name; here he has no memorial, not even a mural tablet, on the walls of Westminster Abbey.

It would appear to have been Count Rumford

who, seeing the strictly scientific character of the speculations and transactions of the Royal Society, first thought out the idea of establishing a school of applied science, which, in his hands, gradually developed itself into the British Institution in Albemarle Street. On its first opening, the Count was what would now be called its "managing director;" and it was he who first secured for the infant institution the services of the great Sir Humphrey Davy, who again in his turn became (scientifically, of course,) the father of Faraday. If the Count had done no more than this, he ought to have been immortalized in Albemarle Street, at least. Is it too late for that institution to do honour to the name of its founder by some memorial more popular and more visible to the public than its "Rumford Medal?"

The Count was past middle life when the death of his wife, whom he had never cared for much, and whom he had never seen since he was twenty years of age, left him at liberty to contract a new alliance. Accordingly, he married a charming French lady, but who cared only for her *salons* and evening parties, and the newly-married couple soon parted. The Count did not long survive the separation, dying at a new house which he had bought at Auteuil, near Paris, in August,

1814. His widow lived on for many years after his death, and was the friend of Guizot and Thiers, and of most of the French *littérateurs* of the generation just passing away.

END OF THE FIRST VOLUME.